S0-ADZ-757

THE CAMERA ALWAYS LIES

The Camera

Always Lies

HUGH HOOD

BIBLIOASIS

Copyright © Hugh Hood, 2015

All rights reserved. No part of this publication may be reproduced
or transmitted in any form or by any means, electronic or mechanical,
including photocopying, recording, or any information storage and retrieval
system, without permission in writing from the publisher or a licence from
The Canadian Copyright Licensing Agency (Access Copyright). For an
Access Copyright licence, visit www.accesscopyright.ca or call toll free to
1-800-893-5777.

Library and Archives Canada Cataloguing in Publication

Hood, Hugh, 1928–2000, author
    The camera always lies / Hugh Hood.

(Reset books)
First published: Toronto : McClelland and Stewart, 1967.
Issued in print and electronic formats.
ISBN 978-1-77196-025-0 (pbk.). — ISBN 978-1-77196-026-7 (ebook)

    I. Title.

PS8515.O49C3 2015   C813'.54   C2014-907971-0
C2014-907972-9

Readied for the press by Dan Wells
Copy-edited by Emily Donaldson
Cover and text design by Gordon Robertson

Published with the generous assistance of the Canada Council for the Arts
and the Ontario Arts Council. Biblioasis also acknowledges the support
of the Government of Canada through the Canada Book Fund and the
Government of Ontario through the Ontario Book Publishing Tax Credit.

PRINTED AND BOUND IN CANADA

MIX
Paper from
responsible sources
FSC® C004071

1

DOWN THERE

1

Three bottles stood beside the telephone, on the table between the beds. The biggest was about the size and shape of a bottle of fifty aspirin tablets, and the others were vial-shaped, cylindrical, and made of a translucent greenish plastic. Each of the vials would hold a dozen tablets. All three bottles carried the prescription label of the same doctor and drugstore, and they had all been obtained in April of this year.

A woman lay on one of the beds at an uncomfortable angle, neither quite on nor quite off, with her feet crossed and dangling awkwardly toward the floor. One shoe had come off. It looked as if she had been sitting or leaning on an elbow and had then slumped down without getting under the covers. Except for the shoe which had fallen off, she was fully dressed. She looked like a piece of the furniture.

Sometimes her chest lifted slightly and the barely expelled breath raised a tiny bubble of saliva in a corner of her mouth that burst with a faint pop, the only sound in the room. Outside, in the motel court, cars could be heard coming in and going out, and voices called across the court with Saturday-night cheerfulness.

"Just before Rutland on Route Seven," said a hearty voice, and "I've been through there," said another. Glasses clinked. In the next suite a radio played. Fair evening light came through the Venetian blinds, striping black shadows across the drugged woman's face and playing on her slightly opened eyes.

Her body stirred. From some source in the brain a signal was flashed to the limbs, moving them so that she rolled onto her left side and got her elbow underneath her. Several seconds passed while she tried to lift herself on her shaking arm. Her eyes opened wider, but she didn't seem to see much. There was a slight film on the eyes.

As she hunched herself up on the left elbow, her right arm began to come across her body, slowly but with purpose. Something animated the cortex; purpose formed the signals and kept them coming; the right hand groped around and then clawed its way up the side of the bedside table, finally resting on the top. As the fingers flicked convulsively open, the forefinger and thumb hit one of the vials and knocked it over, and the light, cheap, greenish-plastic object rolled soundlessly past the phone and fell on the deep-piled carpet. The hand clenched, fingers tightened and loosened, and finally the forearm rolled over and the hand grasped the telephone receiver. Until now the woman's face had been quite still, but at the feel of the cold smooth surface in the palm, her mouth twitched open automatically; she salivated and tried to speak, but nobody could have understood the sounds she made. Her face contorted with an extreme effort.

"...et...et...err..."

She dropped the receiver and fell back on the bed. The receiver swung quietly back and forth at the end of its cord between the beds. In the motel office an orange light appeared on the switchboard. The owner, drowsing in a swivel chair, sighed and leaned forward to put the call through. He jiggled a hook on the switchboard.

"Hello," he said, "Suite Thirty-four?" There was no answer.

At five-thirty, earlier that evening, Rose Leclair had left the Rivoli, where she had been seeing *Goody Two-Shoes* for the second time, and had gone by cab to a parking garage near the Queensboro Bridge, a block or two past her house on East Sixty-first. She had sat in her car for some time, overwhelmed by a wave of shame, betrayal, embarrassment, and defeat.

"Everything O.K., Miss Leclair?" asked the garage attendant after a while. He told reporters later that her behaviour had scared him.

"She's got plenty of go, that one," he told them, "so I knew right away something was wrong."

His words roused her and she made an effort, and spoke to him fairly cheerfully. "I'm fine, Charlie," she said, smiling at him, and he went off shaking his head. Sitting in the car in the shadowy garage, she felt resolution grow more firm in her mind; she rummaged in the glove compartment. The three bottles were there. She had been hoarding them, saving up for three weeks now, and she had a few extra pills loose in her bag. She took the bottles from the glove compartment and studied them, hating especially the feel of the little green vials. There was something faked and betraying about it, like the touch of gunmetal. She put the bottles in her bag and started the car. It occurred to her that she could do it right here, just by rolling up the windows, but it would probably cause Charlie a lot of trouble.

She emerged into the lovely end-of-April light just at dinnertime, feeling hungry and ignoring the impulse. She didn't want to eat something, make herself sick swallowing the pills, throw up, and have to start hoarding them all over again. She was planning, looking ahead, figuring, and ignored her hunger and her beautiful house on East Sixty-first, deliberately bypassing it. She considered driving out to Pelham Manor, where Kate Dixon had rented a house for the run of her show, but decided against it. She picked her way north through the Bronx, and up around Fordham she hit University Avenue, old U.S. Route 1, which she followed aimlessly, detesting the effect of the erosion of time on the scenery, the dirty alleys, rusted bits of bodywork behind service stations, vacant lots of gravel and rank high grass. She noticed suddenly that she had come as far as Pelham; she had no business bothering poor Kate, who had troubles of her own.

She turned onto the Hutchinson River and started north into Westchester, trying to think of a place. At each ramp she read the sign and rejected the town as unsuitable. It was important to be where nobody knew you. She had a vision of lawyers and agents and producers viewing her afterwards, and it made her feel nauseated even without food. Who would want to die in Purchase or Mamaroneck? She made one tentative pass after another at an exit, without following through.

Soon she was into Connecticut on the Merritt Parkway; she had come much further than she'd intended. She passed New Canaan and was tempted by the name, which struck her as appropriate, but she had missed her chance and had to continue north in the heavy traffic to the Route 7 turnoff. She turned north and drove slowly towards Wilton through clusters of eyesores, and about fifteen minutes' drive beyond the town, at a restricted pace, brought her to the Cresta Corona Motel, where she took a suite for the night from Lou Aspinall, the owner. She arrived in declining sunlight, flipped her gloves onto one of the beds, spent almost half an hour swallowing the tablets three or four at a time, washing them down with gulps of water, feeling her stomach heave at the cold flood, and slumped back across the bed a little after nine-thirty.

2

GOING DOWN

1

"In the Rivoli on Easter Saturday?" asked Mr. Callegarini with delight.

"March 25th, 1967," said Bud Horler. "Easter is early next spring."

"It's definite, not a doubt about it, not the least in the world," said Lenehan like a stage Irishman. "Faith, no."

"What a booking!"

"You said a mouthful," said Horler, smiling.

They were sitting on a rooftop patio outside a branch bank on Santa Monica Boulevard, over near the West Los Angeles line, high enough for them to catch the occasional gleam of light reflected off the ocean. It was a clear sunny April day, warm for that time of year, bringing out the indigenous fauna. Girls in abbreviated swimsuits passed and repassed their table, causing Horler, Lenehan, and their confidential secretary Larry Solomon to reflect gravely.

"I've arranged a lot of financing in my time," said Horler meditatively, "but never in exactly these circumstances." They were drinking rum out of pierced pineapples through straws, a sybaritic nuance encouraged by the bank, which inclined more and more towards the Pompeian tone in its conduct of affairs.

Mr. Callegarini smiled. "It is the bank's wish to make finance as simple and pleasurable as, say, boating. It is an error to think that serious actions must be painful. It's very simple. You want money and can pay to rent it. We have money and are prepared to rent it. Why should there be any mystery, or guilt, or hidden fear, connected with finance?"

"Why indeed?" echoed Lenehan, sucking contentedly on his pineapple.

"Like public worship and private prayer, finance, though important, ought to be carried on in a joyous spirit. That is the bank's feeling. We try to create, in our offices, open palaces of sun and air. This is a California bank, founded here in a glad Western spirit, financially strong here; the branch system is our great strength and it flourishes in the California community. Our branches reflect our climate and our ecology, open as they are to sun, light, and the venturesome heart."

"Come off it," said Horler.

"I admit it," said Callegarini, "I'm quoting the official literature. But after all, it makes sense. Jeez, when I was a kid borrowing money was like going to confession. You went into a little cubicle and told your sad story, and they'd absolve you—or maybe they wouldn't—with fifty dollars against a lien on your furniture."

"I remember my uncle's, back in the old country," said Horler reminiscently. "When you went around to put something in pawn, they seemed to see into your very soul. Rather daunting it was too. Drink up."

"That's a firm date?"

"Tell him, Larry."

Pausing to examine a girl's buttocks as she wandered past in virtually nothing, Solomon opened his briefcase. "Hmm-mmmn," he said distractedly, "hmmmmn, here are the agreements. The percentages are specified on page eleven, holdover options on page thirteen, release dates in other key cities, here and here." He shook out the document, and Paul Callegarini handled it with expert and familiar negligence.

"What have you done to this bank? What are these girls?" asked Solomon. They were conferring under an orange-and-mauve beach umbrella, around a glass-topped table to which an attendant brought additional refreshments from time to time. These furnishings were deployed on a small, carefully tended patio of gravel, flagstones, and false-looking grass, with a mock lake at one side and a series of descending levels at the other, down to the street four floors below. There were short connecting staircases from one level to the next; people climbed up from the street and sat on low benches beside the little lake. They brought popsicles with them, and lunches, and the girls went to and fro; the one who had caught Larry's eye was normally a teller, but was doubling as a Naiad for the week.

"What the hell," he said as she rotated her hips indecently though unconsciously. "We don't consider this a part of banking back East."

"California is different, thank God," said Lenehan.

Callegarini seconded him warmly. "Let me tell you guys, when I say 'Thank God for California,' I mean every syllable. I'm not a booster, I just love to be warm, and you got to admit, it is warm."

"Explain these girls," said Solomon, "or we'll think you aren't serious-minded enough, and borrow money somewhere else."

"That's easy. This is 'Banking in Community Life Week,' where we show how our institution fits into the social patterns. We open our entire operation to the public; they can come and inspect the adding machines, inspect the premises, see that we've nothing to hide. This branch had trouble last year, I recall. A widow with real estate holdings in Brentwood got stuck in the vault with the timer on."

"What did they do?"

"What could they do? She damn near suffocated. So this year the time lock isn't activated. We'll probably have a big

holdup on Friday . . . anyway, the public comes and we get to
know our customers."

"And the girls?"

"Scenery, stage setting pure and simple. Did you ever hear
of any operation that didn't run smoother for a few pretty
girls?"

"But the drinks, the garden chairs?"

"That's different, that's the VIP treatment. They sent me
to this conference with instructions that you boys are to be
treated with every consideration."

"Why not just give us the money?"

"You couldn't carry it home; it would weigh too much.
And besides we have to go through the formalities of examin-
ing your position. We have our stockholders to protect."

"But we'll get our dough," said Lenehan.

"Why not?"

Horler asked, "What do you get to drink when you want to
borrow fifty dollars?"

"There's a fountain inside the main entrance to your left."

"I'll have another of these pineapples," said Horler. He
beckoned to an attendant, who came quickly over.

"Can I have a refill?" Horler was a jockey-sized gnome
of a fellow, and the attendant, a small man himself, smiled
down at him as he lolled in improbable sports clothes in his
orange-and-mauve chair. People often smiled at Horler, till
they knew him; it seemed so quaint, even faintly ridiculous,
the sight of this miniature Englishman with the unplaceable
accent, all dressed up like a big producer. His voice had an
elusive charm; what he spoke wasn't cockney or Lancashire or
Yorkshire, or any of the varieties of English accent known in
North America. In fact he came from Nottingham and spoke
with the throaty growl of the area, unfamiliar to Americans
because not often parodied on the screen.

One of his horde of distant cousins had been on the halls
in the teens and twenties, and later on, in the early and mid-

dle thirties, had made a couple of dozen six-reelers under the quota, clad always in baggy plus fours and an ineffably silly expression: Our Cousin Syd. It had been his name that had launched Bud Horler in the trade, at first as doorman in a picture palace in Nottingham in the early 1920s. He had not enjoyed a meteoric rise. He had gone through all of it: doorman, ticket taker, assistant manager, chief clerk in the office of a film-rental business operating in the Midlands, salesman for a distributor, exhibitor. He had inched forward when there was no money to be made in British film production, and precious little in operating cinemas. He had not had an easy time getting where he was, and his smart, vulgar jockey's air concealed immense strength of purpose. What he did not know about the economics of film production would go into a pretty small nutshell. He never said what he thought, except to Lenehan.

Horler had done two years as executive producer on a Crown Film unit at the start of the war, and his name had more or less accidentally been associated with four high quality documentaries of feature length which the unit had produced. Afterwards he had worked at Eagle-Lion, acquiring North American experience in the fiasco. He never forgot from then on that the first thing to be done when producing a feature is to arrange the release dates. He knew, better perhaps than anybody else in the industry, that it is the exhibitor who counts.

He would explain, as his first principle, that there is no point whatsoever in making a film if you can't get it shown. Nothing is more frustrating than the ownership of 8,200 feet of exposed film—an edited print, into which you've sunk sums of money varying between fifty thousand and ten million—which you can't get shown.

"Package the film in your head," he would say. "Put it all together at agency lunches—the script, the players, the director. But spend no money until you've talked to a releasing corporation. Afterwards you can arrange financing by snapping your fingers." He had been so unfailingly impressed by the results of acting on this maxim that he and Lenehan were on the verge of going into distribution themselves, buying a string of six features from a French producer-director and marketing them in art houses, just to get a foot in the door.

Horler had met Dan Lenehan in the late forties, when an Eagle-Lion unit had been shooting in Ireland; they had been sympathetic to each other from the start. Lenehan controlled a number of cinemas in the principal cities of Eire, and Horler was drawn into close relations with exhibitors, like a cat to mice or cream.

"Get to know the indie circuits," he is quoted as saying. "Meet the man who is running a fourth-run house in Boise. Find out what his problems are; that's where the money is. I don't care about the Rivoli or the art houses. Those are specialized matters that we know how to handle. But the big market, the world market, that's the fellow in Boise who has to make money with fourth-run pictures. You can ask him who the stars are, and he'll know the answer. And he's never heard of Jeanne Moreau."

Somebody like Max Mars might object, "Bud, you can't make films on that basis."

"I can't make films on any other basis. The film must play, and people must want to see it a second or third time. I had a friend one time, made a feature for a government agency, in one of the colonies. He shot 60,000 feet of stock, using a modified *cinéma verité* technique. He took six months to get the shots he wanted. He had no script, and no shooting schedule. Then he brought this rather expensive footage—I'm speaking relatively you understand, it cost about a hundred and fifty thousand to get the rough cut—he brought this film back to his government agency and only then did anybody think about getting it shown. It had no audience value of any kind. Nobody ever heard of any of the players. There was no story. When they got a few bookings, nobody came. Nothing, I say nothing, makes me sicker than the sight of the popcorn woman and the ushers and the ticket taker and the projectionists and the manager all sitting around drawing salary, while the exhibitor counts the empty seats."

"What happened to your friend?"

"He is considered the founder of the colony's national film industry, but the government auditors want to put him in jail."

"Was the film any good?"

"Nobody saw it. Nobody knows."

When Horler talked like this, Danny Lenehan would nod his head quietly, in complete accord with his partner. He was only slightly bigger than Horler, with the same gnome-like build. He might have a pot of fairy gold hidden somewhere, you thought, until you'd seen him in action; of the partners, he was the one who played dirty pool. Horler looked after finance. Lenehan handled personnel and contracts ruthlessly.

He claimed that his uncle was a character in James Joyce's *Dubliners* and *Ulysses*, which was perhaps imprudent. The Lenehan pictured by Joyce had been a parasite, without honour, or views of his own, or funds, or visible means of support, a familiar Dublin type, and Danny wasn't quite any of these.

He dressed like a superior squire in the works of Borrow, as though he should smell of horse, and was sometimes troubled in his mind that he did not so smell. To round out the picture of gentility, he kept his handkerchief in his sleeve, his head about him at all times, and he stumped rather than walked.

Neither Horler nor Lenehan knew Paul Callegarini very well, so they let Larry fence with him while they considered what cards they held. What they wanted was around seventy percent of their estimated costs, or about five-and-a-half million. This they wanted from as few sources as possible, and so they came to the bank. The rest of the money would come from their private holdings, with perhaps a little bit from Tommy Dewar, just to keep him honest. The overall strategy was to get the money without surrendering title to the production. It was clear that Callegarini wanted to do business, so they sat and waited for him to come to the point.

He said, "Clears up the release dates all right, for the North American market. What about foreign?"

"We're attempting to negotiate a favourable import status with a number of European governments. There is a possibility of our accepting a limited amount of French or Italian capital in order to qualify. And we're offering to import a number of French features, the Films Vinteuil line. A small producer."

Callegarini's eyes flickered brightly; he took some papers from Larry and went at once to the heart of the matter.

"We can't allow any guarantees to European capital which might in any way compromise our own investment. I'm unhappy about the bearing of this clause." He put his finger on the weakest spot in the agreements, and Lenehan winced and spoke out as if his own flesh had been bruised.

"A purely token statement. We might rewrite it with the inclusion of appropriate options, or with an escalation clause. There won't be a loss in any case."

"So you say, but film production is a gamble."

"Not with us. We've got a record. We've never had a loss."

"Not as a partnership, but both of you have been associated with losses." He named some minor disasters of the thirties and forties, while they stared at him respectfully.

"Neither of us had full responsibility for any of those bombs," said Horler, "but as a production team we've made eleven features since 1955, about one a year. And none has lost a cent."

Lenehan took it up. "*Sailor Take Warning* was ours, and you know the story on that. We brought it in for nothing and it's never stopped earning. And we've got Rose Leclair penciled in for this one."

"But not Lincoln."

The partners were silent.

"I don't insist on Lincoln," said Callegarini, "and I'm thinking seriously about this loan; but I have to know what you've got, and what you'll have to have. You'll be needing an enormous sound stage and very expensive lab facilities, and musicals cost like hell."

"Have you got involved in any?" demanded Solomon suddenly, hoping to startle the banker.

"Not directly . . . not directly. We've been, let's say, interested onlookers."

"You'll have to do better than that for us, Paul," said Danny, "because we've rented the studios and the labs from August 1st, and we've got payments to make."

"Oh, you went in there, did you?"

"Largest sound stage in the world," said Lenehan with pride. "We've never used it before but for *Goody Two-Shoes* we'll need room to swing a cat. We may invite you over for an evening of cat-swinging."

A man came out of the bank and spoke softly to Callegarini. The others waited politely for him to finish. Lenehan drank his drink. Horler craned his neck to stare westward, wishing he were out on his boat this afternoon. Solomon looked from his briefcase to the girls and back. The man went back inside.

Callegarini said, "He's setting up the phones for your conference call. Shall we take it out here?"

"Why not?" said Horler. "Is he putting it through now?"

"They'll be on in a few minutes. Why don't we wrap up as much as we can right now? Maybe I could give you a verbal go-ahead. You've rented the studio space; you've got release dates. What's the production schedule?"

"Fourteen weeks," said Lenehan, consulting some notes. "August 1st to November 4th. There may be some additional editing and even a spot of shooting; you can't tell till you see what you've got. But we generally stick pretty close to schedule. Anyway we have options for additional studio time."

"And you propose to release the picture . . ."

"At the Rivoli, big premiere, Saturday, March 25th, next year."

"Is that enough time for promotion?"

Horler made a solemn declaration; he might have been taking an oath. "We start on publicity the second we get your O.K., whenever you say so. And by the way, it isn't going to be strictly a musical; it'll be more a romantic comedy with incidental musical sequences. Keeps costs down, pleases the Europeans."

"Leading man?"

"Tommy Dewar, with a small percentage."

"Girl? Rose Leclair?"

"On salary, with a small percent of the net."

"Hmmmmn."

"She'll carry."

"She's no Monroe," said Callegarini.

"We'll talk about it. We have a surprise for the public."

"Direction?"

"Max Mars."

"Oh, very good indeed. Dance direction?"

"Jasper Saint John."

"That's quite a package."

"A Lyricart package," said Danny, "which is good because Lyricart can throw weight behind us in so many, many ways for promotion, guest appearances. And it makes the package more economical."

"Does it involve a kickback on commissions?" asked Callegarini sharply.

Lenehan looked at him expressionlessly. "We have no idea what you mean," he said.

"Well it's an impressive package, all but the one thing."

Larry Solomon broke his silence of several minutes. "I admire her. She's a professional."

"Granted, granted, but is she a draw? You've got a big investment here."

Lenehan said, "She has valuable intangibles. She's still married to Lincoln, which has a lot of space value. 'The happiest marriage in Hollywood,' 'Fifteen years of bliss.' All that stuff. Together they get a lot of ink."

There was a silence as the four looked at each other and then away.

Horler examined his fingernails carefully, drew a buffer from a breast pocket and began to polish each quaking fingertip. "Who knows," he said softly, meditatively, "but what they might draw more apart."

"There's nothing better for publicity than a really noisy divorce," said Lenehan. "Just suppose hypothetically that Seth found somebody new, while we were in production . . ."

"The kind of space you just can't buy," said Horler.

Solomon was silent, staring at his shoes through the glass tabletop.

"First the rumours, the short items in columns," said Lenehan, "then the reassurances that all is well between them, then the shots stolen through long-distance lenses, of an incriminating character. The whole bit."

Callegarini grew sharper yet. "It's not the kind of thing you can plan."

"One can but hope," said Lenehan, and he began to laugh. "I saw a little chicken on TV the other night, at an awards banquet, and I checked on her. You never saw anybody come on with sex like that, not on TV. She's with one of the smaller agents—I needn't specify—and would like to move up. She's had two parts in pictures now in release, besides some kind of stag movie she got mixed up in, and is available to us for a flat five hundred a week for fourteen weeks, plus options, say around seventy-five hundred for the picture."

"We'd never get her on those terms from Lyricart and we're grabbing her now," said Horler. "We'll steer her to Lyricart after, and they'll be grateful. Never hesitate to do a favour, that's my motto."

"Cast your bread upon the waters," said Lenehan.

"This girl will support Rose," said Horler. "Rose has the name, and she has the tits."

"Who?"

"My little chicken," said Danny, almost caroling.

Callegarini said, "What's her name?"

"Charity," gurgled Danny. Horler laughed and Solomon gave a thin smile.

"I know who you mean," said Callegarini, growing excited. The 'Hairbrush' girl. She can't be more than eighteen. Charity . . . Charity . . ."

"Ryan."

"That's the girl. A comer if ever I saw one."

"Rose gets the money," Lenehan said. "The little girl has to take small potatoes this time; seventy-five hundred is nothing. And, at that, it's more than she got in her first two pictures."

"She doesn't strain your salary item."

Solomon said "You're all crazy, you know. Rose has plenty of sex, and you're not smart enough to see it. I remember once she was on the cover of *Life* . . ."

"I remember that shot," said Lenehan, "but that was fifteen years ago. We all know what Rose projects, and it's good. It's right for this picture, but we need the other thing too."

"The bitchy slut thing?"

"That's good," said Horler, "I wish we could use it in the publicity, 'the bitchy slut thing.'"

"We'll put it in the press book. Faiers will love it," said Danny, turning to stare appraisingly at Callegarini. "Have we put your mind at ease?"

Callegarini took a stance like that of Napoleon before Toulon. "We will go ahead," he said solemnly. "I am authorizing the loan."

"For the full amount?"

He drew a deep breath. "Yes."

The telephone man came out of the bank with a festoon of phones, which he proceeded to arrange on the glass-topped table. Looking down through the glass, they could see their shoes linked in an amiable circle. Picking up the first receiver to come to hand, the serviceman said, "Operator, this is our conference call. That is correct, four parties here, two in New York."

"Why two in New York?" demanded Lenehan.

"We'll ask him right away. He likely has somebody taking a transcript."

"I believe Lyricart has all incoming calls bugged," said Lenehan, who had a suspicious and brooding nature. "Whenever I talk to somebody there I keep hearing clicking noises."

"You could be right," said Solomon, "that's occurred to me. I never tell them anything I wouldn't want repeated, or anything that the courts might construe as binding."

"You boys from the East," said Callegarini, tut-tutting with his tongue, "you're like a flock of James Bonds."

Horler gave him a dig in the ribs. "Better than a flock of defaulted bonds, eh? Ho ho."

"Oh, we won't lose any money on *Goody Two-Shoes*," said the banker, "and we might make a little."

"Here's your call, gentlemen." They seized the appropriate receivers, and heard the operator's voice tail off. " . . . from Los Angeles for Mr. Vogelsang . . ." There were random clicks and throat clearings.

"Who's there with you, Lambert? Is that Rose?" asked Horler.

"Hello?" said an evasive voice.

"Who is that, please?" said Danny.

"This is Miss McIntyre speaking. I have Mr. Vogelsang for you, operator."

Solomon muffled the mouthpiece and hissed viciously to Callegarini, "They always play this little game."

"Not with me," said the banker placidly.

Danny cried out impatiently, "Jan, put Lambert on, will you? Tell him to pick up the receiver." Vogelsang joined them suddenly.

"Just gone for a piss," his voice came across the continent.

"As long as it's on your own time," said Horler. "How are you, Lambert? Danny is here, and Larry, and Paul Callegarini from the bank's loan-review department. He says it's all systems go, so you can tell the lads in the office to fill their fountain pens."

Vogelsang simulated an effort of memory. "Let's see, that would be *Goody*, wouldn't it?"

"You were expecting maybe *The Adventures of Rin Tin Tin*?" snarled Solomon. "This is Horler and Lenehan, not some jerk on a shoestring, so pay attention."

There was mild reproof in Volgelsang's reply. "Just tell me what you want, fellows, and if I can arrange it, it's yours."

The producers ground their teeth. Solomon stepped away from his phone and took Callegarini by the shoulder. "This is routine. They want to make you feel they're doing you a favour. The fact is, Rose is at liberty just now—not that she's chronically unemployed, she's in demand—but she just finished a three-picture deal and isn't committed for the fall. Horler knows it; Lenehan knows it; Vogelsang knows it; and they all know we're going to bid for her."

"Will he try to rob you?"

"He'll get her the best deal he can, but the going price is pretty well established. It isn't like some nobody like Charity Ryan. Rose has a standard price for a picture, which varies proportionate to her percentage of the picture's earnings. The price moves up and down, depending on how her last picture did, but not in a very wide range. All her pictures do well."

"I've always admired her on the screen," said Callegarini, who had an indifferent wife. "She has a friendly quality."

Solomon said, "I'm very fond of Rose, and you're right about her quality. She has warmth and humanity, but it's all too unobtrusive. She'd be better off if she were more a bitchy slut."

They looked around at the promenading customers of the bank, and at the bathing girls. "Everything fits into banking somewhere," said Callegarini.

"Sex and money," said Solomon. "Bread and butter." They strolled away from the table, their heels clicking on the patio. At the parapet they halted, looked down at the street, offered each other cigarettes. Under the sporty umbrella the two producers swore into their phones, waved their arms, gestured broadly.

A naiad drifted up to Solomon, as he was replacing his cigarettes. "Could I have one of those?" she cooed, and he jiggled the package under her nose. "I haven't seen you before," she said, accepting the proffered light. "Are you new around here?" Callegarini eyed her with nervous disapproval.

"I'm not with the bank," said Solomon. He felt a strong urge to pat the girl's bottom, but refrained.

"That's a shame." She blew smoke in his face and retreated. "See you around."

"Sometimes we have trouble with recruitment," said Callegarini.

"Ah, she's just passing through on her way to stardom," said Solomon. "It's part of the legend, although I never heard of anybody being discovered on the roof of a bank in Santa Monica." He faced the friendly banker. "Don't worry about Danny and Bud. They'll protect your investment and so will I, although I'm not a production man. I'm a legal man, and I keep them out of trouble. They're just a pair of big kids." In the distance the big kids squabbled, shouting angrily at each other and into their phones. "Four hundred thousand and two-and-a-half percent of the net, and an option on her next picture. Want to bet I'm right?" said Solomon.

They got back to the table in time to pick up their receivers and hear Vogelsang make a liar out of Larry. "Four hundred fifty. Suppose we close on that?"

Lenehan raised an eyebrow at his partner, who nodded just perceptibly. "All right," said Lenehan, "with the option. Put an agreement in the mail at once, and we'll send you the contracts. We want Rose on the coast early in July. I'll see you're kept abreast of script developments. I think that's everything, Lambert. Anybody else want to say anything?" Nobody did, and they hung up.

"Why the extra fifty?" asked Solomon, slightly annoyed.

"You said it yourself. Rose isn't a troublemaker, so we'll try to keep her happy."

"Why should she want to make trouble?"

"She won't now. I've got some videotapes to show you boys." Solomon understood, and shut up. They all stood, smiled at one another, shook hands all around, and prepared to leave. "Say," said Paul Callegarini, "who was Goody Two-Shoes, anyway?"

The partners stared at each other. "Jeez," said Lenehan, "I got no idea. Have you, Bud?"

Horler said to Solomon, "Make a note we got to research that," and off they went. Callegarini watched them go. In a few moments the telephone man came out on the patio and started to pack up his equipment. He and the banker looked at each other and grinned. "Where was it?" asked Callegaiini.

"Here." He put his hand on one of the table legs at the top, where it flared out and was attached to the glass surface. He gave a slight pull, and showed the banker the tiny microphone. "It's extremely sensitive," he said.

Callegarini's grin widened. He said, "In matters like these it's important to have some record. Just to help keep things straight."

2

"Just a few more, Miss Ryan?"

Charity put her thumb in her mouth and dimpled. "As many as you like, Jack."

Outside the circle of photographer's lighting, a minor flack laughed to his friend, "She hardly waits to be asked." The friend, who was hanging around the studio feeling thirsty and not specially interested in the production, wishing it was time to go, said, "She's certainly well put together. Are you nearly finished?"

"A few words to say to the press." The publicity man left his thirsty friend and went over to where a clutch of touring entertainment editors were watching Jack shoot Charity. "Isn't she nice?" he exclaimed to them, feeling that his words were somewhat inadequate. He didn't think she was nice in any usual sense of the term. Rose was the nice one, but everybody knew all about Rose, and he had instructions to push Charity as hard as he could. He remembered asking her for a dinner date and blushed.

One of the press party asked, "She's been in what, two features?"

"That's right," said the publicity man, whose name was Eddie Blanda, "but this will be her first really big production. This picture may be the most expensive comedy with music ever made; no expense has been spared, and Horler and Lenehan are betting it will be one of the all-time top-ten grossers." It better be, he thought, or we're all in trouble. "Her first pictures did O.K., but they weren't in this league."

"How is she billed?"

"First below the title."

"That's a break for her, isn't it?" said a lady correspondent for a small string of dailies in Michigan, who didn't seem too pleased at the idea.

"Would you like to talk to her personally, Miss Adams?" asked Blanda. The other members of the group started to complain. "No, wait a minute," he said, "I could arrange a group interview, but it never has the warmth. Would you all like private, individual interviews with Miss Ryan?" All the men in the group quickly said yes. "We could schedule them for tomorrow," said Blanda, "because Charity isn't in the shooting this week. We could give you each ... let's see ..." He counted noses; there were seventeen of them. "It'll take two days, morning and afternoon, and we can give you each forty-five minutes, and we'll have a group luncheon on Thursday, with Miss Ryan there to answer any final questions. Prints of these shots will be available then, and I know she'll want to sign some for you, all you want. How does that sound?"

Only Miss Adams from Michigan rebelled. "I'd sooner talk to Miss Leclair and Mr. Dewar."

"We're visiting the set on Friday."

"Can we have private interviews with them?"

Blanda eyed the group. It was a familiar situation. As the stars were almost always completely absorbed in shooting, especially where complicated musical numbers were involved, it was standard practice to have some kind of substitute available as a stalking horse, a practice which sometimes had the effect of raising the stalking horse's status to that of stardom in the course of a single production. Judging by the male reaction this afternoon, Miss Adams' attitude would not be typical. He made a quick decision, guessing that the men here wouldn't mind too much. "If you're still around next week, Miss Adams, I'll try to arrange something just for you." He smiled at her engagingly. "Is it Rose you want to meet or Tommy?"

"I've met them both."

"Meet again."

"Rose if possible, she's such a sweetie. Does Mr. Lincoln ... Seth ... ever visit the set?" Blanda began to see where he was.

"He's been in a couple of times. The Lincolns don't have a house here this season; they just borrowed something in Pacific Palisades. They live in New York most of the time, I don't know why. I have to go to New York sometimes, but I figure Universal City and environs is God's country. Do you know, one thousand people settle in California every day? Historians say it's one of the greatest mass migrations in history."

"Do they say how many leave every day?" asked Miss Adams.

"I think the net inflow is a thousand."

"And yet Rose and Seth stay in New York. I wonder why."

"I don't know, Miss Adams. I don't feel it's any of my business."

"That's not like you, Blanda. Somebody's been putting words in your mouth."

He almost blushed. He'd been given express instructions not to discuss any aspect of the relations between Seth and Rose, to play down their happy union; he didn't know why. As far as anybody knew, their marriage was exactly what it had been for fifteen years, almost ideal. The instructions had come from very high up. The wisdom of Solomon was what Blanda considered them, and he asked no questions.

He said, "Pure decency, Miss Adams," and smiled. No minor flack around Universal City had ever been in any sense decent. Everyone knew it, but nobody dissented aloud. He led Miss Adams aside, while the others pressed closer to the scene of the action, where the still photographers were arranging new settings. "I'll work you into Rose's schedule the beginning of the week." He was as tactful as he could be. "What's your reaction to Charity?"

"My personal reaction?"

"Uh-huh."

"Saturday night in a Turkish whorehouse."

"Oh, now, she went to Redlands."

"Did she graduate?"

"She was in the music school, voice and organ. I don't think she has a degree."

"Not if she's barely eighteen."

"She's precocious, Miss Adams."

"I can see that. She's anything you like, a bomb, a great new star. I just don't like the look of her."

"Well, if you can't say something good, say something."

"You've got that wrong."

"No I haven't," he said, laughing.

"I'll say something," she promised. They turned and saw that Charity had gone to change. In seconds she was back, in a filmy black bra and bikini bottom, connected by fishnet; the effect was startling.

"Like casabas falling out of a crate," quoted a reporter reverently. Those who heard him laughed, or shuffled nervously. There was a sandbox under the lights with a trident in it. Charity knelt, grasped the trident, and arched her back magnificently; her audience sighed, all but Miss Adams.

"Look up, dear," said the photographer. Lights flashed and Charity's smile widened. The photographer's assistant stepped into the sandbox and rearranged her hair so that it fell across her face.

"Wind-blown," he mumbled, stepping out of the frame. "Pout," he said, and she pouted.

"Oh good, good," said the photographer. "Now stand up, angel, and turn around. Uh-huh. I want you to give us your cute little derrière, sweetie, push it at us, uh-huh, little more, fine. Now look over your shoulder." He spoke to his helper. "Mel, stick that spear in the sand for her, good and hard like she's just rammed it in. That's it." He said to Charity, "Look back and down, dear. Swing your hair back. A little bit savage with the grin, no, don't look at me, look back and down, like somebody was adoring you from behind and below. Atta girl." He made several quick exposures.

The crowd felt the heat; here and there a reporter shed his coat. In the peripheral shadows, Blanda's buddy wished the session was over so they could get a drink. But the photographer decided to work his equipment into some of the shots.

"Like on TV. We'll shoot the crew and the equipment, documentary style, very in. Charity, you stand beside the light standard while Mel adjusts it."

"What'll I do to it?" said Mel.

"How should I know? Anything you like; just look busy. You're only a prop. Now, Charity, look tired a bit, slump, not too much, try to look like you're working. Hmmmmn?"

"He should shoot her lying down," said a voice, and Blanda jumped. They wanted to avoid the whorey image. Charity exuded sex, but the hope on the production team was to suggest fairly clean sex, toothbrush sex as they called it, girl-next-door sex, not the big bomb. He noted that the speaker was a syndicate man called Harper Chandler who was notoriously proud of his adolescent cynicism. Wondering how to make him change his reaction, Blanda went over and put his hand softly on Chandler's shoulder. This time *he* jumped.

"Don't feel ashamed," said Blanda, "we all share the impulse."

"You're too smart for this job, Eddie. Isn't she something? Wouldn't she just melt in your mouth?"

"She's a clean young girl."

"Come *on*."

"Well, cleanish."

"Now you're closer. How do you intend to market this girl?"

"Fresh, unspoiled, naïve."

"I think you're very wrong."

"Why?"

"You're simply duplicating Rosie. Sell her as a dirty girl."

"Do you think she has it? It's very rare. Monroe and Bardot both kidded sex. Who takes it straight?"

"Jeanne Moreau."

"Yeah, but she's the only one, and at that she tells everybody that she's really a man. I don't think this girl has that."

"She has something. You don't like her much, but you want her."

"You might have something. Old Windy Adams hated her on sight."

"Sure, this one is a woman."

"Harperoo, you've given me cause for thought. I'm theenking."

"What are you thinking?"

"I'm hoping you'll be very kind to her."

"Do I write her like a bitch or like a blushing, budding Rose?"

"For the moment, fresh, unspoiled, naïve. I have my orders."

"Haw. Wait till you see these stills." The photographer had tired suddenly and dismissed the crowd. Blanda escorted Charity safely out of the throng and on her way home. Then he came back to pick up his pal and they went for a drink. He was thinking hard.

When the stills arrived he arranged them on his desk, whistled, looked again, slavered a little. Then he picked up the phone and made a formal request for an appointment with the publicity chief of the unit, a very polished pro from New York, originally an Englishman, named Graham Faiers, hard and smooth as they come.

"Mr. Faiers could see you at eleven-fifteen," said his secretary, "for fifteen minutes. Is that satisfactory?"

"It is for me, Miss Glenesk, but I should say that it may not be for Mr. Faiers. I really think I have something for him this time."

"Can you give us some idea what it is?"

"Certainly. It's the proofs on the wire service photo release on Miss Ryan."

"What about them?"

"Mr. Faiers may want to make a change in policy when he sees them."

"Are you suggesting that?"

"No, Miss Glenesk, I am not. I'm paid to take orders and execute them. I just think Mr. Faiers should see the pictures and hear what I have to say before I see our guests at lunch tomorrow." He got the appointment, telling himself that taking crap from secretaries was part of his job, which was very well paid. He was still well inside the limits of his servility. When he came into Faiers' office he even smiled at Miss Glenesk.

"Right to the minute," she said grudgingly.

"I don't want to waste your time or his. I know how busy you must be.

"Very considerate. Go ahead in."

He went through the door, acknowledged the boss's curt nod, and said quickly, "I thought you'd want to see the pictures." He displayed them on the desk and kept his mouth shut. As the silence lengthened and the boss lost himself in contemplation, Blanda crossed to an armchair in a dim recess and sat quietly down to wait. After Faiers had taken a careful look at each shot, he buzzed and Miss Glenesk came humbly in; it pleased Blanda to see how humbly.

Faiers said, "Make a note for an immediate memo to production. At the next publicity conference, consideration of alteration in status of Miss Ryan. When is that conference, please?"

"Nine-thirty tomorrow."

"Get that out at once, please. Suggest unusual press reaction. Suggest we evolve additional angles on her." He asked Eddie, "Who's seen her?"

"This week's press tour, seventeen altogether, syndicates, wire services, and six metropolitan dailies."

"What are you doing for them?"

"They all had the press book before they arrived."

"I should bloody well hope," said Faiers, "considering the trouble we went to to get it out." It was a very elaborate press book and they had worked it up in six weeks, starting the afternoon the producers got their money. They had had to do a lot of research on Charity—there was no standard line on her, as there was for Tommy and Rose. You talked about Tommy's clothes and his delivery of light-comedy dialogue, and you usually talked about Rose's happy marriage.

But Charity's case was like a novel proposition in formal theology. Condemnation of the first proponents, eventual withdrawal of the condemnation, the slow winning of acceptance, finally the triumphant definition of the proposition as dogma. In the same way, Charity would be a glimmer on the horizon, then a meteoric presence, then a glowing fireball, and at last a bright new star, coming into existence like the beginning of a universe. Faiers meditated this novel problem, oblivious to Blanda and Miss Glenesk until their coughing roused him.

He said, "We'll buck it up to the higher echelons. Would you get that memo off, Miss Glenesk?" She went on her way.

"What else?" he said to Blanda.

"She's seeing sixteen of these people, four in the morning and four in the afternoon, today and tomorrow."

"Who is the seventeenth?"

"Windy Adams." Miss Adams' name was Winifred.

Faiers smiled. "I should have known. Whom does she want to see? Not Tommy, surely."

"She likes Rose, and she apparently adores Seth."

"Who does?" asked Faiers, his mind leaping a few connections.

"The Adams lady."

"He's an attentive spouse. He'll be coming around. I wish we had a new angle on Miss Ryan."

They sat silently looking at each other.

Horler idled happily in the cockpit of his big cruising motor-sailer, peacefully moored at the north end of the chain of Santa Monica beaches. Spread across his lap were a number of crucial documents, cost estimates and projections of earnings. He was never happier than when studying such matters. He was more a money man than a production man, and had long since stopped regretting it. He bought and sold production men in accordance with his calculations, but the pleasure was in the pure calculation. His chief artistic and moral principle was his rooted objection to losses.

As he felt his boat rise and fall gently beneath him, quiet in the white August afternoon, in full flood of finance, he compared extrapolations of costs and earnings, and judged himself if not in imminent danger of a loss at least threatened by one; they were spending a lot of money. He thought uncertainly of the musical numbers, especially the Automat dream sequence, now in rehearsal ten miles across town; he thought about Rose Leclair and Jasper Saint John.

"Now Jasper, now Jasper."

"You can withdraw my credit from the titles."

"How do you mean?"

"I am not a hireling. I have worked with Balanchine. In the world of dance I am an important figure."

"We wouldn't have hired you otherwise."

"Then give me dancers to work with, not amateurs."

"Jasper . . . let me ask you this; Jasper . . . listen to me, will you, as a courtesy?"

"As a courtesy, since you put it so."

"Have you worked with the Ryan girl yet?"

"Not yet."

"Wait till you've rehearsed her, would you do that for me as a favour? Would you talk to me again when you've handled her?"

"I need respect as an artist," said Jasper.

"You have my fullest respect. Just give Miss Ryan a chance, give her your full attention. Speaking to you as an artist, Jasper, whose reputation is very valuable to me in terms of this production, I think I can assure you that Miss Ryan will satisfy your demands, as a dancer of course. Will you wait and see?"

"All right."

"You can mold her, Jasper, you can shape her."

"I have heard she is shaped already."

"As a dancer, as a dancer."

"I will do what I can."

"I ask only that," said Bud, wiping his brow.

Letting the breeze cool his sunburnt face, he lay back against the cushions and felt around with one hand for the sexy, almost dirty, pictures. He would have to go into the question when Danny turned up. Meanwhile, if he could just doze for a minute or two . . . He felt the boat rock under him, lulling him into an innocent drowse. He wasn't a young man, though he dressed and tried to think like one. He would be dead tired for the next three months—the first three to four months on a production were always his hard time. Afterwards the others had their turn at bat, the stars, the publicity people. He and Danny corralled the crew, put them in motion, then let them run within the limits set for them. Detail, detail, he felt exhausted; the boat cradled him. His fingers closed on the aphrodisiac envelope.

The boat rocked harder. Horler opened his eyes reluctantly and the sun glared in them. Danny stood over him, a black silhouette rimmed by sun.

"Pleasant wet dreams," he said.

"Huh?"

"From publicity?"

"You've seen them too?"

"They were passing out prints this afternoon at the studio. She's a discovery, no question about it. Let me have another look." They divided the pictures.

After a moment Horler said, "I don't see that there's all that much skin."

"Not a bit of it, not at all, not at all."

"I mean, they could go through the mails."

"She's a decent girl," said Danny.

"And yet . . . and yet . . ."

"It's that 'and yet' that will make her fortune, the darlin' little milkmaid. She bursts out of her clothes. Not many do that, and you can feel the flesh underneath, though you aren't allowed to peek. Look at her, she's a duck."

He seemed very pleased with his find. Horler felt mildly envious and said, "You only tied her up for one picture, isn't that so?"

Danny's face fell. "Quite right, the more fool I. I might have had her for three."

"But not for a long term?"

"They wouldn't hear of it, she and her piddling little agent."

"Has she got rid of that agent?"

"Yes. She's looking around for a new one."

"Lyricart?"

"I told you, she's looking around. She won't decide quickly. She knows a lot, in my opinion too much. I believe she knows how valuable she is."

"That's not good."

"It makes it hard for us to cheat her."

"We can cheat somebody else."

"There's always someone." Lenehan examined some folded estimate sheets while Horler watched his face. The noise of racing powerboats came across the water like the peaceful, unquarrelsome drone of summer bees.

"We'll be a bit short," said Lenehan suddenly.

"You really think so?"

"We're already a day or two behind and it'll get worse." He gestured vaguely towards North Hollywood, far away across town. "Rose is in four big numbers, very prominently, and briefly in a fifth. They're all going to run over."

"Max will arrange things. He can shoot around her."

"He's already talking about back-projections, a whole series of them."

"Can't she dance at all?"

"She's danced plenty. She danced in six pictures when she was under contract at Metro. Do you think I wouldn't check something like that?"

"Oh no, no," said Bud.

"She's like Crosby, who walked through dance routines for years, but nobody would call him a dancer; that was comedy. But Rose can't kid herself like that, no woman can. It isn't a woman's kind of comedy, if there is such a thing."

"We can't have her look silly."

"Max and Jasper will see to that. But I'm afraid her numbers will look obviously edited, no pow, no pizzazz."

"There's a million things Max could do," said Horler anxiously.

"Then there's her billing clause to think about." They sat beside each other in the boat and looked sad, like a stranded vaudeville team.

"There's still Charity," said Horler brightly.

"Graham wants to rewrite all the publicity."

"Not Tommy's too? I'd sooner wrestle a barracuda."

"All but his."

"Including Rose's."

"That's it."

"You know who's an even bigger star than Tommy Dewar?"

"I do indeed."

"Able to cause trouble with our distribution if he feels like it?"

"Quite right."

"We ought to make some kind of overture."

"We certainly ought."

After Seth had worked for the partners, they had wondered who had been working for whom. When he came in the door, followed by Hank Walden, his personal representative from Lyricart, their impulse was to put the lock on the safe and Satan behind them. Three times they had given Seth so much that there was little left for them, comparatively speaking. The one exception to the pattern had been *Sailor Take Warning*, which had starred Seth and Rose and featured Peggi Starr. It had been made when Seth had no real coercive power, and had done much to put him in the front rank. How he had bitched about that picture! He had been on salary with no percentage, and they had kept him to well under six figures by shooting to a very tight schedule, numbered shots, one take to a shot. He had never forgotten that, and when he saw Danny and Bud he treated them with the veneration a horse trader feels for a used-car salesman.

Seth wasn't a drinker, but sometimes he would take a second cocktail at lunch, and would then speak of Horler and Lenehan in very precise language.

"Bandits, assassins, thieves, thugs, murderers, robbers . . . aaaargh."

One day they heard him going on like this to a lady columnist syndicated by four hundred papers, and Danny had had to take the woman aside and threaten her with blackmail.

"Mark it DON'T USE, darling."

She stared at him, shocked that a producer should dare to speak to her like that. "Who do you think you're addressing?"

"That stuff isn't meant for your readers. We don't want to have to bring suit, so why not forget it?"

"Are you trying to intimidate me?"

"I'm not just trying, I'm succeeding." He stared at the woman very hard, without loosening his tight grip on her arm. "DON'T USE."

She felt an extreme anger. "It's columnists who frighten producers. Where do you get off with that crap?"

Lenehan looked at her with a blank level stare, saying nothing.

She rubbed her arm anxiously and tried to guess how much he knew about her, and to remember what she had been doing lately that was disgraceful and disgusting. There was plenty, but she couldn't imagine how he could know about it. He was just guessing, had to be guessing, but she didn't know for sure. She judged it wiser to submit now and plan future revenge. The trouble with Horler and Lenehan, she decided, was that they were criminal only in socially approved ways; that they lied, cheated, and intimidated was only what people expected and accepted.

"If I ever get anything on you, Danny dear . . ." She left the sentence hanging, hoping it would stay in his mind, and hopped off to another table, unwanted and unwelcomed wherever she alighted.

"Mercy me," she whispered to a terrified ingénue, "I haven't seen you since you were drunk in the studio at CBS." She sat uninvited and proceeded to extract intimate confidences from the hapless girl by the identical means that Lenehan had used on her, unvoiced threats of ridicule and exposure.

"You shouldn't talk like that in front of her," said Danny to Seth.

"I say what I like. And every word of it was true. I'm re-dedicating myself, Lenehan, to making you pay me too much money. From now on the lion's share comes to me, or else I won't play." He thought of his paychecks from *Sailor Take Warning* and cursed heartily. "I'll never make that mistake again," he said, and he never did, not that one, though he continued to make certain others.

"I'm damned glad he's not in *Goody*," said Horler.

"But Rose is."

"She's nothing compared to Seth, and Vogelsang is a babe in arms compared to that bastard Walden. We gave her four-fifty and a percent of the net. Think what Seth would ask for!"

"Title to the picture."

"Yeah. And if we start fooling around with Rose's personal publicity, he may want to make trouble."

"Does he care about Rose's personal publicity?"

Horler said, "Why do you think we're playing down the husband-wife bit?"

"I thought we might work it hard at Christmas."

"For God's sake, Dan. Are we making a family picture or an adult picture?"

"*Son of Flubber* grossed over seven million."

"But we're spending over eight. I think we've got to make a dirty picture. Not too dirty, so we have any trouble with the decency lobby, but good and dirty." He poked at the pile of photographs. "Sex it up, in short."

Lenehan said, "Up the Princess Margaret Rose," and giggled.

3

In a rented rehearsal hall in North Hollywood under the oppression of deep August heat, sweating in half-darkness, the *Goody* dancers prepare the Automat dream sequence, which Jasper hopes to block this morning. A crew member makes marks on the floor. With his chin cupped in his hand and a worried look on his face, in sweatshirt, tights, and ballet slippers, Jasper examines these guidelines as they are drawn. Next he watches the boy and girl dancers practicing steps and lifts at the other end of the hall, and finally he looks at Rose, who is off in a corner doing a set of limbering-up exercises he has given her. She wears a beige leotard which is unkind to her figure—she isn't very tall, but will seem taller in her dream headdress, all plumes—and a pair of soft, scuffed slippers. Like everybody else in the hall, she looks hot, upset, uncomfortable, and overworked.

Charity isn't in this number. The Automat stuff is mostly Rose's, and is important to the story line, which is why it has been scheduled early, when everybody is fresh, particularly Rose. They are going to have to lead her through it shot by shot, and a number like this is the hardest thing in the world to do. You have to make a non-dancer look great, while concealing the fact that the real dancers are creating the whole effect. Jasper has four boy dancers backing her up in this number, any one of whom could handle leads in all but the very best companies in the world, really technically accomplished people. It's no treat for them to work at half-speed while the nominal star is lousing up the routine.

Jasper calls the boys over for final instructions.

"We'll take it from B, and you'll be on this line, doing that shuffle I gave you. Can you show me that again? Walk through it, all of you."

The boys do a complicated sequence step in which Ray leads off with two fast bars, Elmer joins him for two bars of duet, Gene comes on to make it a trio, Harry is in for the next two bars and HERE Rose is supposed to spin and fall backwards into Harry's arms. This will run for ten seconds if we ever get it on the screen; the whole number is timed for close to five minutes. The sets, the score, the arrangements, dancers, musicians will send the cost of this five-minute strip of film way up into six figures, and this is the way we put it together, ten seconds at a time in this cheesy rehearsal hall, with everybody terrified and afraid to say anything, because the person on whose shoulders rests the responsibility for getting people into the theatre, the name, the box-office factor, is just barely staying in the number.

"One more time," says Jasper. "That looks clean."

They whistle through the pattern again, faster than before and with perfect precision; it looks superb. One of them, the tall blond boy named Ray Waites, perhaps the best male dancer on the Coast, has come on from several seasons as the male lead in the Royal Winnipeg Ballet and a subsequent stint on TV. Strictly speaking he isn't in the chorus. He's more or less bellwether to the flock, in all the numbers. The chorus learns the routines by watching Ray—he's very highly paid. Nobody who sees the picture will know he's in it, and yet the dance numbers would be ineffective if he weren't there. Jasper walks Ray off to one side, while Billy B. Jay, the assistant dance director, goes over to where Rose is standing by herself huffing and puffing. He nods to the rehearsal pianist, who strikes up a waltz. Billy seizes Rose around the waist and whirls her away from the walls onto the marked floor.

Dancers creep out of the gloom to watch Billy, a great dancer, for years a sensation in clubs with a partner who died a couple of years ago. Nobody waltzes like Billy B. Jay. He can even make Rose look fairly good. If you saw her in a dance hall somewhere on a Saturday night, you'd think her a pretty good dancer, certainly better than average. But put her in the arms of somebody like Billy or Ray Waites, and the difference between amateur and pro becomes apparent. It's the same in all the professions. Ray and Billy aren't as good as Rose at being movie stars, but they're better dancers.

Billy does what he can with Rose. They laugh together, and Jasper feels more hopeful. He looks around the vast old barn, once an armoury, and decides that despite the miserliness of Horler and Lenehan, and the inadequacies of the star, they may make something of the numbers after all.

It's dim in the hall, dusky, dusty. There are no windows at ground level, just tiny slits in the wall that admit scarcely any light, crusted over as they are with the dirt of decades. High up towards the roof in small classical wells, daintily recessed from the main walls, are the little windows that let in what light there is. Outside, the sun sizzles on the metal roof; passersby shade their eyes from the glare. The day is intensely hot; we haven't been on the picture more than ten days, and we're already feeling the heat.

Down in the great expanse of space under the metal crossbeams, pretty much in the dark, Jasper calculates. He asked the producers for proper equipment for the dancers, but there is none, not even bars to get loose on. He asked for a mockup of Rose's headdress from Wardrobe. If she's going to wear plumes nearly a yard long in the fantasy parts of the number, she should have something like them to rehearse in, to accustom her to the weight and to the drag on her head and neck, which will affect her balance. Trust Wardrobe to ignore all such requests. He still has no idea what the dancers will have on their feet. Probably patent-leather fake oxfords for the men. He doesn't know what for the girls. Girls in Automats are often cashiers. How do you fantasticate a woman cashier in a dream musical number? What does she wear? He looks at his watch. Nearly time for a midmorning break, and they haven't done anything apart from reassuring Rose, and he isn't even sure he's managed to do that. She and Billy make a last turn and come to a stop in the middle of the floor; the company dutifully applauds and Jasper steps forward.

"I want Rose, Ray, Elmer, Gene, and Harry down here, please. Billy will take the rest of you over your marks. Learn them as fast as you can, I beg of you. If we can rough out the number today, we might be able to think about shooting it next week. Supposing, that is, that they have something for you to wear. I can't have you cavorting about in the nude."

"I don't know about that," says Billy B. Jay.

"I'd love it, myself," says Jasper, looking at the girls and caricaturing lasciviousness. "But would our audiences love it?"

"Yes," shouts the assembled company.

"Then why don't we do it?"

Everybody groans.

"Let's take off all our clothes and run around in the lewd lewd nude."

Nobody moves.

"Built-in censorship," says Jasper mockingly.

Watching this byplay, Rose marvels at the loyalty the little director elicits from his people, like some pygmy king. In pictures, the dancers are a race apart, with their own kings and queens and hierarchies, like an obscure hiving system or pecking order.

In this complex society Jasper ranked at the top because of his gifts, his knowledge of what he wanted, and his really extraordinary talent as a teacher. Time after time he had worked miracles with unformed dancers, untrained people.

Rose knew that he had been engaged principally to work with her and lick her into shape, and she was ready to go just as far as she could with him. In the ten days since production had started, and for weeks before, she had worked, how she had worked. Driving out to Pacific Palisades every night, she was so stiff and tired she could hardly handle the steering wheel. Her thighs ached, and her buttocks, and her shoulders, and, above all, her calves and ankles. Many times she was sure she'd broken or chipped an ankle, the pain was so severe.

She had listened to everybody's advice, had gotten her weight down, started exercising months ago, slept a lot—the whole health bit. She had never been a party girl, and for the last few years had felt less and less wish to get around on the social circuit. When she and Seth were together in the evening nowadays, the most they would do was open a really good bottle of wine and drink a couple of glasses each. So she was feeling pretty good physically.

But she still couldn't manage Jasper's choreography, and didn't seem to be getting any closer to it. The girls in the chorus whizzed effortlessly through the air around her, as though they had steel springs for legs. They seemed to hang in the air as long as they willed it. She couldn't do it.

"Let's go, Rose," said Jasper, and she snapped to attention. The chorus was at the other end of the hall, boys and girls chasing each other in complicated Bacchic coils, typical Jasper Saint John direction.

"They look good," said the director as he walked her along towards the piano. "It's going to be a sensational number. Now just watch me, Rose, and I'll show you. Easy now."

The pianist began the dream music and the familiar theme made Rose feel nervous. She nodded at Jasper obediently.

"All right," he said, "it's up to Max to look after the frames that bring you into the situation in your street clothes. You walk along the serving areas looking at pieces of pie through the glass. And then you see from your reflection in the little windows that you aren't in street clothes any more. You're in spangles and a plumed headdress. Your eyes pop. I love the way you pop your eyes, Rose dear, it makes you look about twelve. THEN we cut to Medium Shot, and the boys leap up behind you on that chord. Give her the chord, Mitch."

The pianist hit it good and loud.

"They're standing behind you—Ray, Elmer, Gene, Harry, in that order from left to right. You whirl and face them. I'll show you the twist I want. It has to come very sharp and fast and you hold your arms stiff like this. Energy and menace, force, the left thigh cocked out forward like this, see? Point the toe, stab it out! Hard. That's better."

She made the whirl a couple of times.

"I wouldn't be surprised if they use a shot of you in that pose for most of the publicity layouts. They can shoot it from a low angle and you'll look taller. And remember, you'll be wearing that headdress; be ready to cope with that."

She nodded, docile and willing.

"Now watch me," ordered the director, standing in front of her with his arms jabbed stiffly in the attitude he'd described. He was a wonderful mime. Instantly, with no change in his clothes or manner, he became a girl, his movements were exactly those of a young girl dancer, his timing, the whole nuance of his body line. He did a little strut and then stuck his tongue between his teeth and jumped, BANG. There was Rose, or his idea of Rose, standing in the Automat; you could almost see the spangles and the plumes. He did the twist he showed her; another chord from the piano and he fell into Harry's arms, sure that Harry would catch him, with just the sureness that Rose didn't have. She wasn't getting to the right place at quite the right time . . .

. . . and the plumes held her back and the boning in her spangled bodice felt uncomfortable and irritating after days and days of unrestraining rehearsal clothes. When she tried to soar, the headdress dragged her down, making her an ungainly and unimpressive figure on camera. On the colossal sound stage the music crashed in on multiplex stereo in ultradimensional fidelity with tiptoematic voom and the rest of it. They would mime, shoot, dub, mime again, shoot again, try for something like a decent sync, again, again. It's a crazy costume, she thought, flipping along the line of dancers, rolling from Harry to Gene to Elmer to darling old Ray, her mentor. She loved Ray, who had guided her through this, step by step, who would guide her through four more numbers the same way. She smiled at him as she came up from the last turn of the four and he made the lift, planting his broad palms softly but firmly at the top of the hipbones and with a smooth and immensely strong motion of his forearms moving her forward and up to where she must sparkle and look gay. He lowered her and she ran, with what dignity she could manage and as gracefully as possible, between two rows of ostensibly singing choristers dressed rather romantically as customers, some waving pieces of pie, others with trays of prop dishes, still others with parcels and boxes.

On the prerecorded tape the inane lyrics of the number blared out in a complicated crescendo in quadruple counterpoint plagiarized from Bach. Male and female customers, and Automat employees, forming a conventional S.A.T.B. choir, were supposed to be singing:

SOPRANOS:	Quarters, dimes and nickels,
	Jingle in your pocket.
ALTOS:	Jingle in your purse,
	Jingle in your purse,
TENORS:	Just a little piece of change
	All alone in old Manhattan.
BASSES:	Gonna go from bad to worse,
	Gonna go from bad to worse.

This number, "A Little Piece of Change," about which Max and Jasper have been sharing grave doubts, has somehow evolved into the principal musical spot in the picture.

Barbara has come uptown from West Tenth Street alone, for the first time since she and Goody hit town. They have been quarreling, and wonder if they might not enjoy themselves more if they broke up, so they won't be competing for the same men. Barbara has been looking for modelling work all day; now she's tired, footsore. Maybe a change would be the best thing for both sisters. She realizes that it's time she had something to eat, because she is faint with hunger and very dispirited. She sees the big electric sign: AUTOMAT, standing out like a dream image among a cluster of lights. She stops in the middle of the sidewalk to count her money; all she can find is seventy-five cents, two quarters, two dimes, and a nickel.

CLOSE-UP: the silver in her palm. Cut to:

MEDIUM LONG SHOT: Barbara going through the doors. We see her through the glass. Chorus up under with the verse of "A Little Piece of Change," and we cut to:

MEDIUM CLOSE SHOT: Barbara wandering along the row of little windows, looking at the food and the prices. She sings, recitative:

A little peace. A little change.
Gotta get away from Goody.
The best way out for all of us.
Just a little piece of change.

Max hasn't been too happy about these lyrics. He's been making a lot of remarks about the good old days in Berlin with Bert, Kurt, and all the boys.

Barbara looks from the money in her hand to the window with the pie behind it.

And

POW into spangles and plumes—the dream sequence—as she takes the fall into Harry's arms and rolls along the row and UP UP, EASY NOW, UP. Ray boosts her outward and down and she runs between the chorus rows. Chorus chants:

Gotta get away from Goody,
Gonna go from bad to worse.

Down down down to the back of the set; we see her tiny figure sparkling and shining in crossing bands of different coloured lights. Now the chorus is ranked along the serving windows, which flip open and shut, and we get a good feeling of thirties comedy, something from *Modern Times* perhaps, the automatic restaurant, the man in the machine. The chorus starts to feed the slots with coins; they seize the food. Some are eating and others run in a long circling line past us into the background, where they dance around tables and chairs.

We see Barbara running along an enormous steam table, kicking the lids off the holes, with a manager in a cutaway chasing her, followed by cooks in tall white hats, busboys with trays, dishwashers. We see that she is carrying a platter with a whole turkey on it, tripping and cursing to herself as she accidentally puts her foot into the steam-table holes, instead of just kicking away the lids .

"Christ, she'll never do it. Look at that."

"Who choreographed this?"

"Never mind that," says Jasper indignantly. "Who thought up the idea for the number? Not me. I've done the best I could."

Rose tries her run along the steam table for the fifth time, carrying a light metal disk painted to look like a platter, with a papier-mâché turkey glued to it. I'll break a leg in one of those holes, she thinks—and just misses doing it. What the hell am I doing here, in this ridiculous getup, at my age?

Things are getting very fugal:

Gotta get away from Goody.
    (Quarters, dimes and nickels
    Jingle jingle in your purse.)
Just a little peace, a little change.
    (Just a little piece of change,
    Gotta get away from Goody.)
Gonna go from bad to worse.
A little peace
    (A little piece of change.)
A little change
A little piece.
    (All alone in old Manhattan
    It's the best way out for all of us.)

And into a choral "Amen" on "Manhattan."

SOPRANOS:	Ma, aaaa, aaa, aaa, haaa, aaa, aaa,
ALTOS:	Ah ah ah ah, ah ah ah ah,
TENORS:	Maa, aa, aa, hat, ha, aaa, aaa, aaa,
BASSES:	Ha, aa, tan. Ha aa, tan tan. Ha aa tan.

And soon.
"We'll have to back-project that."
"Or a mat shot."
"Yes," said Max, "a traveling mat."
"Oh my poor number," said Jasper, and he wept without restraint, while Ray, Elmer, Gene, and Harry, one to a limb; caught Barbara as she leaped off the end of the steam table in front of an enormous blowup of one of the little windows with a sign over it saying: STRAWBERRY PIE 15¢ SLICE, The four boys swung Rose forward and she came whizzing down a ramp like a piece of Automat pie, headfirst out of a window on her stomach, wearing a triumphant grin. But being swung like that made Rose sick to her stomach; no matter how many

times they did it, she couldn't muster up the necessary grin of triumph.

"Never mind," said Jasper at the last, "I'll fix it. I'll fix."

4

Max Mars studied the writer's instructions to the art director, and after a while felt satisfied:

> . . . the interior of a basement apartment on West Tenth Street, featuring a pair of folding doors or French windows which allow access to a tiny front patio below sidewalk level and screened by wrought-iron gratings. You could put a couple of small tables out there. People can go back and forth from apartment to patio quite easily. Any such apartment would cost like hell, of course, but it shouldn't look that way. It should look like the kind of place two ignorant sisters from Canonsburg, Pa., might accidentally find, a real jewel.

It would be hard to set up for, because of the goings-out and comings-in off that damned patio. But the patio falling-in-love scene had so much charm they had decided tentatively at last Friday's story conference to leave it in. Max shuffled his papers while the crew moved the wrought-iron gratings. He checked the synopsis:

> . . . while Goody is in the living room dancing quietly around, Barbara wanders out onto the patio, before which all New York passes sooner or later. We see polished shoes, trouser legs. We are eight or ten steps below sidewalk level and we watch with Barbara's eyes as a poodle

happens along at the end of a leash and puts a friendly nose through the grating. She says, "Hello, poodle," or something in character (see dialogue sheets) and the dog kisses her. We see that she is lonely and glad to see this friendly, if woolly, face. A voice above her says, "I'll be glad to stand in for him, if his nose is too cold," and then we see dog-walking Dino (change the shot???) on the other end of the leash.

What Max was after was a distinct tone, not *chic* and not New York sophistication, but the unique Max Mars dry witty gravity, which was completely adult and whose last lingering impression was of an extraordinary sadness. Horler and Lenehan, who knew nothing whatsoever about direction, or how films are actually conceived and made, had never understood him. Max figured if they knew how sad a man he was they would never have given him this assignment.

His pictures were like certain wines, having as many as four distinct effects on the palate, at first light and sweet, then heady, then bitter and cutting, and finally vanishing, evanescent, haunting, whatever the word was for some lost intense pleasure now irrecoverable. When a Max Mars comedy registered with you, you felt at first exhilarated and joyful, then intoxicated with laughter, then struck and self-critical because of the moral overtones, and then suicidally depressed.

Maybe not quite suicidally. He didn't want his audiences running to the sea like lemmings; he wanted them to be oppressed by a sense of loss. All Max Mars comedies tried for this fourfold effect, and often got it. He was a serious artist.

He said to the cameraman, "Shots 106 to 114 can be handled with two cameras, but for shots 98 to 105, and for those after 114, down to 120 in your copy of the shooting script, we will use three, eh? There's no need for more."

"Number Three on the boom?"

"Yes. On the patio a pair of angles will do; we'll choose between Rose and Tommy when we edit. But for the interior we'll want variety. We'll try some three-shots from crowd distance to get emptiness and aloneness."

"That sets up the party."

"Right. On the patio we'll try for a tunnel effect with Two, set it up on the patio and shoot in, do you see, so we get distance and intimacy, like looking through a keyhole, a nice effect."

"Eavesdropping?"

"In a sense. Every moviegoer is a voyeur, eh?"

The cameraman wandered off to think this over, and to set up the patio shots. Time wasted, Max thought. About one-third to half the time it took him to make a film, he realized for the thousandth time, was spent standing around waiting for several different groups of people to finish their work. Directing a movie was like conducting a battle from an unhandy command post, except that a general had a staff and an intelligence service and a logistics team to supply his wants, whereas most of the co-ordinating on a film had necessarily to be planned by the director, who decided what the unit would do today and what they would do tomorrow unless it rained, in which case they would do something else, or something else.

He wasn't looking forward to tying in the musical sequences, which he'd sooner have omitted completely. That decision, at least, had not been his. Officially they were producing a "comedy with music," which wasn't a musical comedy, or just a comedy, but a hybrid. Like most hybrids, Max thought, the form had the defects of its parents without their virtues. He hadn't told Horler and Lenehan that, and he intended to make an excellent picture, though not exactly the picture the partners had projected.

In a spaghetti-like nest of heavy cables in a corner of the sound stage, Rose, Charity, and Tommy were reading lines.

He watched them from a distance and marveled, as he always did at the sight of actors at work, that three people could share the same professional psychology so plainly, the actor's need for attention and love and his hysterical need to verbalize and dramatize, and nevertheless in such totally distinct ways.

Tommy never made a waste motion when he was working, and the rest of the time he dawdled and idled, saving himself. He knew how old he was.

Rose kept trying to be a good person. A word he hadn't used in decades crossed Max's mind, virtuous. That's it, he thought, Rose is virtuous. If she had just a bit more talent, she'd be a great woman.

Charity. Blotting paper. Never took her eyes off you if you could teach her something. She was watching everybody on the sound stage with total absorption, entranced with the way Tommy read his lines, with Rose's professionalism and her status . . .

. . . *he's here every day or he has been, and it looks like he will be, whenever Rose is working. You'd think that she'd introduce us, not that she isn't nice, and she couldn't possibly have anything on me. She hasn't thought of it, that's all, she's so sweet. Everybody says she's so sweet, you get sick of hearing that. I'm not nice. I wonder exactly how old she is. The date is in her official biography, 1933, but she might be older. She doesn't look older but you can never tell with the stars. They get all the attention, the best appointments at the hairdressers, more fittings than anybody, better numbers. She'll have twice the footage I'll have, and look at the way Max Mars treats her, as though she was a queen and I was one of the peasants. I wish I could hurry it up. I'll be a star pretty soon. One more picture if I'm lucky, two or three at the outside. I can feel it. There he is.*

He sits in the shadows like he was scared or something. Why wouldn't he just come right out and speak up? Whispering in the corners with his wife. His wife. I wonder what they do together

when they go home. What do you do? When you're in your thir-
ties, although he doesn't look it, he looks in his late twenties and
hardly anybody else does. And he's rich, boy, is he rich. He owns
scripts and part of a recording company and he has money in
the agency. What about that agency anyway?

Mama says to display myself and I'm ashamed to do what
she says; it's immodest. But I guess I have to; that's what I'm
going to be, a sexpot. I wish it was different. I wish I could be a
lady like Rose. She isn't a great lady of the screen, like Deborah
Kerr, but she's a lady, you can tell it a mile away. I wonder what
they do alone together. Would they go to nightclubs? I've been in
the movies two years now, counting "Hairbrush," and I've never
been to a nightclub, why is that? I'd like that, but I don't have
the time. If they're going to bill me as a sex bomb, they ought to
start letting me get around a bit, because it would help with the
promotion.

There he is, looking at me. Think I can't tell?

In the dark like he's hiding something. And there's Tommy,
Max always calls him dear old Tommy Dewar when his back
is turned. Some kind of joke. He must be a million years old,
and he's the boy star . . . isn't that a laugh. Imagine with him . . .
imagine . . .

". . . we're ready for positions," Max said, crossing to them.
"What about walking through some of them, just for size?"

Tommy was notoriously slow with lines, and he looked
worried. "Are we shooting before lunch?"

"Yes, the patio shots, numbered 106 to 114 on your script.
We won't get them all in this morning, naturally, but we might
get three. It's all on this week's schedule, Tommy."

"I know, Max, I know. I don't have too much to say anyway." He looked more hopeful.

Charity said, "Mr. Mars doesn't believe in improvisation."

One of her credits, the first, was a famous subterranean
film made on 16 mm just before she left Redlands, a comic

study of sado-masochism in the adolescent female—she had wanted to be spanked by a series of dominant types—which had not of course had commercial distribution and which had been improvised as they went along by a group of friends. It had a certain impact on any audience and prints had drifted East by this or that illicit route, to provide Charity with a reputation before she made a commercial film. It hadn't exactly been a dirty movie, though it was undeniably provocative. It was just a piece of experimental art with the unquenchable innocence that much of that kind of art has. There were some fresh angles in the film and some beautifully composed frames.

Max spoke a little dryly. "I've had my European training, Charity. I knew Murnau and Lang in the twenties. Do you know what I call improvisation? I call it UFA 1930. Everything recurs." He noticed, while he was talking, a tallish, thinnish, wry-looking, dark-haired man, standing at some distance from them, a little diffidently, as though unsure whether he ought to be on the set or not. He shouldn't, Max thought, but there he was.

Charity said, "Just because it's been used before doesn't mean you can't use it again."

Tommy Dewar said, "It's harder than learning dialogue, if you ask me. I couldn't ad-lib a fart."

Charity turned on him fiercely, very young and strong. "Have you ever tried?"

"Certainly. When I was in my twenties, forty years ago, I toured with a concert party as compère and feed, and we used to invent blackout sketches on standard situations; we made them up as we went along and audiences loved them. But you can't do that on a sound stage."

"Oh, you always say that; somebody always starts to talk cost."

"It's simply a question of what effect you want," said Max. "If you want informality, poor picture quality, and constantly changing sound levels, to give you the 'just-shot' effect, then by all means use a hand-held camera on a street corner. You may get a wonderfully actual feel. But if you want to do an elaborate musical number, or tricky special effects, you need a stage and a lab and a movieola with five screens."

"Five screens? Is there such a thing?"

"Charity, Charity, you're the experimentalist, not me," Max said. "Anyway this sound stage is costing Bud and Danny thousands per day, so let's apply ourselves to our duties, if you'll kindly step this way." They wandered over to the set, and as Max passed Rose, he took her gently by the arm. He said, "Seth is over there. Would you do me a favour? Tell him we're all set to go. If I can get a couple of good takes on three shots we can break early for lunch, and we can all talk then. I'd be glad if he didn't interrupt us right now."

"He knows the name of the game, dear. I'll be right back." She trotted over to her husband, put her arms around him, not demonstratively, and kissed him. Max watched them talk, and in a few seconds Rose turned away from Seth, let go of his hand unwillingly, and came smiling towards the director.

"All he said was, 'The lower the costs the bigger the net.' Seth is a real pro."

"I like Seth," said Max, quite truthfully, leading her onto the patio. "You've wandered out here," he said, "while Goody is looking over the rest of the apartment. Now you're alone, and this is where we begin to establish your quality."

"What is my quality?" asked Rose, smiling at him affectionately.

"That sounds like the New Testament. Who is my neighbour?"

"Well, who is? I mean, what is?"

"You are warm, womanly, whimsical."

"I'm the letter 'W' in fact. Witty, wise, wonderful, womblike."

"Let me come to it slowly," he said. "You are not, repeat not, to hide your light under Goody. You come across slower, but in the end you eclipse her, you have a fineness. Anyway we get you stepping out onto the patio; we hear you humming to yourself; your voice is warm and womblike and all that, an Alice Faye quality. Twilight is coming. We change the shot, and we see the legs going by; we're over your shoulder. Goody says, 'Oh, Barb, it's simply heaven,' off, and you say, 'Heaven,' pause for two beats, 'Heaven eight steps down.' Shot of the poodle through the grating. Two-shot, you and the poodle, set up from two angles I have in mind, very sweet, very beguiling. Then the shot of you, the poodle, and dog-walking Dino's legs and feet, and into the dialogue. O.K.?"

"Got it."

Max gave Charity a few exercises in the living-room set to get her used to its proportions. She had never been in New York. "Is this set authentic?" she asked.

"A little romanticized, but yes, you might find such a place on West Tenth."

"It doesn't feel right to me."

"No, but then you're not the designer, and it's not your worry."

"Right, chief," said Charity, saluting. She began to work hard.

Max went back to the patio, squared off his actors, and made a few takes. Things went very briskly so that they had three short shots in printable form just before noon. Patience, Max thought, *patientia*, the waiting game, slow work. Out of all that, they might have a minute of screen time, if they were lucky. Some days went better, some not so well, and their shooting schedule was getting tight; they were supposed to be out of the sound stage by the first week of November but they weren't going to make it. It wouldn't be his fault, and wouldn't cost him any dough. His percentage came off the gross, though his cash fee was smaller than, say, Rose's, and it wasn't directly in his interest to keep costs down. He was therefore easier to work with than in the old days when his own money had been at stake and when he had been a one-take demon. Nowadays he would shoot twenty takes if necessary, to get exactly what he had in mind. His pictures reflected his imaginings more accurately than formerly, and they had lost a certain spontaneity. Max thought this a positive gain in his work; it was more formal, more finished.

But some of his critics, mainly in France, mourned the old slapdash Max Mars of the days of his collaboration with Brecht. Max didn't. He often said with his charming smile, "I like to eat well and live comfortably."

"We'll break for lunch," he told the crew, and strode off the set.

Seth Lincoln was sitting in a corner out of everyone's way, and he was puffing meditatively on a cigarette and turning the pages of a paperback book when Max approached him.

"Do you want to eat with us?"

"All together?" Seth had known Max for twenty years. He displayed the cover of his book, *Around the Mountain*.

"You should read these."

"Nobody reads short stories," said Max. "The food here isn't bad."

"We were going to anyway. Rose likes a slow lunch."

"Then we can use my table. Let me see, there's you, me, Rose, Tommy, that's four."

Seth looked aside delicately. "Aren't you forgetting . . . ?"

. . . he's staring, wouldn't you think she'd say something, she knows I'm in the picture after all, even though we haven't done much together. "Oh, Barb, it's heaven," off camera, and she gets all those close-ups. You'd think Max was in love with her, the way he gives her the play. What I need is a song. If I just had a song or a dance number of my own. I know what I'd wear, one of those sort of beach-pajama outfits, only in satin, and I'd have them drooling. That's awful, I shouldn't think like that, but they keep telling me to show it off.

Lines, look at him sweat, the old bag. I can learn twenty pages in under an hour, and Tommy wets his pants over five lines, what a pro. But his delivery, mamma mia, what a style he's got, and it doesn't much matter how you learn lines if you can read them like that. He's got that over me, and she has too; she speaks up nice and plain. I'm your big sister Barbara, Good-dy, and I'll look after you, Good-dy. So clear and sharp. I never knew there was a California accent, but that's what I've got. A sexpot with a California accent. Shit.

Look at the way Tommy moves, so smooth, you can hardly take your eyes off him, and the way he wears his clothes, the only one who's any better is Rex Harrison; he has beautiful sweaters, Tommy has. They both have. But Tommy really has wonderful sweaters. I wonder why men don't sweat in those sweaters, even with the sleeves rolled up. They look so bulky . . . satin beach pajamas. I'll show them.

I wish Mama would stay away from the set, she's going to get us in trouble if she isn't careful. She doesn't know as much as she thinks, and anyway from now on I can arrange my own contracts, and nuts to her. She's the one got me started as a California sexpot and I've got to get away from that sometime or I'll never really make it big. You can go just so far and then they start to laugh at you, like poor Jayne Mansfield. I don't want anybody laughing at me.

. . . looking at me . . .

I want to get away to New York maybe or to Europe, get some good clothes, get away from the surfers. I've got to make people forget I was ever in that beach-party stinker. Lines, boy, can he read.

"Forgetting what?"

"You're putting me on, Max."

"Charity eats with her mother."

"Ask her to join us."

"I'll have to ask her mother too."

"Is that so bad?"

"Yes."

"Oh," he looked foolishly disappointed. "In that case, do as you like, Max, it's your table." He turned away to Rose, who was gabbing happily with Tommy as they came up. He watched his wife closely; he had always rather liked her work, and she was going to be very appealing in the straight scenes, though maybe not in the dance routines. Max can get her through, he thought, if Jasper will co-operate. He took her arm. "Lunch with Maximilian?"

"Oooooooo, with the boss," said Tommy. "Goody."

"Speaking of Goody," said Rose, and then she was interrupted. A stout woman with beads and red hair bore down upon them, announcing herself with enthusiasm. Rose squeezed Seth's arm secretly.

"Dear good people," said Mrs. Ryan.

"You should see her with Lenehan," whispered Rose.

" . . . to ask my daughter and me. We'll make it a party, Mr. Dewar."

"Oh, that'll be delicious. Not too much of a one though, because we all have to work this afternoon."

"Naughty," she said, "naughty. I haven't met this gentleman."

Rose choked down frantic laughter. "Ah," she said, "sure now, and ye've often seen him on the silver screen."

"I have that, but we've never been properly introduced."

"Mrs. Ryan, may I present my husband, Mr. Lincoln?"

"You may."

"Seth, this is Mrs. Ryan, Charity's mother."

He considered her and the bachelor's myth that the daughter will grow into the mother. Would lissome Charity ever become slab-sided Mrs. Ryan, thickening and becoming intimidatingly loud? Christ, what a mother-in-law, thought Seth. He said pleasantly, "How do you do, Mrs. Ryan."

"May I call you Seth?"

"Oh sure, sure."

"I feel as though I'd known you all my life. I believe I've seen all of your pictures, especially those you and your wife made together. She's such an essentially sweet person, isn't she?"

"Essentially, yes."

"So fine."

. . . Rose is good too when she reads lines. I don't know where she comes from but she really sounds like somebody. You can tell she's had people waiting on her for a long time. She has that smoothness and you can't buy it. I think I could develop it after a while, but then I'd be as old as she is. Men make me laugh. When she moves or reads, she comes over sharp and fast, and yet they think that I'm the sexy one because I bounce around the way I do. All right, Mister Mars, I'll bounce and let's see if you can spot it. Jasper would catch me right away, but he isn't here. Now Jasper I can work with, my God, what a dancer.

Lunch already? We haven't done anything. Oh-oh, here comes Mama, and she's got him. I haven't seen a thing. I'll just go along ahead. I know what he's thinking about, standing there in the dark watching me jiggle. Little Good-dy knows, baby, yes she does. What's everybody having? Lettuce leaves and tea, no cream, that figures. That's no meal to work on, I'm hungry, I want to eat, I'll have five dollars' worth of studio food, ham, strawberry pie.

I could have him in two minutes.

What's she want?

"Seth, this is Charity Ryan."

Rose had gone ahead with Tommy, and he was glad she wasn't present. He thought the situation grotesque, but his cardinal principle supervened, never offend a fan—a reflex, wholly subliminal. He let himself be borne along on Mrs. Ryan's flood of rhetoric as they came to the commissary. Looking across the room with relief, and with the sense of having endured much, he saw that Charity was sitting at their table between Rose and Tommy. He crossed the bright room quickly, with Mrs. Ryan trotting behind, and came to the table in time to give his order with the rest.

As usual Rose had asked for lettuce, low-calorie dressing, carrot slices, and tea with lemon. He saw with a curious sensual pleasure that Charity wanted ham and potatoes, and pie for dessert, and yet her skin was unmarred. She must dance it off, he thought, and he lowered Mrs. Ryan into a chair beside him, turning to her and smiling.

Rose said, "Seth, this is Charity Ryan."

"I'd already guessed," said Seth, looking from one to the other, making comparisons.

5

Though of Russian extraction and temperament, Jasper Saint John was wholly Americanized and an ardent baseball fan. He drew many analogies between baseball and the dance, considering them equally rhythmic and stylized, and equally dependent on exact timing.

"Those neat flannel clothes," he would exclaim, "so turn-of-the-century. You people don't appreciate your game." He would mime the pitcher's motion to first. "Delicious white or gray on green shadows, and the exact proportions of the diamond." He loved boxing too, but baseball was second only to the dance in his heart. When he complained about Rose, it was by comparison with the decline of the great DiMaggio.

He sat in the darkened screening room and they all heard his voice go on. "I tell you how it is. In 1951 the book on Joe D., the World Series scouting report for the Giants, had the whole story: 'Reflexes gone. Arm gone. No longer gets around on the ball.'" They all felt that there was justice to Jasper's complaint. They had just watched rushes of the apartment-party number, originally designed as a showstopper, with four dozen dancers and the principals executing a very complex routine in a television-sized set, an almost impossible problem for Jasper which he had almost brought off. Watching the results, he was heartbroken.

"Do you see what I mean? She's swinging late. Look, look, there, do you see? The dancer is there, ready to make the lift, but she's two steps away from the base. There is no way for me to correct that. It is not my fault." He kept up a running commentary, and Danny, Bud, Max, the projectionist, and Paul Callegarini, visiting the set in the role of amateur—or so he said—listened to the gifted little man and believed him.

"I love her," said Jasper, "but she can't dance. Now watch, here's the little Ryan."

His audience was enchanted as Charity whizzed through the air to land precisely at the appointed spot in the arms of a dancer in the working clothes of the New York Fire Department who carried a prop nozzle. Charity made a funny face as she saw the nozzle, patted it affectionately, smiled incandescently at the dancer, flipped his enormous helmet down over his eyes, whirled away and executed the rest of her routine.

"That's not classic dancing," said Jasper. "She has not had the classic training and her ankles and thighs are not up to really heavy work, but she can do what you give her. You can even give her quite a lot to do, and the dance talent is there, which is rare amongst cinema people. She could work her way into a ballet company if she wanted. I don't believe that she could ever dance leading parts, but she might. Anyway that's not her business. She's an extremely talented musical-comedy star."

She had everything but humour. She had enormous sex; she could sing right in the middle of the note, and awfully loud. She could dance, and could read lines better than adequately.

Best of all, she had the irreplaceable thing. She bounced out of the screen at you, and no matter what she wore, you sensed instantly the flow and the smooth firm texture of the flesh underneath. It was a killing vitality, an almost smothering health. They babbled about it among themselves.

"Let Mr. Saint John go on with his story," said Horler.

"How I worked on this routine! Every dancer knows just what he has to do. Nobody has done this before, in a film musical, handled so many people in such a small space. Similar things have been done on television, but out of necessity, not as free design. It is a highly ingenious conception—and my star is letting me down."

"Where is Tommy?" asked Callegarini.

"Oh, he's a joke. The whole world knows that Tommy can't dance, so we simply have him fall over his feet and retire to the patio."

"He doesn't dance at all?"

"He did forty years ago," said Lenehan, "but he doesn't attempt it now. Have you ever heard him sing? He's not at all bad, a pleasant light tenor, but he doesn't do it in pictures. Not his business. Tommy is very shrewd."

"Shrewder than Rose," said Callegarini, who might not have paraded it publicly, but who liked Rose a lot. Lenehan had introduced them at a party, and the banker had afterwards invented a lot of excuses to come out to the studio pretty often. His motive seemed clear, and the partners often snickered about it.

"When the bankroll loves the star, the producers grow fat," Lenehan would say, although he was sure that the bankroll would never confuse love with money.

"She shouldn't try these things, like poor Joe D.," said Jasper.

Horler said, "Does anybody think she's actually hurting the picture? She's a pretty solid draw."

"Let Jasper say what he thinks," said Max.

"He has the most at stake," said Horler.

"I would not want it thought that I was unable to stage these numbers properly."

"Isn't that obvious?"

"Even if it were, you don't want bad numbers in the film. A quarter of the footage will be devoted to them. They're the most important aspect of the picture. I have my reputation to consider, and you have a big investment to protect. Rose is equally inept in all five numbers. Let me show you more."

He went onto the narrow apron in front of the screen and his head and shoulders stuck up into the arrested picture so that he was in glorious colour almost to the waist, with the pompoms on Rose's slippers projected on his upturned face. He had a pointer in his hand and with it drew attention to certain parts of Rose's anatomy, as revealed in wide-screen aspect-ratio. He couldn't quite reach the parts in question, but was able to lead the onlookers' eyes in the right direction.

"Look at her bottom," he said, pointing.

"What about it?" asked Max. "It's cute."

"Too much of it."

"I think he's right," said Danny.

Callegarini kept silent.

"The whole point," said Danny, "is that Rose can't carry this picture. I blame myself for this. I'm only glad we've got something to fall back on, which I'm also responsible for and which partly gets me off the hook."

The others went on listening to Jasper.

"Here again, just over the kidneys. Look at that bulge. No glamour, no sex. She doesn't come across."

"I can't agree with that. I've seen many of Miss Leclair's pictures, and she comes across to me," said Callegarini.

"Paul, you're a gentleman and a scholar," said Horler with some impatience.

Callegarini knew that he was neither, but was pleased to be so described.

Horler went on. "Naturally she would appeal to you or me, safely married middle-aged men, and we buy tickets, but not enough tickets."

"What is the audience of this movie anyway?" demanded Lenehan rhetorically. "It's the audience that likes a little smut for breakfast, lunch, and dinner. The sex audience. We have made market studies on each of our features before general release, and in our experience the predicted audience and the actual audience coincide."

"He means that we know who we're talking to," said Horler.

"Yeah," said Lenehan. "It's not enough these days to say, 'I'm making a woman's picture,' or maybe, 'I'm making a surfing quickie for teen-aged jerks.' You have to research your market precisely."

Max felt drained of all resources. He had been carrying much responsibility for several weeks now, and was looking around for somewhere to lay it down. It angered him to hear Danny going on like this, because in all ages and climates practical men of affairs have talked this way to artists, that is, through their hats. He knew that Rose had qualities that, properly handled, could make her a much bigger star than she had ever been, but that wasn't his assignment.

"I have an extrapolation here, showing exactly what proportions the projected *Goody* audience will have," said Lenehan, taking some papers from an attaché case.

"Don't read them now," begged Max.

"Let Mr. Saint John continue his story," said Horler.

"Right," said Callegarini, resenting their treatment of his views. He wasn't a judge of talent, and he supposed he should mind his own business. And yet, his was certainly a reaction, not an expert reaction but a reaction nevertheless. Producers always said, "All we want is a quick reaction, Paul." Then they would make their pitch and go away, satisfied or not depending on whether they got the money. The quality of your judgment doesn't change, he thought, once the money changes hands. But he knew that effectively it did. As long as you retained coercive power your counsels were heeded, but only that long.

"I have nothing further to say," said Jasper from the stage apron. "I don't want to knock Rose. Personally I like her much better than the other girl, but it isn't a personal matter. With Rose starring in the musical sequences, without some change in their handling, the film will be a dull failure."

"Do you agree, Max?" asked Horler, as Jasper sat down.

"I think we have to decide the bias of the picture once and for all," said Max. "We can't split it beween the two girls. Those who like one will hate the other. Maybe I should say those who love one . . ." He felt embarrassed and didn't say anymore.

"Aha, aha, aha," said Lenehan.

"Yes, what do we do about that? Should we give it to the press and ride it for all it's worth, or do we try to sit on it for a while?"

"Is it good for us?"

"What do we think of it officially?"

"What will our predicted audience think of it?"

Callegarini, Max, and Jasper said nothing, feeling slightly disgusted. Two of them, at least, were subtle and sensitive men, who did not like to cause pain.

"He's on the set daily, and everybody in town knows it. They've been seen together repeatedly," said Lenehan.

"They make an attractive couple," said Horler approvingly.

A strange, oppressive panic filled the screening room. Strong passion appalls us; we quail before it, cannot contain its effects. At the idea of that immense genie and that little bottle, at the notion of Seth, Rose, Charity, the newspapers and the wire services and the television broadcasts and the columnists, they became frightened and unsure of themselves. Callegarini was silent, but thought the more and felt profoundly disturbed. Max and Jasper were sorrowful. Horler was judicious and fearful, and Lenehan was exultant at the thought of all that space.

"Let's sock it to them hard," he said. "It could add millions to the gross."

Everyone present felt the air of conspiracy and assassination around the producers—the dagger concealed in the fold of the cloak, the smiling handclasp before the sudden lunge and jab. In the dark ambiguous room, brilliancies of coloured light crossing above them, stilled music frozen on the glittering screen, the atmosphere of tragic betrayal thickened grotesquely.

Max thought: making movies is like that. It takes place in secrecy and darkness and is all illusion. The real moviemaking is when you sit in the dark and change the natural order of things by cutting and juxtaposing unrelated actions. It has nothing to do with real people who suffer. It is an art of excision and splice, like surgery or butchery, with the sadistic psychopathology of those arts, and with the incidental murderous blood. He would make cuts and excisions, and would tie in, with bold and safe ligature, new parts, new anatomies, and all would hold firm and be organically one; but what "drops horribly in a pail," the excised part, would decompose and stink.

It is (he thought) a confusion of multi-reals, illusion laid on illusion, Rose's bright slippers on Jasper's anxious face. A film is an arranged reality, a composed reality, made in womblike darkness. The motor purrs, the dancers move and strut on the movieola screen, three inches high, Charity's perfect swelling breasts little insignificant mounds not more than a millimetre in size, prisoned in the mechanical device. Max thought of his masters and of certain bright mornings in 1927 in Berlin, where he had learned the craft, and he felt like crying for the great dead and for their broken promise.

There is something wrong with the cinema *ab intrinseco*, a lie built into it. Far from authenticating the real, from dragging phenomena into undeniable life, his cinema was turning out to be destructive. It crossed his mind that theologians have sometimes condemned acting as a profession deleterious to the personality, and he wondered if the cinema might not fall under a similar condemnation, as being in essence the product of lies, connivance, and darkness.

Meanwhile a banker lurked at Max's left hand and Elizabethan assassins at his right, while outside there was October sunshine and the promised outing on Horler's boat to follow the dark session of conspiracy. He waited quietly, and in the darkness his friend Jasper gripped his arm fearfully. Jasper would regret what he had started; he was innocent and honest, devoid of guile or malice, as the instigators of revenge tragedies often are. He would not want to harm Rose, but he had his reputation to think of, his wish to work in New York again, his own life. Jasper yanked at his sleeve, but Max wouldn't face him.

"Enormous publicity," said Lenehan, "and it will make Charity a star even before *Goody* opens. It's like getting a four-hundred-thousand-dollar star for seventy-five hundred."

"We'd have to shoot additional footage, for which she isn't contracted," said Horler.

"What kind of additional footage?" asked Max sharply.

"Just a little bit of promotional footage, Max. We aren't telling you what to do."

"Spell it out, or is somebody afraid to say what he thinks?"

"Not on this unit," said Horler softly. "None of us need be afraid to say what he thinks. We think that Seth is seriously involved with Charity. And you can't blame us..."

"...we certainly can't be criticized for wanting all the publicity we can get," said Danny. "If Charity is going to be the best thing in the picture, I don't see that we have any choice."

"That's right," said Jasper, "they don't have any choice."

"So you propose to leak to the press, or simply perhaps to publish in a publicity handout, a story of stories glorifying a romance between Charity and Seth. In short, you intend to break up Rose's marriage to publicize the picture."

"What's wrong with that?" said Danny.

"Max, all you have to do is make the best possible picture," said Horler.

"I can make a good picture around Rose. Or I can make a good picture, which will make more money, with Charity as the star."

There was a short, nasty silence.

I ought to come off the picture, he thought. These men are killers; they don't care what they do to anybody. But he had never come off a picture in his life. Once started, it rooted itself and flourished in his mind so that he couldn't bear to quit it.

"What about it, Max?" said Horler levelly. "We will shift the emphasis of the production," said Mars all at once. "In any future conferences or shooting or editing, I will treat Miss Ryan as the center of attention, apart from Tommy."

The projectionist switched on the lights in the screening room, and the screen went blank.

6

"They that live by the sword shall perish by the sword," said Peggi Starr to Charity. "I used to hear that and a lot of other proverbs all the time on WWVA, 'The Voice of Wheeling,' when I was growing up at home."

"I wonder what it means," said Charity. They were waiting to be called for their big scene together in which Peggi, playing a blond whore, hard as nails, named Daisy Fay, finds little Goody sitting on a gritty bench in Washington Square, deciding to go into prostitution on a professional basis because of a fight with her sister over the love of dog-walking Dino.

Charity, as Goody, opened the scene with a new song that had been written into the script for her, "All I Do On This

Green Earth Is Dream," during which she wandered around the arch and the park benches, holding the hem of her miniskirt in her fingers and trying to look like a lost little girl. The track had been recorded several weeks before, and was currently moving well as a pop single on 45. As the scene looked as though it would be much more important in the exploitation of the picture than had originally been estimated, it had been left almost till the end of the shooting, with the idea of building it up, perhaps writing in some additional dialogue, and giving Charity major exposure early in the print.

Peggi didn't like the scene, for rather unprofessional reasons. The script made her Goody's buddy, as over against her sister Barbara, whereas their real relationships were the reverse. Still, laugh-clown-laugh, and all that sort of thing. She tried to look as if she loved little Goody, her coat being so warm and all, and as though she greatly mistrusted her coolly worthy elder sister Barb.

Off camera, she spent a lot of time needling Charity, who didn't get the message half the time. It wasn't so much that she was unperceptive; she was simply flushed with triumph, so full of her access of good fortune as to pay attention to nobody but Seth. She and Rose had no more of those awful scenes together. Rose was effectively out of the picture, her scenes complete, her dubbing finished, and the problem of Seth apparently decided. It was now established that when he appeared at lunchtime it was Charity he came to see.

"It means that those who screw other people get screwed themselves in the end," said Peggi.

"That's the place," said Charity brightly. They had both spotted Seth waiting for her.

Peggi asked, "Are you satisfied with the scene? This is key dialogue. Do you think we've got it right?" With all her assets, Charity wasn't in the same league as Peggi where comedy dialogue was concerned. A slight adjustment of tone in Peggi's lines could make the scene quite disagreeable. Once or twice, reading through the lines, Peggi had caught Max gazing at her over the rims of his glasses. He hadn't said anything, but she got a distinct impression that if she could get the scene away from Charity, it was hers for the taking. The opening part was Charity's by default; she had the song and the pathetic situation, and was alone on camera. When Peggi came on, it was possible for the scene to take a different and much more acid turn, so that pretty little Goody seemed like a spoiled brat. Peggi could insinuate in her lines that prostitution was honest hard work and that Goody wasn't equal to it.

Secretly Peggi thought that Goody might not have what it took for big-time whoredom, but that her live equivalent had already made it big in the business, on a high level of accomplishment for one so young.

"Where did you get a crazy name like that?" asked Charity offensively. "Peggi Starr. That's a joke name."

Ostensibly without knowing it, she had touched Peggi's sorest point.

"I got it because I was young and stupid," she said, only just not adding the obvious "like you." "Young and dumb as they come. When I got out here, I had this crumby agent, a real nothing. He's running a used-car lot in North Hollywood now, so you can imagine. He thought he was pretty smart, the way some of us do. He didn't like my real name, which was Marge Stoner in case you want to know, and he changed it. He said, 'We'll call you Peggi Starr. Starr by name and star by nature, get it?' That was a long time ago, when I still thought you could get something for nothing."

"Of course you can get something for nothing," said Charity.

"Don't be a silly little bitch. Everything costs. I got some cheap publicity and I turned myself into a joke. Maybe if I'd stayed a bit thinner, and didn't have a whisky voice and dance-hall-girl looks, I'd have got better parts, but I don't think so. It was the name that did it. In the end everything evens up."

"You could have changed it back," said Charity, alarmed by her tone. '

"Some things you can't change back. They who live by the sword shall perish by the sword. You may steal and cheat and lie your way to the top, but it all comes back on you sooner or later."

"I don't believe you."

"Look, I asked you a question. Are you satisfied with the scene or not?"

"Sure I am."

Then you're crazy, Peggi thought, because I'm stealing your pantie girdle off and you don't even know. Wait till you get into a movie with your darling Seth, he'll crucify you. Without expecting any results, she said, "Why don't you leave Seth alone?"

"What an optimist."

"No dice?"

"Nope."

"We'll go over the dialogue," said Peggi, and they began to throw lines at each other like BB shot. Peggi did better with her lines than Charity. It was a mismatch.

7

One afternoon before Christmas, when she'd been safely back in the city for several weeks, Rose came in from a quick shopping trip to find Seth, just in from the Coast, standing in the hall with Macha helping him to hang a picture, a big black and yellow abstract oil which she liked on sight; it made her want to laugh. When Rose came in, Macha smiled adoringly at her and disappeared, leaving her to handle Seth.

"I like that a lot. Where did you get it?"

"Over on Fifty-seventh Street on my way uptown; it's an early Christmas present," he said quietly. This alarmed her because Seth, though not at all ungenerous, had never been exactly lavish in his gifts to her, and the painting was obviously expensive, maybe very expensive. They had several paintings in the house, but until now nothing sensational.

"What's it called?"

"'The Lights on Saint Hubert Street.'" He smiled at the incomprehension in her eyes. "He's the hottest ticket in town. I'm doing you a favour." He stepped down from the folding kitchen stool which Macha had given him, and standing back he gave his gift a thorough assessment. "I hope you get a lot of pleasure from it," he said, and she felt greater alarm. What he was saying had a valedictory air about it. As she had for weeks, she felt now as though she were being torn from him bodily, flesh ripping. He had never been a philanderer. There had been a couple of trivial side glances at sexually stimulat- ing girls in his pictures, but she had refused to take offense. He was an attractive man—she knew better than anyone how attractive and in what ways—in a peculiarly exposed posi- tion. It would have been demanding too much to look for total fidelity and chastity. Yet till now his chastity *had* been total, or nearly—she had never conducted any investigation of the facts. There might have been flickers in his brain but not bodily extravagance; they had loved each other. She had helped him, and she was utterly certain that he would some- time remember that, perhaps at great cost.

This Christmas everything was endangered. Long after she had come off the picture, long after he should have gone back to work himself, he had lingered on the Coast, seeing Charity and causing newspaper gossip. Rose set no store by columnists, but she knew that this time it was serious. She was in grave trouble.

One of the things she had loved about Seth was his sta- bility. He would wobble emotionally once in a while—who doesn't?—but he had always come right back to his level bal- ance. Talking together alone at night, they could voice each other's professional problems in perfect harmony, of one mind. She had thought they were perfectly united, and forever. She had meant to let him be perfectly free, to trust him, in the wise hope that Charity would prove an incident like the others.

"We'll both get a lot of pleasure from it," she said, turning to take her coat off.

Then he gave it to her. "No we won't."

She went right on taking her coat off because there was no point in turning round, and she felt her knees tremble and almost buckle under her. She had never felt anything like this in her life. She could predict everything that was coming, the reasonings, the wish to remain friends, she could see it all, and it didn't begin with numb shock; it began with awful pain before the first speech was out of his mouth, and it was going to get worse.

"Seth, look Seth, don't say anything right now, please don't. Take some more time, all you want."

He looked at her, she felt (and her perceptions seemed to her to have become terribly acute), as though she were a heavy chair to be pushed aside, some blocking piece of Victoriana. "It would be better quick," he said, moving as though he meant to embrace her, and then restraining himself. "I can't help it," he said, "I'm sorry."

"We've been married fifteen years. I don't mean to wave it at you like a club, but we've been very happy together, really happy, even at a distance, even when we were apart for months."

"I'm still happy with you, Rose, but it isn't the same. It just isn't the same. It's got something to do with passion . . ."

The injustice of her situation washed over her like breaking surf, all foam and confusion. Their chances weren't equal. It was a widespread popular misconception that modern young women like herself, on the pill, free from the obligation to bear children, could pick up and go from one affair to the next with the lightheartedness of the male. It wasn't so. She knew no woman who had done so, and would never be able to do it herself. She'd be left alone with the best of her adult life ripped out of her. All that time, all that expense of mutual confidence gone. What was worst was that she was sure he couldn't see clearly what he was doing. So they hadn't had children. That had been their mutual decision because of the demands of their work. But they had had some sort of real union, which she had never had to think about and couldn't name.

"Haven't we anything to show for it?" she said. It was going to hurt plenty, all right.

He said, "It's over. It's over."

She could read hunger, not just sexual, more a moral desperation, in his face, and still couldn't feel anger. She wanted idiotically to set him straight, save him from a disastrous error. "But you can buy girls like that."

"That's enough, let's drop it. I want you to promise me that you'll file as soon as you can establish residence. Would you do that, please?" He paused and then made a terrible thrust. "It would make a nice Christmas present for Charity."

This last remark made it clear that he was unable to be rational on the subject. How can people go around saying such things to each other, calmly, without the words blistering their lips? She would have put the question, but saw from his fixed stare that he had no sense of how he sounded.

"How much was the picture?" she asked, throwing him off balance.

"The picture? Oh, you mean this?"

"Forty-five hundred."

"And you're giving it to me."

"If you want it, yes."

"That's about three hundred a year. I didn't come high, did I?"

"That's a bad line."

"I'm not reading dialogue. I'm trying to say what I feel."

They had lived together, on the average, about six scattered months of every year, and as no single stretch of cohabitation had been longer than a shooting schedule, she wasn't sure just what it was she'd lost.

8

Horler normally spent a lot of time on his boat, but it wasn't adequately heated. That year, when December arrived, he shivered through sleepless nights under extra blankets in an already cramped berth, and finally decided to have her crewed around to his Baja California hideaway, where it would be warm. Meanwhile, missing his boat, he was sleeping around in the homes of his associates. They kept telling him to buy; he kept saying no, a house in California was a contradiction in terms and against nature. He and Lenehan had about closed out their local operations for the winter. There was a final conference to hold, a last decision to make, and then they would base themselves in New York and London, and really go to work on the promotion for *Goody*.

Today, a couple of weeks before Christmas, with no place to hold a conference; unwilling to spend time in sparsely furnished and depressing rented office space, he had simply hired a limousine and a driver for the day, picked up his associates, and driven around and around L.A. for a couple of hundred miles; it was a peculiarly rootless and sharply distressing meeting with the four of them huddled in the rear of the car and the freeway signs and direction arrows whizzing anonymously past. It was like a conference in an alien new world, much like hell. Mile after mile on the elevated highways they sped along, over endless rows of stucco apartment houses built in 1947, of four-room bungalows which seemed as much of the distant past as the Spanish coastal missions, reminding the producers of certain skirt lengths and hair styles seen briefly and forgotten on the late late show, the trim and execution of these little houses survivals of a system of manners infinitely remote.

They flew on, the hired chauffeur grim and inattentive in the front seat, cut off from them by a glass panel, his shoulders hunched and sinister. They never remembered his name; he was simply an inchoate hump of darkness up front. Over expansive parking lots with straggly yellow lines defacing the sheen of blacktop, with rickety supermarkets in the distance, insectlike shoppers darting hither and thither across the immensity of parking lot. Soon now all of Southern California will be blacktopped over.

They flew on, past flagged and bannered used-car lots, their draperies proclaiming the openhanded, almost lunatic, generosity of the proprietors, past campuses of obscure colleges, past morticians, past airports; on the ground, above the ground, and under it, the limousine bore them on this mad ride. Now and then one of the conferees broke his chain of thought or argument to gaze with mute revulsion out a window, and each time he turned back to the discussion with a horrified shrug. It was an inhuman landscape, too much, too long, too wide, too far. Christmas at the end of the world.

At last, frightened, Max Mars asked Horler, "Where are we going? Where are you taking us?"

"Nowhere." This was a visibly upsetting answer. "I mean we will drive around a little longer, have a meal somewhere, and drive around some more."

"That's no way to live," said Mars.

"Soon we'll all be gone," said Lenehan, who had a tendency to car sickness. He felt better on a horse, he thought, though he had not been near a horse in thirty-five years. "I'll be in New York. Bud will be in London for a while."

"I'll still be here," said Mars, gloomily. "There's a lot to be done."

Lenehan said, "For a rough cut . . ." and stopped. The others stared at the director.

He said, "It's money in the bank."

"Yes, yes, but we can do better."

"Haven't we done more than enough?"

Larry Solomon, who had said nothing for the first hundred miles, finally spoke. "Tell him to stop at a gas station. I would like to urinate."

"That's the worst of these freeways," said Horler, and there was a chorus of agreement. The limousine sped on for another fifteen minutes and Lenehan demanded, "Are you in pain?"

"No, not pain. I have a certain amount of foresight, and there are no pissers on freeways."

"True enough," said Lenehan. "I have no prostrate problems myself . . ."

"Prostate," said Solomon.

"What is that?"

"Prostate, not prostrate. And my case is not prostatic. I have a small bladder, that's all, and we've been driving for hours."

"And getting nowhere," said Max.

"Oh, we are, we are," said Horler, "we just went through Buena Park. We're nearly in Anaheim."

They all started to complain. "We've been into Anaheim once already this morning," said Solomon. "I insist we stop."

They had said nothing to the driver, but telepathically he now swerved into an exit ramp, and they descended into less futuristic realms. The car halted beside a light traffic flow, and then the driver put it in motion and headed out Commonwealth towards Fullerton. Then he slowed and turned into a gas station, coming to an abrupt stop at the pumps. The imprisoned filmmakers leaped out like four Jack-in-theboxes, and made as one man for the washroom.

" . . . while you were lolling on silken cushions," mumbled Solomon reproachfully, standing up to the urinal. He had been sitting on one of the jump seats.

"Not lolling," said Horler indignantly. "I was brought up never to loll."

"Like the Royal Family," said Lenehan.

"Quite. A small self-discipline but it impresses others, a dignified self-control."

"I've seen you loll," said Solomon rebelliously, as Horler eyed him.

"And this is the fruit of your upbringing," said Max Mars, peering through a gray and unwashed lavatory window. "A luncheon in Anaheim."

"Fullerton."

"It's all the same," said the director, hungry and out of sorts.

They left the lavatory and went into the lunchroom adjoining the gas station. There they found their chauffeur, a morose man, sitting at the counter—there were no tables—trying to drink a cup of disgusting bitter coffee. They sat in a row beside him, and the juxtaposition made them all reflect.

"That's the thing about life," said Solomon, "no matter how much money we make, we wind up eating in places like this." This fell rather chill on his companions' ears. They placed cautious and rudimentary food orders, and resumed their interrupted discussion.

"It's as good a cut as you can expect," said Max. "I've done just about everything I can." He spoke as one haunted by an oppressive sense of having done wrong.

"You've done just right. You've laid the emphasis just where we meant."

"I'll tell that to Kitcheff, he'll be pleased. In effect, though, I'm my own editor."

"It's the new thing," said Lenehan, "we might play it up in the promotion."

Max wondered if he could be kidding. "The new thing? Every great director has done his own cutting and editing when he was allowed to, from Eisenstein on."

Horler winced. He said, "When I hear that name, I think of losses."

Max answered him. "Doctor Goebbels said something similar. 'When somebody mentions culture, I reach for my club.'"

The partners felt the latest in a series of misgivings. Aren't you happy with this undertaking? they wanted to ask their director. Have you second thoughts about our approach, what is wrong? They sensed a peculiar masked rebelliousness in his talk, and although it was not a typical employer-employee relationship, which they regretted, they often wished that they could take a club to Max Mars.

Always with the artistic conscience, they thought, or with conscience pure and simple. Why can't he drop it and act like everybody else? What's so special about his conscience? Is it so fine?

"I feel a certain solidarity with Eisenstein," said Max, more kindly. "And I learned much, stole much, from his pictures."

"But you mostly do comedy," said Lenehan. Sitting beside him, Larry Solomon put his head in his hands and Lenehan caught him.

"What the hell," he said sharply, "have I been stupid again? I know I'm not one of you intellectuals."

Max felt glad the production was finished. "We're all on edge, but the picture is complete, and it isn't bad."

Horler said, "It's certainly Charity's picture. You'd hardly remember there was another girl in it."

The counterman heard the word "picture" and came alive. "You guys in the industry?" he asked, leaning on the counter and wiping it with a dirty rag.

"Oh no, no," said Horler quickly, "we're salesmen, just out checking the territory, ha ha." They all got up and moved to the door. Solomon paid the check and they went out and got in the car.

In a few more minutes their chauffeur arrived, wiping pie crumbs from his lips, got into the front seat, and without asking for directions retraced his route, got back onto the freeway, and headed northwest.

"The trouble is, anybody can see it isn't the picture we started to make. Every stinking little reviewer in the country will say it. I mean otherwise why is Rose in it at all? That's what they'll say."

"That won't bother audiences, Danny."

"It needs another gimmick."

"We can't cut her out of the picture entirely."

Solomon said, "If we did, she might have grounds for a suit."

"Maybe a little lawsuit would help the picture, maybe that's what we need."

Horler recoiled. "The divorce is enough and a lawsuit helps nobody. First thing somebody hits you with an injunction, and you're powerless to act. Let us, by all means, avoid litigation. I think she might be able to sue us for violation of contract if we left her completely out of the picture."

"And in some states for damage to her professional reputation," said Solomon. "We have to leave her in the picture, and besides, her name is worth something, especially with the divorce coming up. That isn't hurting us."

"But there's the artistic question," said Max, "Danny's problem. We really have two pictures here, not one, coexisting in strata, like geological formations one on top of the other, like the nine cities on the site of Troy. There's the clean healthy family picture we started out to make, and there's the Charity Ryan vehicle we seem to have arrived at, I'm not sure how. These two strata coexist very nervously, and anybody can see it. We want something to ram the sex home, a great big signal that Charity won the battle."

Horler said, "If the divorce goes through early in March, don't you figure it'll get us a lot of mileage in the press, right before we open?"

"Yes, but that isn't in the picture, and won't keep it running."

They drove for a while in silence, and then Lenehan said, in a tiny little voice, "That thug Faiers has a suggestion which is worth considering."

"What?"

"There's all the promotional material. And there are the titles."

Max said, "I thought you were having them done by Animation Associates; those are the ones I've seen."

"We have those, yes," said Danny. "But the Faiers proposal . . ." He seemed happy to father it on Faiers. ". . . the Faiers proposal is that we give Charity several minutes of solo footage with the titles over, a whole big new musical number with her alone on the screen, or just with the chorus, something that wasn't in the stage production. He even has a title."

"What?"

"Mini-Goody-Go-Go."

They all laughed nervously.

"Catchy," said Max. "Have Donat and Reynolds done the words and music already?"

"No, Faiers has been afraid to go quite that far."

"Who can blame him?" said Solomon.

"Nobody could claim that the titles are legally part of the picture," said Horler. "They're simply an announcement appended to it by a polite convention, and are entirely at our disposal as long as we observe the billing clauses. If we want to use a sequence with Charity on the screen by herself, as part of what is essentially an advertising device, that is within our rights. Isn't that so, Larry?"

"I think the courts will so rule."

"You want me to shoot an entire new number around Charity?"

"We're not getting the idea across. It'll be just Charity, with the chorus purely background; they won't have to do anything much. Charity appears, sings her song, performs a few simple calisthenics designed to show her off—nobody could manage it better—and then the titles come over. The song lyric relates to the titles perhaps, or to the storyline. After all, she has the title role. And she'll be twenty-feet tall in a close-up. It's an unparalleled opportunity."

"I'm beginning to read you. You want straight display."

"We want all of Charity that you can get on the screen right out there in plain view. We want to ram her down their throats. The soundtrack should be very loud."

"'Mini-Goody-Go-Go,'" said Max. "It swings."

"Wait till you hear it," said Danny.

"I thought it wasn't written yet."

"Well, it's just a little bit written."

Max blanched. "You people are awful; you really are awful. You have the psychology of ward politicians. You do everything with a low stratagem. What did you hire me for? I am not your enemy; there's no need to go behind my back. I want the picture to do well, as much as you. But in the meantime, I would like to get out of this car. I'm getting carsick, or anyway sick."

"Are you agreeable to the Faiers proposal?"

"Anything you like. Send Jasper a memo to work up some little step for her, and a running order. We can shoot it in a week. Have somebody send me a score of the arrangement so I can read over it, to get the feel. Would you ask this chauffeur of yours to let me out?"

"Don't go away mad, Max."

"Who is mad? I have my fee and my percentage. I never complain as long as I'm paid. I'm an artist. You want this bitch on the screen twenty-feet high, that's what you get. You want to stupefy them."

Horler pronounced it like a benediction. "To stupefy them."

Max stood at the curb, by the open door. "They'll never know what hit them."

9

"So. I'm paying for the party?"

"Horler said they would."

"They should, God knows."

"No, Rose, it's customary for the star to do it, or something like it, you know as well as I do," said Vogelsang a few days before the premiere, "but because Seth is . . . Seth is . . ." He had some trouble verbalizing it.

"Since Seth has flown the coop and I'm all alone, a bereaved divorcee, I don't have to pay, having no husband and no means of support, apart from what generous producers pay me; that's nice. Will they pay me rent on the house, and a fee for insurance against breakage?"

"Rose, Rose."

"Pooh. Pooh to you, Lambert. They're simply using me and my house."

"Somebody has to give a party."

"Let Tommy Dewar give the party. He's as much involved as I am."

"It's more gracious like this."

She shrugged in amused disgust. "And just who is this French creep they've unearthed for me? Boy, have I ever had foreign producers."

"Jean-Pierre Fauré? Rose, dear, he's very big in France, and on the art-house circuits. Films Vinteuil is his production unit. *Feu James Dean* was his first success. It's supposed to be the first real new-wave film."

"Fauré, as in foray. He's after money like all the rest of them. Art-movie producers are all alike, and he's been after Horler and Lenehan to buy his pictures for the States for nearly a year. He's just another of their creatures, like Max and Jasper."

"Have you met him?"

"No, but they were always talking about buying his line of goods and getting into distribution. They haven't done it though. They haven't got the guts or the brains."

"He's a director, Rose, more than a producer. He paid for his first movie himself."

"It can't have cost much, if he used his own money."

Vogelsang said vaguely, "With those pictures made at a price you can sometimes get it back quick. I heard he did very well on his first two. He's just a kid."

"What's he doing in New York? He must be after money."

"Distribution. Name stars."

"He better not fool around with Horler and Lenehan or they'll swipe his pictures from him, also his shirt, coat, pants, and anything else he might be wearing." She felt angry. "So one of their parasites is going to be my date? Believe it or not, I prefer to arrange my own dates. I don't need Danny and Bud to procure for me."

"Aw, Rose. Danny just thought it would do us all some good to have you seen with a new man. He thought it might put you in a more glamourous light . . ."

". . . instead of the unglamourous light of the wronged woman, not a very juicy part. You're as bad as they are, Lambert, you just want to use me. So. What does this Fauré look like, anyway?"

"Now there you won't have any complaints. He's a nice-looking boy, dark, tall for a European, around six feet. I'll tell you who he looks a bit like, Henry Fonda."

"So does Seth. In fact Seth is the one who wasn't Hemy Fonda, perhaps on a smaller scale."

"I think of Fonda as essentially a stage actor," said Lambert.

"What are they after?"

"They just want you at the premiere with a presentable man."

"To show that I'm not dead yet."

Vogelsang did something he almost never did; he showed a trace of impatience. "Will you go with him or not?"

She said, "Have them tell him where to come. Have them get a decent car for him. I'm not going to jockey mine in and out of the garage."

"A limousine," her agent promised.

"It damn well better be."

When he turned up the night of the premiere, he seemed very Americanized, his clothes, his cigarettes, everything but his haircut, which was very long on the sides and combed low on the forehead, flopping in his eyes. Like Belmondo, she thought. Belmondo was the only French star she knew much about, and she'd enjoyed several of his pictures.

Her feelings were crazy, ridiculous, teen-ager stuff, as she looked down at him from the top of the stairs. He stood in the hall, perfectly quiet and well behaved, and gave his dark top-coat to Macha, who took it away as though she did this all the time. But Rose hadn't been out with anybody but Seth, except on business dates, for fifteen years.

She had to steady herself against the staircase wall, feeling the way she used to at sixteen when her mother had been lining up dances for her, with potential college men, before she left Bristol, Connecticut. She, hard-bitten Rose Leclair, who had been through it all. My God, she thought, how ridiculous, meeting a boy for the first time. I may blush.

And to her great surprise and embarrassment as she came down the stairs, seeing that Jean-Pierre Fauré was a couple of years younger than she was—though he might not grasp this all at once—and seeing that he was tall and really quite good-looking, she found herself blushing; her cheeks grew very hot. She knew that her colour would show because she could produce it at will for pictures. She hadn't blushed involuntarily since her adolescence.

He turned from calling some politeness after Macha in a pleasant murmur, and looked at her with a serious expression, an almost placid look, very calm, very composed. His face had none of the anxiety and none of the driven, compelled set and tension of the conscious careerist, a look which she had noticed sometimes in Seth's face over the last few years.

Seth and Jean-Pierre Fauré might each resemble Henry Fonda in his own way, purely physically; but they didn't look like each other. What caught her envious attention immediately was this rested and restful quality in the French director; she didn't feel invaded or threatened by him, which was rare with men in the picture business. Usually they tried at once to put you down, to show that they were more important than you were, that their salary was bigger, or that if it wasn't, this was owing to some incomprehensible lapse in the front office. Rose was known in the industry as a big earner, and a lot of men sheered off from her because of it; they didn't dare compare incomes.

Jean-Pierre Fauré had made money from his early pictures, those he'd financed himself and therefore owned outright; but he couldn't possibly ask Rose's price per picture. No French star or director could, with a single possible exception, not Belmondo or Delon or Moreau. The market just wasn't there. He might be holding more capital, but he didn't make her salary. She took a second look as he came closer. Quiet, he seemed quiet.

She asked him if he'd like a drink and he refused.

"We have a few minutes before the car comes around," she said.

"Could we sit down and talk?"

"Yes, certainly," she said jumpily, "come in here." On the ground floor of the house to the right of the front door there was a small conservatory with plenty of light and some comfortable chairs. Rose thought it the most agreeable room in the house, and as the rest was all polished up for the party, she led him in there.

"Have you seen the final print?" he asked casually.

"Just a couple of rough cuts. I've been very busy, I'm afraid."

This was a real curve ball for him to handle. She had been very publicly busy, in a rather noisome, and noisy, situation. She had spent the time from mid-December to early March getting her decree, and seeing Seth and Charity safely and irretrievably deposited in each other's arms. It was all dreadfully, uncomfortably, indecently—what was the word—odiously, horridly public property. She was the betrayed wife, the drab homebody, the superannuated ingénue, everything dully pitiable, and he must be aware of this; it had been in all the papers, all winter.

"Getting a divorce," he said surprisingly.

"That's right."

He smiled for the first time. "Where were you married?"

"In Palm Springs." She remembered her father's regrets, and blurted out, "In the middle of the night by a little man in a nightgown, a justice of the peace or something."

His smile grew broad. "Not in a church?" She suspected that she was confirming his worst prejudices against the tone of American life.

"No, not in church."

He stood up suddenly and looked at his watch. "Time to go." He picked up her wrap and walked her to the door and out, off the plank.

Going very deliberately across town to the premiere, in the big anonymous hired car, with passers-by putting their faces to the windows to see what dignitaries were inside, Fauré seemed to have divorce and marriage and churches and that sort of thing stuck in his head. Perhaps he had panicked and couldn't avoid the subject out of pure tactlessness. She had a distinct impression that he'd read up on her background in some file before coming to pick her up, maybe even before agreeing to date her, so she put a leading question. "Why do you ask specifically 'in church?'"

He grinned. "We've only known each other fifteen minutes."

"Oh, say twenty."

"Twenty, then. As we only met twenty minutes ago, I have no right to question you, I know that. But I'll ask anyway because I'm incurably inquisitive. Besides, a star is public property."

"No, she isn't," said Rose automatically.

"Oh yes she is! You're entitled to reasonable privacy, but you must always concede the public the right to curiosity. That's why I have the right to mention your divorce; it's a matter of public record and interests me because I'm one of your fans, and I buy tickets. I own part of your life."

"Isn't that awful?" she murmured.

"I don't think so. You probably like it; anyway it's inescapable. You are rich, famous, beautiful, admired, and in return for this you sacrifice your privacy, but only to a certain extent. Some things the public needn't know; but they will talk about your divorce. When was it?"

"I got the decree about three weeks ago. It was kind of a shock."

"But you're not in mourning."

"I haven't lost a thing."

"A Nevada divorce?"

"Yes, perfectly legal anywhere."

"I'm sure it is, otherwise I wouldn't be here."

She laughed at him; he wasn't her idea of a Frenchman. "Aren't you a prig!"

"A prig? I don't know the word."

"A snob, a puritan, one of the hundred-percenters."

"I see. *Un snob, un Tartuffe, des bien-pensants . . . les honnêtes gens.*"

"I think you've got it."

"I don't believe in casually entertaining other men's wives," he said, "but that's not entirely to the point because, equally, I don't believe in divorce. I think that after the first marriage there is no other. If you are once really, sacramentally married . . ." The look on Rose's face stopped him. "What is it?" he said.

"Are you religious?"

"Of course, I'm a Christian. It's possible to be quite intelligent, you know, even quite modern, and religious as well."

"I didn't know that."

There was a lot of noise outside the car, coming closer. He laughed at her, and his laughter mixed with the crowd's. "The religious question is still open," he said with assurance, "because the evidence isn't all in. Certainly I believe that marriage can only be dissolved by death, once it is really effected. This is, there's no such thing, morally and psychologically, as a divorce. Maybe you were never married at all."

"Because I wasn't married in church?"

"No. It isn't the priest who marries you. You marry yourselves. In your case there might not have been a fully formed intention, on one side or the other."

"This sounds silly."

"Correct. Nobody talks like this nowadays. But it's a perfectly logical attitude to love and marriage, once you allow the notion of a sacramental union. Also it makes marriage and sexuality, and sexual love, very valuable, very important, crucial, holy, like getting born or dying. None of the most important things in life can be done more than once: birth, growing up, aging, dying, choosing a profession. And marriage is the same. It seems to me an advance on the idea that it can be accomplished an indefinite number of times, depending on the state of one's glands. It makes it worth more."

"Is sex that important?"

"Sex isn't the whole of marriage, but it's the necessary condition. I'd say that sex, as the physical consummation of mutual love, is of enormous importance. It's as valuable as religious practice and art, one of the three most important things we can do, of vital importance. I can't express the value perfectly, but that's what my films are about."

"But you aren't married."

"No. I've been foolishly promiscuous."

"That seems inconsistent."

"It's worse than that, it's wrong. I mean bad. I shouldn't have done it. I hope not to do it again."

Nobody had said to her for years that what they had done was wrong and that they regretted it.

"You likely had good reasons," she said, trying to be helpful.

"There are no good reasons for bad actions," he said.

Rose was horrified at this view. "Oh, but there are."

He gave a negligent laugh, plainly not taking her answer seriously.

"Don't patronize me," she said. "I'm just as clever as you, and more important."

The noise around the car was shocking. "See?" she said. "Nobody in that crowd knows who you are; they're screaming at me."

He had to raise his voice. "You're quite right. You're much more important than I am, both here and in France. There, your pictures earn more than mine, even though mine are the native product."

"Are the earnings the only measurement?"

"Earnings are probably the most accurate measurement of a great film, over the very long run. I don't want to make coterie films. I want to be seen by the great public; that's why I'm looking for a star."

Their chauffeur turned around and spoke. "This is as close as I can get, Miss Leclair. The cameras are over there, and the interviewers are in the bullpen, up back of the foyer. Mr. Lenehan is with them, and he asked me to ask you not to speak to anybody till he sees you. He has it all planned."

The crowd was calling for her in cadence. "We want Rose; we want Rose; we want Rose; we want Rose." As she stuck a leg out of the car, she shouted to Jean-Pierre over her shoulder, "They've got it all planned." She caught his answering grin and the encouraging nod of his head, and then she launched herself forward into the uproar.

The first thing she saw was an enormous horse's behind, a horse's enormous behind, the horse was enormous, his behind was enormous, the noise was enormous, so was the occasion. This horse had somehow jockeyed between their car and the curb, and there was a mounted policeman on it with some kind of bullhorn or megaphone in his hand. He waved this cone, looking down at Rose, and then hailed her through it, and this sound too was very great.

"GO AROUND BEHIND ME, MISS LECLAIR."

She did as she was told. Coming out from behind the horse's ass, she stepped into a huge pool of coloured light. They had rigged floodlights over the entrance, which changed colour constantly, and there was a crazily mixing and blending wash of colour at her feet, green orange red blue yellow, on the pavement and sidewalk. Together with the noise and the intrusive horse and the shoves from behind that Jean Pierre gave her, the whole impression was that of a blurred confusion.

Her dress was simple and not hobbling; she'd picked it on purpose to allow freedom of movement. Sometimes in a premiere crowd you had to make a quick change of position, and if your dress had bits of stuff hanging loose here and there you might in an instant be stripped bare. So she wore a simple sheath and no expensive accessories which might be grabbed at close quarters by souvenir hunters and carried off, to her financial loss.

She could walk easily in her sheath, and run if necessary, and felt no special hesitation about mounting the sidewalk at her handsome escort's side. She looked around through the maze of coloured light for the TV cameras and placed two of them. There must be more, she thought. You're here to be seen, so be seen. Where are the others? Aha, aha. Now she had four of them, and that was par for the course out here. More inside. She took Jean-Pierre by the arm; he stood storklike on one foot, then on the other, and she knew exactly how he would look in the TV news clips, awkward and unused to his evening clothes. They always did, even people in the business, when they weren't used to performing. Her own training, more than fifteen years of it, made her move and hold herself firmly erect, exhibiting herself, her modest décolletage and the fit of the sheath over her hips, and her very feminine stride. She walked and turned, lifted her breasts, smiled, pulled poor Fauré here and there, as though she were the director and not he.

"Over here, Rose, over here," people shouted. She glanced at the police lines; they had barricades which looked fairly firm. It was not an insurgent crowd, and there was no anger in their cries. People strained at the barricades and beckoned beseechingly at her. It was allowable on these occasions to approach the cordon and sign a few of the nearest autograph books, so that the photographers might catch the gesture, making you look good in the fan books. This was a big picture, a major release date, a world premiére, and the stars were Tommy Dewar and Rose Leclair, and there were other gay and vivid personages to be glimpsed, a couple of Kennedys, Senator Dirksen, Mickey Mantle despite the upcoming Yankee home opener, one of the Gabors, Ed Buchanan. Nobody was missing Charity, Rose decided, and in all this noise perhaps nobody would think to wonder where Seth was, or remember that he had just got rid of her. She realized suddenly why Horler and Lenehan had supplied this convenient, if offbeat, Frenchman; he had that faint resemblance to Seth. The public were used to seeing her with a tall thin man who looked like a younger Fonda. He was, in short, an unconscious stand-in, and she felt a bit embarrassed for him.

"Over here, Rose, over here."

Rose had perfect eyesight, and all at once, as if she'd zoomed in with a special lens in her eyes, she isolated an elderly motherly woman with an enormous satchel over her arm. She wore glasses and her mouth yawned open, disclosing ill-fitting dentures. Like the rest of the crowd, she was shouting happily with no idea of being noticed or addressed. Rose looked deliberately straight at her, caught her eye, and smiled as politely as she could. The woman drew an excited breath, aware that she had been noticed. A quick human communication passed unspoken between the two women. Seized by a sudden impulse, Rose grabbed Jean-Pierre again and drew him with her as she went up to the fan. As she came near the barricades, a lot of waving arms stretched out like tentacles from an aquarium tank. She evaded them, refusing to go within grabbing distance. She called to the woman.

"How do you like it?"

The woman dug frantically in her satchel for an autograph book, which she suddenly produced and held mutely forward, delighted to be spoken to. Rose felt ambiguously like a queen; she took the book.

"What's your name?" It was necessary to yell.

The reply came slowly, as from a long distance. "Mrs . . . . Mrs . . . Thelma . . . Sloper."

"What? . . . WHAT?"

"Sloper . . . Sloper."

Aware that the cameras were on her, she opened the book to the first empty leaves and quickly wrote, "To Thelma Sloper at the 'Goody' premiere with best wishes from Rose Leclair." She hastily added the date and handed the book to a surprised

Jean-Pierre. "Write in French," she said, and he scribbled, "*Meilleurs voeux*," as though it were a Christmas card. She took the book and leaned towards its owner. "Are you staying for the picture?"

Thelma Sloper smiled beatifically: "I'm coming tomorrow."

Rose handed her the book; she opened it and read the friendly inscription and you could see her melt with pleasure. The fans applauded cheerfully, and Rose felt mixed gratification and self-disgust.

It was time to go inside, and their cries grew louder and a little desperate as she turned away. Other stars and celebrities were arriving, and soon the picture would begin. She and Jean-Pierre walked into the theatre and up past teeming shoals of photographers to where Bud and Danny stood like little Caesars among a horde of interviewers who, transistorized tape recorders in hand, clamoured with insistence for direct speech with the star, the real thing.

"Here, luv, here, over here, dear," called Danny, beckoning. He held a small sheet of paper, and four privileged choices were ranked next to him.

"We're giving you to these four exclusively, two TV and two tapes for network radio. Do thirty seconds apiece." Rose thought he was pretty peremptory, but this wasn't the time or place to take him up on it.

"I'd love to, Danny, who's first?" A cadaverous TV interviewer put his apparatus up close to her and said, looking at his watch, "Three seconds, O.K." He turned to her, smiled expansively, and said, "Are you glad to be here, Rose?"

"How are you, Barney? Yes, it's one of the happiest evenings of my life. I'm looking forward to seeing the picture very much."

"Haven't you seen it yet?" A stock gag.

"You know how it goes, Barney, you see a bit here and a bit there. This'll be the first time I've seen it through, and I can't wait."

"Look, Rose (over here, Tommy, over here), Rose darling, it's been a pleasure talking to you and to . . . uh . . ."

"Monsieur Fauré."

"Yeah, to Monsieur Fauré, and I think you've got a great picture going for you, a real contender for picture of the year. Congratulations."

"Thanks very much, Barney, I hope so. Bye for now." She stepped adroitly out of the picture and moved to the next man.

". . . she is everybody, the sweetest kid, one of the top stars in the business, and the really big attraction at tonight's premiere, Rose Leclair. Hello, Rosie."

"Sandy, dear. Glad to see you."

"Awfully glad to see you, baby, and I'm sure the picture will be a sensation."

"We all hope that, Sandy. Can I say hello to the people?" She smiled brilliantly at the camera. I hope they zoom, she thought, make a good shot. "I hope everybody enjoys seeing *Goody* as much as we enjoyed making it."

"Aw, gosh, thanks very much, Rose. Nice having you."

"Nice to be on, Sandy." Out of it and on to the next. She could see Jean-Pierre watching this routine; she was going through her hoops pretty well, like a well-disciplined little circus pony. Now they were taping, ". . . for seven hundred syndications across the nations it's JUBILEE at the *Goody Two-Shoes* opening, your reporter Harry Goldston here now with *Goody* star Rose Leclair, looking radiant in . . . what is it, Rose?"

"Why, Harry," she said, "it's nothing very special. It's a fairly fitted sheath, I guess you'd call it, in a raw silk. In a café tone. The girls will know what I mean."

"So will the boys, sweetheart, it looks divine. And this is . . .
"He looked at Jean-Pierre, slightly puzzled.

"The French producer-director Jean-Pierre Fauré. We're conferring about a picture." She said this out of simple courtesy, and could sense his shrug and lift of the eyebrows.

"You're keeping pretty busy, Rose, way to go, sweetheart, aat'sa way. We'll be coming inside in just a second, dear, to report on the picture, and congratulations." She moved on, did a very short fourth interview, and found a young man from the production office at her side.

"Your seats are right over there, Miss Leclair," he whispered, leading them along. "Next to Mr. Mars. Then comes Tommy with Miss Starr, then Mr. Lenehan with a lady—I don't have her name."

Rose slid along the row. "Right here?"

"Uh-huh. There you go, Mr. Fauré. Is it all right, are you comfortable? Here's the special souvenir program with places for your friends' autographs."

"Thanks for your trouble. What's your name?"

"Eddie Blanda."

"Oh sure, you were on the Coast. I knew I'd met you before. Are you coming back to the house?"

"I haven't been asked, Miss Leclair. I don't want to seem to be hinting around."

"But you aren't at all; be sure you come along. You know the address?"

"Yes."

"I'll be expecting you. This is Jean-Pierre Fauré, you know."

Blanda pulled a rabbit from a hat. "I know. I saw *Les bonnes petites filles* when I was in Paris, and I loved it."

Rose said, "There, you see? In the long run you're more important than I am." Jean-Pierre shook his head, and Blanda stared. "A family joke," she said, a little wryly. By this time Horler and Lenehan were seated, towards the other end of the row. It grew quieter. Blanda went away and the house lights came down. No cartoons, no trailers, right into the feature.

The vast screen lit up instantaneously in a wash of peachy-rose light. In the 2.5:1 aspect-ratio, it looked like a long slit out of a ballroom, or like a theatre cyclorama when the sets have been removed. In astonishingly lifelike sound, strings were bowed rapidly, around and behind you in low urgent figures. Horns in. All at once a gigantic Charity Ryan appeared alone on the screen in a medium shot, dancing à gogo. The anticipatory strings stopped abruptly and the soundtrack crashed into a dreadfully loud orchestration, a solo for Charity on the grandest scale. As though she were running on a treadmill up a low hill, she advanced upon the audience, belting out in a roar a song almost nobody had ever heard before:

> Honey baby sweetie cutie little dolly-bird,
> Brand-new girl in old New York and haven't you heard?
> Who's the teeny-bopper swinger everybody wants to
>   know?
> Mini-mini-mini-mini-Goody-Go-Go.
>
> Ring-a-dinger real swinger everywhere in town
> Downstairs, upstairs (BOOM BOOM) putting everyone
>   down,
> Hipster, mister, take-a-tripster, man you gotta go
> For mini-mini-mini-mini- (BOOM BOOM)
>   Goody-Go-Go.

The boom-booms came from a fleet of bass drums tuned in a simple chord. The scoring was all drums and brass on top, with strings under, very up-tempo, insistent drumming. In front of you, frighteningly, loomed enormous GOODY, dancing and shouting to this insistent BOOM BOOM.

> Teeny-bopper swinger-clinger, man you gotta go
> For mini-mini-mini-mini- (BOOM BOOM)
>   Goody-Go-Go.

Charity wore a skintight beach-pajama top which left her forearms bare, and a blazing tartan mini-skirt about thirteen inches above the knee. Her breasts, thighs, and buttocks might as well not have been covered at all, so prominently displayed were they, and so mobile. There was much vibration, and all over the theatre you could hear through the great blasts of music awed and reverent sighs, in-takings of breath, half-spoken exclamations. That it was a distinguished black-tie audience made no difference. Men predominated in about a 60-40 proportion, and their reaction filled the auditorium. Seats creaked. People shifted from ham to ham, suddenly feeling a bit crowded.

The mauve beach-pajama top had curious fins or flaps at the sleeves, probably along the seams, long strips of material which were agitated partly by Charity's undulations and partly by an invisible source of air current; they must have had a fan or a wind machine on her, because these little fins blew backwards in the slipstream giving her an oddly machined look, like a piece of radiator sculpture from the early 1950s, a smoothly streamlined chromium quality. All her curves had this same combination of smoothness and hardness, as though she had been die-cast in chrome. Her hair tumbled wildly behind her as she gyrated, caught in the artificial current from the fan. She strutted, turned right, left, trotted rhythmically the length of the screen, flopped on her back in a tight close-up, fifty-feet long, kicked up her thighs and bicycled briefly, her legs glistening in their bath of peachy-pink light, and all the time the thundering orchestration allowed no respite. Then she jumped up, arms akimbo, and threw her head back and her breasts at the camera with gorgeous insolence.

The light changed from peachy rose to bright sunny yellow and up behind her came the singing and dancing choruses, all the boys and girls from the L.A. company, Ray and Elmer and the rest, dressed like members of the Sanitation Department, with wheeled carts and stiff push brooms which could be used like majorettes' batons. Eight dancers, running wildly around with these brooms, did a complex routine where they fenced with the broom handles, then twirled them, tossing them in the air and catching them, then rode them like hobbyhorses while Charity stood in their midst and laughed.

When the screen was full of street cleaners, after about two minutes of the number, the titles came over. TOMMY DEWAR . . . ROSE LECLAIR. There was a big laugh at this. They got top billing all right, all right. Ha! Then, timed to coincide with her doing a split and sliding towards the camera, the words AND INTRODUCING CHARITY RYAN as she held the split and threw her hair forward, cascading over the camera lens in a warm furry wave. Enormous letters: AS GOODY TWO-SHOES. Cut to ranks of dancers and super the rest of the titles over the third chorus.

Titles, Charity's solo, the dance routine, came to about four minutes, and there seemed to be strong feeling in the audience that this was the most taking set of titles, the most memorable, of the year. If they gave Oscars for titles these would win, as being chemically pure sex. As the last members of the production staff received their acknowledgements in small lettering, the lighting went to pink peach again. Under PRODUCED BY BUD HORLER AND DANNY LENE-HAN, Charity retreated from the camera, blowing kisses, for God's sake. Then she turned, stuck out her bottom under DIRECTED BY MAX MARS and gave a very solid bump as the sequence ended. The audience cheered, and it isn't often they cheer the titles.

Good as it was, the rest of the picture was an anticlimax. The colour was less fantastic than in the titles, more lifelike, and the soundtrack not so strident. When Tommy and Rose were alone together, the music grew almost quiet, but these moments were few. The editors had simply taken the whole stinking picture and handed it to Charity on a platter. Max had obviously done the cutting and editing, or overseen it. so he was to blame for the final cut. But who was to blame for the titles?

Rose was in shock; she couldn't straighten things out. After the longest four minutes of her life, when she saw exactly what they had chosen to do to her and how the picture would be twisted, all she could do was grip convulsively whatever came into her hands—she nearly took the armrests off her seat. Tears flowed from her eyes and her face twitched, but luckily she was in darkness and nobody could see. Beside her in the dark, she was sure, Fauré would see what they had done. You take a big star and rub her nose in the dirt; when she's been given top billing you allow her the footage of a minor supporting player; you cut her numbers to nothing and hand the picture to an unknown, exalting her above the star in every way—what can you expect? Rose cried bitterly in the darkness.

Her nice little scene with Tommy, where she kissed the poodle, which had been so good, so warm and humorous in the rushes, was almost gone, cut unrecognizably. In its place was a reprise of "All I Do On This Green Earth Is Dream" with that bitch acting as if she was a pure fifteen-year-old. No wonder the song was a hit; they plugged it like the "Ave Maria" or something. The good little scene with the deep blues and warm greens, and the sweet feeling of twilight that she and Tommy had liked so much, the pleasant atmosphere of West Tenth Street, something quite spontaneous which they had enjoyed and done well, just about gone.

The Automat stuff was worst of all. The audience couldn't help seeing that Rose Leclair was such a shitty dancer she had to go. The number made no sense. They had contrived so many sudden cuts and tricks and evasions that you were left with the impression of a big nothing, a lot of choppy shots of people waving their arms in a bizarre setting, with no star to pull it together. That last swing and slide down the chute, which had made her so afraid, through which she had shut her eyes and hung on tightly so many times, didn't even get into the picture.

The number was a senseless bore, making no advance in the final story line. Rose was sure that everybody must know.

She looked at Jean-Pierre surreptitiously several times, but he continued to stare in front of him, his eyes averted because of friendly feeling or embarrassment, certainly not because of his absorption in the movie. He must see it, she concluded, and writhed with shame. She had been coming on like the big star, the queen of the premiere, and this film, of all those she had made, had to be the one he saw right after her big-star act.

I should have policed the production, she thought, or had the agency do it, while I was getting the divorce. It was a mistake to hide away like that. Why couldn't they have come to me and said "Rose, dear, it isn't working out, your dancing isn't right, you aren't right for musical comedy, we're cutting your footage and we'll bill it as a guest appearance or a cameo." They could have done that. I'd have gone along with that. She cried some more, a bit more noisily, and felt her escort's hand on her arm. I wonder how much screen time I got? Twenty minutes, tops? It couldn't be any more. That she got Tommy in the closing frames made no sense—she hadn't spoken to him more than half a dozen times in the picture. The new footage was all lines for Charity or new songs or new arrangements like those damned titles.

Every time Charity was on, the producers' decision grew more obvious and humiliating. Rose knew that she was still pretty, that she kept herself shapely and in good health, that she maintained her stock in trade, her looks and good humour and appeal, what she traded on, by diligence, skill, practice, and, considering her age, she was in wonderful shape. She was a marvellous thirty-four, and that's young. Young.

But every time Charity appeared she rolled over the audience like a division of mechanized infantry. She had physical presence, health, prettiness, bloom, sexual power that simply steam-rolled you. In the final cut they only had about ten minutes together, and in that time she completely eclipsed Rose, who had imagined that she was pretty much of a woman, a nice piece of ass; but seeing all that spread out beside her, pushing and oozing and pulsing, made her feel like a peanut-butter sandwich beside a platter of prime porterhouse. The comparison, and her own loss of face and force, was acutely depressing. Worst of all, she saw that it was her own fault.

It had been up to her to shine like a star, and she hadn't sparkled, hadn't glittered, hadn't come across with star quality. She had been as nearly invisible as the moon at noon. *Noon Moon*, a great title for a Rose Leclair vehicle. She squirmed in self-abasement. Oh God, she prayed, just let me get that girl on my own home grounds, in a black-and-white comedy without music, and I'll take her apart.

But she had a terrible feeling that this wasn't so, that Charity in black and white would be the same or worse, that Rose would still look old and tired and not very interesting.

The slow pressure on her arm steadied her; otherwise she might have run from the theatre in tears, and you can't do that in this business. She felt that he held her in her seat by sheer force of sympathetic will, this supposed creature of her enemies. She sat it through with his help, feeling like a boxer drunk with punishment whose reflexes and marvellously conditioned legs keep him in there and erect under the blows of a superior opponent. But she had to sit and take it; she couldn't stick and move, bob and weave. She had to sit and take it, sniveling into a useless handkerchief and worrying about her eye makeup. Thank God it was a long picture; there was time to decide what to do. She had no previously prepared position; she'd been fool enough to absent herself trustingly while the assault was being prepared. Now she had to retreat and retrench, fall back, make new defenses. And then she remembered, as trumpets shrieked from the screen, as Peggi sat and initiated Charity in the film, and made her look stupidly adolescent with the lightest of touches, Rose remembered the party.

From whatsisname, the publicity man Blanda, on up, there would be a hundred and fifty people coming along to see what she thought of it all, not counting the uninvited who always showed up at these affairs. They would all want to know what she thought of the picture, the dear loves, and of dear Charity and dear Seth.

Her mind froze and she watched the screen as Peggi took the short scene in Washington Square away from Charity without the little giant's being in the least aware of it, so smoothly and with so little apparent effort that Rose laughed, the only person in the big house to laugh at that point in the picture. Along the row of seats, Peggi caught Rose's laugh and felt better. Peggi could handle herself in the corners. Charity had been camping it up with cute snaggle-toothed grins since the titles, and while the audience loved her body and could have swallowed her on the half shell, they might just have been beginning to feel like something tart. Max Mars was quite smart enough to work in old whisky-voiced Peggi, who with her effective lines and very sure comedy sense could grab any wandering attention and refocus it on herself. Rose saw Peggi do what she should have done, saw her friend's moral competence move her easily out of danger. She dried her tears then, or rather let them dry on her face to avoid smudging. Tears lay stiff on her face as she waited for the lights, exposure, time to go . . .

. . . one very seldom dared to ignore a directive from Graham Faiers, because he might lash out at you insultingly in front of anyone. He might say in silken tones, "Stay in line, Eddie," and you would be humiliated, as you had been before, in front of secretaries. There was a limit to what one would swallow, but it was hard to tell where the limit lay; the money was good.

So Eddie obeyed orders. When the picture began he retired to the back of the house, where he assumed the posture of a superior usher, greeting late-comers, some of them household words and some of them nobodies. He gave smiling and polite attention to all, because he now knew he wasn't a good judge of when and how a nobody might turn into a somebody. He had had the bad luck to meet Charity Ryan when she was nobody, and had treated her as such, with mitigated contumely and contempt. He knew that she would always remember him and never forgive him, and that he could not work successfully around her again. He was glad that she was in Europe with Seth, because otherwise he couldn't have handled the opening.

And yet, he said to himself as he moved briskly about from one level of the theatre to another, squiring this or that pretty notability to the lavatory, and yet it was I who brought those pictures to Faiers' attention. And then he blushed enough for an observer to notice; he had momentarily concealed from himself the plain fact that if he hadn't noticed Charity somebody else would have. You can tell lies without thinking them; don't kid yourself, he thought.

Coming back from a ladies' room with an incontinent starlet, showing her where to sit, treating her like royalty, he vowed never again to make the mistake he had made with Charity. He had treated her as somebody of no importance, like himself. He had asked her to eat with him the day after he showed the publicity pictures to Faiers; he had felt an obscure relationship with her and meant to tell her what he had done for her.

She had looked at him slowly, taking him in from his heels to his crown before answering. "I can't be bothered," she said. He'd turned away, closed his mouth, gone on working for her. What else could he do?

The starlet reseated, he came back to his original post, and saw with surprise that the picture was nearly finished. He left the darkened auditorium and went to the main lobby, where he found the dispatcher and some attendants. He had orders to keep the cars coming fast and to clear the sidewalks around the entrances quickly. The dispatcher had a list which identified the limousines, and a pretty good idea how to move them out of there.

"I can get rid of them in twenty minutes," he said earnestly.

"Great," said Blanda, going out onto the sidewalk. One or two curious fans still stood idly about, but most had gone. As ushers opened doors, passers-by began again to line the barricades in the hope of seeing somebody important.

The first to straggle out were faceless nobodies who went off ignominiously in cabs, the dispatcher sparing them hardly a glance. Blanda, still relatively new to the business and eager to train himself, tried to guess from their behaviour whether the picture was a hit or not. He was supposed to concentrate on getting the crowd out, not on noting their reactions, but if he could come up with a quote that could be worked into publicity, it would be much to his credit. Or if he could spot a new reaction, something that hadn't appeared on the preview cards, it could earn him a small raise.

The preview cards had reflected the slant of the picture towards Charity. "Let's see more of Charity Ryan" had been the usual comment, but there had also been a sprinkling of cards here and there asking, "What happened to Rose?" These were probably from people in their thirties and up, not the largest potential market for the picture, but one which shouldn't be completely ignored.

When Eddie read over this sprinkling of pro-Rose reactions, it had seemed to him that there was a kind of picture she could make and an audience she could satisfy which *Goody Two-Shoes* missed. When he named this obscure segment of the market to himself, he always thought of them as "decent people," but the phrase wasn't quite right.

She and the French director came out first, and Eddie stared at them attentively. There had been alarm at publicity HQ (Faiers' phrase) about Rose's possible behaviour when she finally saw the picture. Some people thought she might leap up and shout a torrent of filth at the producers—a legitimate response in Eddie's view—but he and Faiers and Lenehan had been of a different opinion.

Mr. Lenehan said, "She's been around, she knows what you do and what you don't do. Besides, she owes us a picture. She won't make trouble."

It comforted Eddie to reflect that everybody had to take it from somebody. He took it from Faiers and Lenehan and Charity. Rose took it from the producers, and they took it from God. And at that she had noticed him and asked him to the party, which gave him great pleasure.

She and her date stood at the curb while the dispatcher called, "Limousine for Miss Leclair and . . ." He looked at his list, ". . . limousine for Miss Leclair and Mr. Four."

Rose took the dispatcher by the arm. "You pronounce that 'Foray,' like a small raid."

The dispatcher called again, "MR. FORAY'S car please. Limousine for Miss Leclair and MR. FORAY." The car rolled silently up; it was a very fine car, Blanda noted with relief, one he had seen somewhere before, maybe in a picture. It was such a fine car that it looked rented; nobody owns such a car; they are only used at the openings of eight-million-dollar movies. Rose and her companion got in and the door shut behind them with a luxurious THUNK. The car moved away.

Blanda thought she looked out on her feet, and decided to risk Faiers' displeasure and go across town to East Sixty-first when he was through at the theatre. He had been invited by the star herself, and maybe he could be useful. He had a sharp sense for discord among intimates. If she takes it badly, he decided, there'll be trouble.

There was no doubt that the picture was a hit. The audience was one big smile as it poured out the opened doors, and there was plenty of agreeable high-pitched chatter and genuine laughter.

". . . ever seen anything like the dancing?"

". . . that little Ryan girl, well, my dear, Edward couldn't take his eyes off her, *could* you, darling?"

"I just love him, he's so suave, and he never smokes his cigarette all the way down."

"Just divorced, yes, a couple of weeks ago, wasn't it?"

"She's a little bit *passée* of course . . ."

"It'll gross twenty million easy."

"Whatever happened to Rose Leclair?"

Finally the theatre was empty and the crowd dispersed, the sidewalks around the theatre as clear as they ever are. The cleaning staff came out and dusted off the sidewalks; inside the lights went out, the velvet ropes were rearranged in the lobby, and the theatre prepared for a long run. Blanda looked at his, watch, knew that he would have a job tomorrow, the picture was home free. He would never have to sit through it again. He started for the party, wandering along, taking his time, over to Madison and up. He whistled "All I Do" as he strolled; he considered it the hit song of the picture, and suddenly remembered Charity's pop single. When he thought of her he felt that he was in a servile and inhumane peonage, and he blushed and distrusted himself as he assessed the sexual quotient Charity's image stirred in him, a wish to power, and a wish to be scorned and humiliated, very mixed.

He turned onto East Sixty-first, feeling as though the turn signaled a switch in allegiance. Soon he saw the paparazzi at a distance, or what one would have called paparazzi in Rome, not many of them and nothing like the Continental type. Just a group of half a dozen freelance photographers who hoped to come in range, by good luck, of some celebrity in a compromising or at least titillating attitude, drunk perhaps, or with somebody else's wife or mistress, anything that was potential trouble. It was never officially understood how these poor men knew, say, that Rose Leclair was giving a small party for the hundred and fifty most prestigious people at the premiere.

Eddie had handled the "leak" himself, simply calling some people known to the New York office and passing on the information. Those who were interested got the message and showed up, looking especially for gag shots of Tommy Dewar and his new girl. Everybody knew all about Tommy, his very considerable age, his tastes and habits, and the "Tommy Dewar's new girl" story (no, really, Mr. Dewar and I are friends, no there's no engagement) had become over the years a columnists' in-joke. A shot of Tommy with his tie up under his ear, with some careerist of seventeen, would always sell to the European agencies. Charity would have been hot copy too, especially if she had been there with Seth. But they were safely installed on the Avenue Kléber, apparently for good.

Three of these freelancers knew Eddie from before he went to the Coast. They aimed their lenses at him, then chanted, "Not him, guys, he's nobody."

"I am not," he said, "I'm somebody."

"No, no," said a special buddy, a name in his field, "you are a nothing, a little faceless man struggling to hang on."

"I'm Eddie Blanda," he said emphatically.

They were standing on the sidewalk in front of the house, with a uniformed security guard lounging by the entrance. He was supposed to keep the photographers in line, but did nothing except bum cigarettes off them. To enter the house you went down some steps into a small court where you faced a solid, heavy black door with brass fittings, such as you might see in Mayfair or Westminster. Inside on the ground floor were the hall, a small conservatory, the housekeeper's office, the kitchen and other domestic arrangements.

From the hall you ascended a broad straight staircase to the first floor, which comprised a hall and two enormous rooms that could be made one by folding back the doors between. Seth's decision to give almost all the space on this floor to a single main enclosure had been a handsome and just choice; it allowed what you hardly ever got in midtown Manhattan, a feeling of space and freedom of movement.

As Eddie stood outside the front door, it swung suddenly open before him. He lost his balance reaching for the handle and almost collapsed into the arms of his boss, Graham Faiers, who stood just inside with blood on his dinner jacket. He reeled slightly as Eddie came in.

"What the hell," said Eddie. He leaped forward and slammed the door shut behind him, nearly severing a photographer's leg. An attendant came over to help and together they leaned on the door and bolted it; voices outside indicated great displeasure. They had seen the blood. "What goes on?" he said to Faiers, who seemed about to faint, putting his arms around him and helping him to a low bench which stood beneath a large and beautiful abstract oil. Faiers moved uncertainly on the bench.

"Max Mars hit me," he said, keeping his hands to his face. Eddie looked for the attendant, but he had disappeared. There were a couple of other people on the stairs and in a room off to his left, but for a moment he couldn't spot a servant. Ah, there she came, silently and efficiently, a dark young woman with a damp white kitchen towel padded in her hand. She proffered this and Faiers took it with a low curse and dabbed at his eye and forehead. A mouse was forming below the left eye. He pressed the towel to the bruise and removed it, wiping off most of the blood. He was going to have a black eye, and there was a superficial cut above the cheekbone.

"I think he must have been wearing a ring," said Eddie.

"Quite right," said Faiers, and then in a lower tone, "I disapprove of jewelry on men." He laughed surprisingly. "Especially when they hit you with it." He handed the towel to the silently waiting girl and stood up, drawing Eddie confidentially towards him. "Who's outside?"

"About six of them, Lisle, Gelinas . . ."

"They know me?"

"Yeah, but Mr. Faiers, apart from the cut there's no story. If you put a Band-Aid on that, or even a little piece of toilet paper, and go out as if nothing had happened, they won't pay any attention to you. Don't wait around till your eye comes up black and blue."

"You're right," said Faiers. He asked the girl for a Band-Aid and a fresh damp towel. These applied, he felt ready to chance controversy.

"Could I ask what happened?"

"Nothing really. All I said was that Rose would have to get rid of this place when people noticed she was slipping. For some reason Max got very upset; then he hit me."

"Did you hit him back?"

"Don't be ridiculous, he's a famous director. In our business you can't go around hitting famous directors."

"I guess not."

Faiers said, "You're young and you've got a lot to learn, but thanks for the moral support. And keep an eye on things for me."

Eddie felt that he had made an impression. "Yes, sir," he said in clipped accents as he walked Faiers to the door. As it swung shut behind him, Eddie heard him fending off the freelancers with practiced deftness.

He climbed to the top of the stairs, where there was a dense crowd and much laughter and gossip. Eddie was fairly tall and could see over the heads of most of the people in his way. Rose was standing down the hall with a fixed, determined expression on her face; she was pale and seemed tired and nervous.

Peggi Starr and that French director stood beside her, and the three were chattering to each other, and to people who came and went around them. Eddie recognized many of them, and in particular Kate Dixon, whose show had been running for eight months with no sign of a drop-off at the box office. Kate was that rarity, a real star of stage and screen, with equal facility and star appeal in both media. She had once costarred with Lincoln, which was probably why she knew Rose.

Rose had no stage experience, Eddie remembered. Thinking of Faiers' conviction that she was slipping or had slipped, he decided that she would probably have a try at the stage this summer, a standard gambit of movie stars whose careers are in the doldrums. Maybe she would take a new play around the summer-theatre circuit, and bring it to New York in the fall. But he couldn't see her for the stage: not enough presence.

Kate Dixon was standing close beside Rose, talking to her very earnestly. It was interesting to see them together, because Kate had the gestures and voice of somebody long accustomed to projecting without electronic aids, and she made poor Rose seem even paler. Blanda averted his eyes the way you cover your head at the end of some Greek tragedy or other, as a ritual act of pity. He passed from the crowded hall into the *salon*. At the other end of this big room there stood an elaborate bar, at which an associate of Eddie's presided, brought in specially for the occasion by the producers, a highly skilled golfer and bartender whom the producers retained to entertain bankers and distributors. He had white-jacketed helpers who obeyed his barked commands. You expected him to cry "Fore" as he launched the olive or the onion.

Eddie and this golf player would have been sworn enemies if they had had any contact. Eddie hated this man because he didn't know publicity or production, and wouldn't learn. He hoped to be on the scene when the tall Texan's golfing skills deserted him, and his suavity and pouring arm, but unfortunately it seemed that a good golf swing could be preserved over an unreasonably long period. The golfer poured, and poured again, and Eddie decided to have the single discreet drink that calculation allowed. He moved towards the bar, ears at the ready to eavesdrop as he went. He sidled cautiously past Mr. Horler and Mr. Lenehan, hoping they wouldn't notice him and give him some orders. They were standing with Max Mars, who bore no signs of physical combat except that he was breathing a little faster than is normal for an unexcitable man in late middle age.

His collar point, the left one, which was long and Californian, had gotten bent backwards and had climbed up over his lapel in a way that reminded you of the late S. Z. Sakall in some movie about Vienna; an endearingly rumpled quality was suggested. But there was really nothing endearingly rumpled about Max Mars tonight. Eddie knew by the director's tone that he was gravely displeased about something. But all he heard as he passed was a single harsh phrase.

" . . . swine, all of us."

That would do, Eddie thought, that covered things. He saw that the partners were shaking their heads in unison like mechanical toys, in dissent from whatever developments of this strongly stated theme Max might adduce. All passing or past, thought Eddie, reaching the bar, where it took him some time to catch the attention of his golfing associate.

"A Scotch," he said finally.

The golfer poured a stingy little drink, slopping in an ice cube with a hole in it which suggested the imperfectly constructed igloo of a bored Eskimo. He handed Eddie the glass, and Eddie took it and turned away. He was right at the back of the house and could see his hostess through a hall door, still receiving, but unable from fatigue or other distress to smile. He wondered how she felt, and decided that whatever her feelings were they would be intense and painful. He wanted to go and speak to her, to take her hand, thank her for asking him to come, perhaps comfort her. His glass was slippery and his palm perspired. He was not learning his business hanging around watching this comedy.

His drink was all water. It struck him as he swallowed it that he had had a bellyful of this miserable existence, and he thought of going back to Akron and going to work in his father's menswear store, but he knew he wouldn't do that; he finished his drink and prepared to leave. He crept through the hall door and was suddenly moved forward and to his right by a wave of late-comers whom he politely evaded. His side step brought him immediately in front of his hostess; they gazed silently at one another, without communication. Eddie had the feeling that he was looking at a still close-up; all the detail was there, the flaked lipstick on dry lips, the network of faint lines under the lower eyelid, some hair escaping above an ear. Below, coffee-coloured silk lay smoothly on white skin; her bosom rose and fell silently. He pushed past her and went downstairs and out the door.

Rose remembered the publicity man, but not his surname. He had certainly looked her over pretty closely, she thought, but she was used to being inspected like a side of beef hanging on a hook, and thought no more about it. The crowd in the hall thinned, the guests had all arrived, and it was time to go inside. She made a tentative move, but Peggi restrained her.

"Why don't we get rid of these creeps and talk?"

"How long would it take?"

"From now? An hour, starting with this guy." Peggi grabbed a mousy little fellow who came trotting down the hall with two drinks in his tiny paws. Despite his pace, he spilt not a drop. "You must have been a bartender in a previous existence," she said, and then saw by the man's change of expression that she had hit a long-concealed target. "Who are you, and who invited you?" she asked with controlled savagery, bullying him.

"I work for Mr. Solomon. I'm a statistical analyst."

Peggi was placated. "And when were you a bartender?"

"At C.C.N.Y. during the Depression, and after I graduated. I've been poor," said the man defiantly, "and I'm no freeloader. I was invited. I did all the extrapolations on the grosses. Aren't you Peggi Starr?"

"Yes. This is Miss Leclair."

"I know. I know. I didn't hope I'd get to meet you, Miss Leclair." He said an astonishing thing. "I'm sorry about the picture. I liked you best."

"That's all right."

"I hope you make a lot of money."

"I hope so too. Have a good time, won't you?"

"Yes, I'll try." He turned to go but Peggi held him relentlessly.

"The party's over. Why not drink your two drinks and go?"

"All right, Miss Starr. We were just going."

"That's the spirit." She released him and he scuttled away. "I'm unhappy about statistical analysis," she said. "I think they take things too much to heart."

They were an isolated trio now, the guests seeming glad to leave them alone. Peggi said, "Aw, Rose." She took the other woman's hand. "Aw, Rose!"

Rose began to cry quietly and helplessly. She cried. She said, "Do you know Jean-Pierre Fauré?" She laughed and cried together, but then cried harder, looking for a place to go. The noise from the salon was loud, and hid her crying. There was a powder room just at the end of the hall and they took her there, leaving the hall empty. There was nothing to sit on but a small towel hamper and the toilet, so they stood and looked unhappily at each other.

"She should rest," said Jean-Pierre. Behind him the door swung open. A male guest stuck his head in, said, "Excuse me," and went away.

"I'm all right." But she continued to cry. "The victim is always the last to know, right?"

"I thought it was me, slipping," said Peggi, "when they didn't ask me to come in for a screening. Now I know why."

"I had seen it," said Jean-Pierre. They stared at him angrily.

"Why didn't you warn us?"

"I only met you at eight o'clock tonight," he said defensively.

"It seems longer," said Rose. "How much screen time did I get?"

"Important footage, about twenty minutes, more or less."

"They cut her to bits," Peggi said. "What a stinking trick. Take them to court, Rose, that's what I'd do."

"I didn't watch you make the film," said Jean-Pierre, "but I'd imagine that Rose originally had three to four times the footage, isn't that so?"

"How can you tell?"

"From the editing. You can see at once where cuts have been made and new footage cut in, and as for that business with the titles . . . it's effective, I see that. They want you to see her all at once, and you do."

"Would you use her in a picture?"

"No, it's not a type I like."

"Who's like her in France?"

"Perhaps some of the yé-yé girls. She's beautiful physically, I grant you that."

Peggi said, "Rose is more beautiful." They were silent and the cubicle was full of disinterested affection. She went on, "Sit here, sweetie, and we'll go and clear the bastards out." She led Jean-Pierre away.

Rose looked at her streaked and dirty face in the mirror, feeling the dawning of an urge to throw up. She sat on the toilet and put her head down, and the nausea temporarily passed.

10

Back from London, Lambert Vogelsang came into the Lyricart offices on a Thursday. The switchboard girl smiled at him apologetically, which alarmed him. He walked far back into the ranks of smaller offices, along a dark, windowless corridor to his own room at the end of the floor, where he sat down suddenly and passed a palm over his forehead. He was very tired from the flight. When Miss Mcintyre bustled in, he flinched.

"Miss Leclair has been trying to get you all morning."

"Does she say what for?" They both laughed sadly.

"I suppose we can guess, the poor thing." Miss Mcintyre had felt much sympathy for Rose during this mess; they were about the same age and had always gotten along together better than most chance acquaintances. Rose had been coming into the Lyricart offices ever since her first trip East, oh, years and years ago, to help promote one of her earliest pictures. At that time Miss Mcintyre had been just a girl in the pool, who now and then took dictation from Mr. Vogelsang among others. Rose had spoken to her with cheerful politeness one afternoon when she had come into the room to transcribe the details of a contract. Miss Mcintyre had been glad to be treated like a person instead of an appliance, and now she was sorry to see her friend all upset and deserted, and she wanted Lambert to do something.

"There isn't much I can do for her, Jan," he said. "I spoke to Horler yesterday and he says there's absolutely no question of preparing alternate prints of *Goody* and I must admit it would cost him a flock of dough to do it."

The phone rang insistently. "You better take it," he said. "Say I haven't come in yet." It was Rose all right. He watched with anxiety as Miss Mcintyre picked up the receiver.

"Hello again, Miss Leclair. I'm sorry, no, he hasn't appeared. What?" She covered the mouthpiece and whispered to Vogelsang, "She says the operator told her she saw you." He nodded, cornered at last, and she spoke into the phone. "I'll just look along the hall, if you'll hold on a minute. Perhaps he stopped to speak to somebody." She put the phone down again and said quietly, "I don't like the way she sounds, Lambert. I think you'd better talk to her."

"How?"

"She sounds pretty disturbed. She says she's been alone for days."

"She can't have been drinking, or anything like that."

"Well, she never has, that I know of."

He sighed. "I'll talk to her."

Miss Mcintyre said, "Miss Leclair, he's just coming along the hall, if you'll hold on. I'm so sorry to have kept you waiting." She handed him the receiver and he held it for two counts and spoke, hoping that what he heard as a ghastly false heartiness would come across warm and kind.

"Rose dear, how are you? I just came in this minute. We had a bumpy flight and I didn't sleep much." He had always forestalled the complaints of others with his own, and hoped that if he acted miserable enough Rose might feel sorry for him instead of for herself. "I'm too old for these quick trips," he moaned.

Miss Mcintyre was certain that the familiar strategy wouldn't work this time, and was pleased to hear Rose's voice, sharp and insistent through the instrument, cutting off Vogelsang's lament. He listened silently for thirty to forty seconds, his face at first calm, then worried, then seriously alarmed.

"Don't talk like that, you'll make fifty more features before you're through," he said, but the tirade went on. He was convinced now, Miss Mcintyre saw, that there was real trouble to come.

She wished she could help Rose, remembering the sight of her on the night of that disgraceful party. The only people who had stood up for Rose were Lambert and Peggi and that nice French director. The whole business was a shame, and the worst of it was that Lyricart had clients on both sides of the fence. They would all have to be very careful about declaring where their sympathies lay, especially Lambert. She followed his words carefully as he spoke with great circumspection to the angry and disappointed star.

" . . . know how you would feel. I've thought about nothing else all this month. I'm racking my brains for ways to help." A pause. "Yes, yes, I spoke to him. But Rose, can't you see what you're asking? To do that would be to make a whole new picture. They may have destroyed your original footage by now, probably have. Be honest with yourself . . ." He listened to her reply. "Legal action?" he said into the phone with a voice full of horror. He raised his eyebrows at Miss Mcintyre. "You'd have to change lawyers. No," he corrected himself, "I forgot you'd done it when you got your decree. I don't know anything about the new firm. I can never remember the names of law partnerships." He laughed as she recited them. "I've never heard of them, maybe they're too exalted." He allowed her to explain who they were, waiting for an opening. "Would they fight this out for you? They'd have to throw a lot of weight downtown. Oh, they *do* throw a lot of weight downtown? How much? Oh. Oh, him. Well, that might do you some good in Washington, but I don't see how Washington comes into this litigation. Look, let me talk to you before you see them. Yes, today, now. The usual; when did we ever eat anywhere else? I couldn't digest my food off Fifty-eighth Street. In one hour precisely. Uh-huh. Uh-huh, bye-bye." He was shivering slightly when he hung up, and Miss Mcintyre felt sorry for him because they were all in a difficult business together which exacted heavy withdrawals against dwindling balances of nervous credit.

"This is impossible. What'll I say to her?"

"What's wrong?"

"She has the idea that the agency sold her down the river to protect themselves with Seth."

"She's right."

"Sure she's right, but I can't admit it to her. Lyricart couldn't exist without sometimes putting one client's interests ahead of another. Naturally I'd sooner Rose got the best deal every time, but we have more important clients, and they come first."

"What are you thinking of for her?"

"A TV series, a situation comedy; she'll go great in it, and she may make some real money for a change."

"Would she do TV? She never did before, and Seth doesn't."

"She'll have to. She got the house in the settlement. She has to earn a hundred thousand before taxes to run that place."

"As much as that?"

"There's a full-time staff of four, with tax contributions, Social Security payments, accident insurance, and all kinds of other charges, their food for instance and uniforms. The taxes are unbelievable, and the fire, theft, and casualty run very high. Painting and repairs and general upkeep run to thousands a year. She has to pay into a private police organization the people on the block subscribe to. Shall I go on?"

"She could sell it, I suppose."

"She would sooner die."

"I'll call Mr. Charles, and say you'll be in."

"Would you do that, dear? I'd appreciate that." He moved around the small office whistling tonelessly, putting this and that piece of paper into a briefcase. He scratched his head, just at the hairline. Dandruff fell on his desk blotter.

"Fatigue does that," he muttered absently, "nervous fatigue. Call them, will you, and I'll go along."

Going up Madison in a cab, he took out Rose's agreement with Lyricart, *not* strictly speaking a contract, but a written presentation of an agreement, a piece of paper with ambiguous legal status. He could not have said, on the spur of the moment, to what degree Rose was bound by it, if at all. It was part of his job at Lyricart to intimate at all times the dire consequences of any breach of this agreement, without actually making any definite threats. He might recount gothic tales of how so-and-so's billing had shrunk at another agency, or how somebody else had foolishly priced himself out of the market while trying to avoid paying agency commission. He might suggest that while Lyricart was no longer actively involved in production, all producers were its natural allies, and would go along with its policies and discipline. This was not factually correct, and had never been so, but it was his job to elicit fear of the consequences of disregarding his instructions, to keep the client as much as possible in the dark.

"Corner Fifty-seventh all right?" asked his driver.

"Yeah, I'll walk from here." He paid the man and got out, walked a block north and turned east. He was a little early, and wanted Rose to be seated and composed when he came in. He could trust her not to make a scene in the restaurant, for she was a friend of the owner's family; she wouldn't make a scene in any restaurant. She wasn't a temperamental girl; he had handled other women with much less status at the box office, television actresses and the like, who were infinitely more troublesome than Rose Leclair. As he sauntered along, he saw her coming from the east; she'd probably walked over from the house, almost the only one of his clients who ever walked anywhere.

She was in good shape—he remembered that she had a lovely little body. He had seen her on the late late show a couple of weeks ago in a movie about the twenties, in which she wore a period dress in gold lamé with beads, a very cling-ing effect. She still had most of that, he thought, watching her enter the restaurant. He walked the short remaining distance half-reluctantly, and then steeled himself to go inside. He went to his customary table, where Rose sat chatting with one of the waiters; she laughed at something he said as Lambert came up.

"Philippe comes from the Marais," she said pleasantly, "where Jean-Pierre was born."

"He must have been a poor boy like me," said the waiter.

"Where is that?" asked Vogelsang.

"East along the *rue Saint-Honoré* near *l'église Saint-Merri*, that's our church. It has a famous organ."

"I'll ask Jean-Pierre if he remembers it," she said. Philippe took their drink order and went off, coming back almost immediately. He put their drinks in front of them, and Rose hesitated a decent interval before diving in. She had never been a problem in that way, but there was something wrong with her which might have been considered the effect of drink if she'd had any track record. She seemed stunned. They ordered food, and again she showed extreme restraint.

"You've given up eating?"

"If I eat a boiled egg it slows me down for three hours. A piece of toast divides, and one half speeds directly to each hip. Do you know what I have to do tomorrow? I spend all day— all day, mind you—first with Madame Sylvie, then in a reducing *salon*, then the last part of the afternoon working out in the Goulmoujian gym. There's a day shot to hell."

"Why don't you take a couple of months off? You needn't work so hard."

She gave him a quiet friendly look, and he felt pity and embarrassment. Her eyes wrinkled very attractively at their corners and she communicated a quality that was never evident in her pictures, which would have been worth a lot of money if anyone had ever caught it, a spontaneity, warmth, courage, that are unpurchasable. Only one or two of the greatest stars have had it. Seth didn't have it. What made him big was his nervous, edgy penetration and intensity, something that stirred his audiences at once. Vogelsang much preferred this elusive quality of Rose's, but could never catch it long enough to record it. He smiled at her in genuine friendship, relaxing, or pretending relaxation, as they ate.

"You're an awfully nice woman," he said, "and you've got a great career still to come." Maybe this wasn't too well phrased.

"What are you lining up for me?"

"I could make you a lot of money in TV."

Her face stiffened, and he went on quickly: "An awful lot of money if the show catches on, fantastic residuals, enough that in a few years you'd be independent and could do what you like."

"I've heard that argument before," she said, "and all I know is what I see. The ones who've gotten rich on residuals make another series right away. They don't go back into films and pick and choose; they try for another quick strike, and then they're marked as TV stars and never do anything afterwards. I can name a dozen who've gone like that. I'd sooner be a second-rate movie star than a top TV personality any day. Any day."

"I don't know what prompts that choice."

"*C'est une question de ma gloire.*"

"Have you seen much of that fellow?"

"You ought to know. You threw us together." Then she relented. "I haven't wanted to bother him. It can't be much fun for anybody to have to cope with me in this state. We've had a couple of dinner dates, but we actually got acquainted at the party."

Vogelsang shuddered. "What's the name of that law firm again?"

"Zaslow, Reichert, Bickersteth and Folsom."

"Crazy name. What did you do, pick them out of the book?"

"They were recommended to me."

"And you feel able to trust them?"

"More than I do you."

"I suppose I had that coming."

"Yes, you had that coming. Do you realize that I've been on Elavil for three weeks? Largactil. Sodium Amytal. You name it, I've been taking it."

Her face was white and strained. "Rose," he said.

"Don't 'Rose' me. The only people who've come near me are Peggi and a total stranger. Imagine! Jean-Pierre Fauré, whom I'd never met before, has been kinder to me than anyone except Peggi. It's humiliating to have to go for help to somebody you met an hour ago. I can only get to sleep, if at all, under sedation. 'A potent anti-depressant with distinctive anti-anxiety properties.' It's humiliating." She finished her food quietly.

"Then see them downtown."

She said, "Yes, I intend to."

11

No legal recourse, big help, Rose thought, no recourse. She laid a dozen stills on Madame Sylvie's desk. They were mostly black and white shots from *Goody* but as a precaution, just to show what she used to look like, and what she looked like in straight comedy, she had included some bathing-suit shots from the mid-fifties, a gag picture of herself and Seth as Lady Aminta and Sir Grishkin, in which she wore a flowing kirtle with a good line, and two drawing-room shots of herself and a male ingénue in her picture before last, a black-and-white sex comedy in which they had all been falling over low divans. She held one of these up and looked at it critically. She had been wearing slacks of some abominable stretch material that clung so close you could see the edge of her panties. It shouldn't have done that, she thought, that's too stretchy. That wasn't my fault, that was the material, nobody could get away with a pair of panties under that, not even Charity. No recourse, said Mr. Bikersteth, nothing at all we can do.

Madame Sylvie had the other pictures spread on her desk and was looking at them with the highest professional interest.

"It's a slow deterioration," she said.

Rose felt insulted. "I haven't deteriorated."

"You don't understand. I'm referring to the behaviour of muscle tissue under aging conditions and loss of tone. Everything is just a little lower down. The band of muscle that attaches to the cheekbone and supports the jaw, for example, will stretch eventually and nothing can be done about it, even if there's no fatty deposit, along it."

"Nothing?"

"The process can be retarded, but that isn't my business. For that you go to Goulmoujian."

"That's exactly where I'm going when I leave here. I've got to be in the *salon* at two and the gym at four. What can you do for me?"

"Why have you never consulted me before?"

"I never had this problem before. You've had my measurements for years, and you've made all my bras, at least those the studios didn't make."

"And the rest of it?"

Rose blushed. "I've been known to enter a department store."

"That's all right, my dear, we all do, but department store girdles won't solve your problem, will they?"

"No"

Madame Sylvie shuffled through the pictures. "Let me try to sum up the situation. You haven't put on much weight, but you've put on some hard fat, which comes off only after a death struggle. I can tell you exactly how many pounds." She held up one of the first publicity shots of Rose ever released, showing her looking lovingly down at a baby lamb with a bottle in its mouth. She had ringlets, and the only bare flesh visible was her arms. Madame stared hard at the arms. "When was this taken?"

"In 1951."

"And you were then . . . ?"

"Eighteen."

"And at that time you weighed between a hundred and two and a hundred and five, mostly around a hundred and two to three."

Rose stared, and Madame Sylvie laughed. "There's no magic to it. I can see the flesh on your arms in the picture, and I can see your bone structure as I sit here and watch you. In your stockings you're what, five feet, three inches?"

"Exactly."

"And you have—forgive me—a big rump, or at least apparently so?"

"Have I ever!"

"It's more appearance than reality, and proper designers would deal with it. We'll get to that later." She eyed the other pictures and said, "Give me the one you're holding. Ah, yes, this is from last year."

"Late in 1965 actually. That picture was released in 1966."

"You were in your early thirties." She put a finger on the line of Rose's thigh in the picture. "There," she said, and Rose winced, for she had put her fingertip precisely on the place where the edge of her panties showed.

"You can't blame me for that. Nobody on earth could have gotten away with those slacks, and I don't know why I let them put me into them."

Madame stared at the photograph. "You see what I mean about deterioration? In 1951 that wouldn't have happened. But you weighed a hundred and ten in this picture."

Rose said nothing.

"More?"

"Oh, the whole thing is so boring, so horrid. Is it for this that I'm alive? I weighed three pounds more than that. I can't eat a thing. A cocktail is deadly."

"A hundred and thirteen?"

"And a half."

"Then don't appear in this stretch material if you want to seem to have the same figure you've always had."

"Well, do I?"

"My dear, I don't know. Why did you come here?"

"I guess I do."

"You are not Twiggy or Jean Shrimpton. You don't need the high-fashion figure. At your height, you'd have to get down to ninety-two pounds, and at your age you couldn't do it."

"I was never even close. It's these hipbones."

"No, the hipbones aren't the trouble. A hipbone is a good thing to hang a skirt on, that isn't the point. But you're not doing modelling, and in your work they don't simply use you to show the line of the dress. You don't need the figure of a coat hanger and you couldn't have it."

The notion of the endless and hideous self-sacrifice involved in losing twenty pounds made Rose quail. Systematic near starvation and constant energy output, sweat suits and grinding bloating constipation as a way of life. "I don't want that."

"Of course not. What you want is the figure of the woman of thirty, a perfectly good figure, simply not that of a young girl."

"I'd like the young girl."

"Impossible."

"What do you think I should do?"

"You must combine nature and art. You must lose eight pounds and improve your muscle tone, and allow us to do what we can for you."

"What can you do?"

"We can help you to correct your most important figure defects."

"What are they?"

"You've asked about your hips and *derrière*, and about your bra cups. To start with, you're short-waisted, and this is the most troublesome and least obvious problem because it is so simple. Nothing troubles the designer like a short waist. It is innate and unchangeable."

"Show me."

Madame took up a picture of Rose in costume for the Automat dream sequence in *Goody*. She wore a sequined leotard with some boning in the bodice, net stockings, and that screwy headdress. This attire made the juncture of leg and hip uncomfortably obtrusive.

"Look," said the great *corsetière*, pointing. "See the jut of the bone shelf here? See how short a distance to the beginning of the rib cage?"

Rose nodded wonderingly. No designer had ever told her anything about this. Obviously it had all been said behind her back.

Madame Sylvie said, "Between the lowest rib, where there is bony protrusion, and the top of the pelvis, bony again, there ought to be a regularly proportioned length, depending on your height. In your case, the distance is disproportionately small, and you have a slightly heavier pelvis and a considerably deeper chest than most young women of your height. The muscled area over the kidneys and liver is shortened and thickened and crowded."

"And it bulges."

"Exactly. The virtue of such a figure is strength and durability; its defect is dumpiness, as the English say."

"Am I dumpy?" said Rose sadly.

"No, not at all, but you are insufficiently self-critical. Now watch. Lean on me." She supported Rose. "Swing your left leg free," she ordered. "See how it moves in the socket? When you stride or leap, as in dancing, the pelvis lifts and swings and the abdominal wall is lifted; there is a momentary bulging action, not ugly when you're sitting down, or standing very erect, but evident when you walk or dance. You will always seem less slim in motion than poised and still, and in your business you can't stand still."

"Not for long."

"Then what is to be done? Very much can be accomplished with a *combiné*."

"A *combiné*?"

"A full corset in a stretch fabric, with a mild cinching effect. It will encourage you to lift the rib cage out of the pelvis, and it will not allow swift and ungainly movement. Half the beauty of the Edwardian type was in the slowness of her pace. And you will notice that in the twenties, when by reaction the uncorseted girl came in, every dress was long-waisted, with the attention focused on the hips, often by an obvious stratagem like a broad stripe or a bow."

Rose suspected that she had missed a lot in life.

"But one can't go about in sportswear fully corseted," said Madame, pursuing her reflections.

"I started out as a sportswear model at seventeen."

"Precisely. At seventeen one does not worry about her corset."

"But at thirty-four . . ."

"I will design a line of foundation garments especially for you, in several models and colours, that will control your abdominal muscles and minimize their bulk, and I'll tell you when to wear them. I can't make you long-waisted, but I can help your designer to create that illusion. Another thing: don't wear two-piece outfits with strong colour contrast at the waist. I've seen you in them, and they're very unflattering."

"I had a lot of those in *Goody*," said Rose. "Very peculiar."

Madame wasn't listening. "The other matter is easier to correct. You complain that one breast is smaller than the other and that therefore all your bras are uncomfortable and a bad fit. That's silly. Any difference in size would be minimal and extremely hard to measure. The only means I can imagine would be to immerse the breasts separately in water to gauge the displacement."

"Can't you do it with a tape measure?"

"My dear child! Only very crudely, as crudely as with the eye. There is no significant difference in size, I assure you. The trouble is fortunately simpler and easier to correct. You're consistently holding your left shoulder lower than the right, I suspect to minimize the size of the left breast."

"Maybe."

"I think so. You've acquired a habit of swinging the left shoulder low, by a quite perceptible distance, and this is affecting the shoulder straps and cup sizes of any bra. You probably find that the right cup binds and chafes slightly under the breast."

Rose admitted the fact.

"But if the left were actually larger, it would be the one to bind."

"I guess you're right."

"You know I'm right. This is a matter for your trainer. Get that left shoulder into place with exercise, and we can fit you as your skin fits you, and there'll be no more chafing and binding. That's a promise which I can keep."

"That will be a nice change," Rose said.

When she came in, the *salon* was noisy with the cries and squeals of women in, if not torment, at least quasi-sexual agony. Out the window across the frivolous and lovely avenue she could see the consulates of several nations, and somewhere near, she remembered, the Cubans, until fairly recently. She wondered what had become of the leisurely gentlemen with perfect manners, cigars, and double-breasted suits who used to be seen on sunny mornings killing endless time in front of their prestige address. All dead? All in the hills of the Oriente province?

She swayed, staring out the window, in her leotard and tights, in a slower rhythm than her companions, most of whom seemed to have abandoned themselves to the species of corybantic ecstasy dear to the heart of S. J. Perelman. They stood, these devotees of the nine-hundred-calorie regimen, in front of a line of iron posts that looked like parking meters and vibrated like some sort of trick in a carnival fun house. To these shaking posts were attached broad belts of webbing which shook and pulled unpredictably, depending on which part of the body pressed against them. Slap, slap, slap, SLAP, SLAP, they resounded all along this line of girls, mixed with a deafening mixture of giggles, squeals, attempted conversations, protests of pain as the webbing struck too sharply at hip or thigh. A national fetish, thought Rose gloomily, for those who could afford it. In *salon* or studio, from New York to Terre Haute and beyond, these same machines racketed and vibrated.

Next to her an aged harpy with a ruined torso, still feebly resisting the inroads of six decades, shook and stomped in ritual earnestness, turning from time to time to those on either side of her to demand, "How much have you lost, dear?"

At first Rose made no reply, but at the third application she felt that politeness required speech, at least, if not information.

"I'm just trying to stay even," she said somberly.

"Oh, my dear, with a figure like yours, I can see how you'd want to. Aren't you slender, lucky thing! What do you do, dear?"

Rose pondered a number of answers, under the banging and shouting. "I'm a housewife," she said finally. Nobody even knew her.

"You must do your own work, to stay so slim."

"Quite a lot of it."

"Roger won't let me lift a hand. I tell him that's what's wrong with me, but he won't listen. You know how men are."

Rose said, "I may not know, but I suspect." The other woman had swayed away from her, and didn't hear. The band of webbing rubbed and slapped at her abdomen, wrinkling the cotton jersey of her leotard. She was quite certain that no real results were being effected. The only way to get rid of it without diet and real exercise, she thought, is with a knife. She switched the vibrator off and let the webbing drop in front of her, nodded and smiled politely at her neighbour, who had now commenced an obscenely rhumba-like oscillation, and went across the room to a device whose design had always amused her, a metal drum about two-and-a-half-feet wide, with a broad rectangular opening cut in the top. Inside was a series of irregularly shaped spindles, like chair legs, which could be made to rotate at varying speeds.

There were handles at the sides, and the whole thing could be adjusted to various angles. You could lie across it belly-down as though you'd just been saved from death by drowning, or you could mount it in any one of a number of somewhat suggestive attitudes, so that the spindles bumped solidly against the inner thigh. You could even lie sidewise across it, and so get at the spare tire over the kidney.

Once Rose had been at work on one of these machines when the next girl down, a dancer whom she had seen a number of times on television who was vainly trying to diminish the dimensions of her thighs, had looked up with a vague smirk of pleasure, caught Rose's eye, and said involuntarily, "Cheap thrill, eh?"

There was certainly a sexual aspect to the machines—whether sadistic or masochistic, or more probably both, she wasn't equipped to say. In a recessed compartment elsewhere on this floor there lurked an affair of rollers, surrealistic in conception, straight out of Kafka's penal colony, which was actually quite hurtful, and dangerous if misapplied. Rose had used it only twice. It marked her sides, Seth complained, and she gave it up.

She decided to have a go at her stomach muscles, even though they were in better shape than the rest of her, firm and rock-ribbed. She lay across the rotating spindles, gripped the handles, and gave herself to the machine's caress. It hurt slightly, there was no denying. She had eaten a piece of Melba toast and drunk some skim milk after leaving Madame Sylvie, and there could be no question of her stomach's being overfull for this exercise. There was nothing in it; there almost never was. Nevertheless she felt slightly sore across the lower abdomen, as though faintly nauseated or bilious. She associated this feeling with sleeping pills and tranquilizers, suspecting that they deranged her normal body chemistry; but what could she do? She had to get some sleep somehow. She wondered how long it would be before she could get off the pills; they always left that taste in the mouth. Her doctor swore that they couldn't possibly leave a taste in the mouth, but she knew they did, and then there was this faint abdominal distress.

I should just lie awake, she thought. But when she tried this, it was awful. She lay sweating and tossing until dawn, and finally dozed for half an hour to jump awake, aware that sleep was impossible for another day. Stretched across the barrel, thinking of real sound sleep, she almost drowsed when all at once she felt a terribly painful pinch on her belly. It went through her like a knife wound, and she cried out loudly. She let go of the handles and was thrown forward on her face on the other side of the machine.

She rolled onto her side and began to cry helplessly, feeling babyish. Her stomach hurt badly. She plucked at her leotard, but as it was all in one piece she couldn't find the wound. She sat up with her legs askew and went on crying.

One of the girls in attendance rushed up and yelled, "Did you hurt yourself, Miss Leclair?" Rose felt the united stare of a hundred eyes converge on her. Round pale blobs, the faces seemed, curious and unsympathetic.

"The barrel pinched me," she sniffed, "and it hurt like hell." The attendant helped her up. "You ought to warn people about them; they bite," she said, and went to the lavatory to examine her stomach. She stood in one of the cubicles and rolled her leotard down till she found the mark, an angry red welt an inch wide and four inches long. The machine had caught her with one hell of a pinch, just where the spindles moved in under the outer cylinder. Her flesh throbbed sadly, making her feel like giving way to helpless tears again. She stuck her arms back in the armholes of her leotard, shrugged the material into place, came out and stood in front of the mirror, looking despondently at herself.

She wished that the convention about the man calling the girl didn't inhibit her. She wanted more than anything to telephone Jean-Pierre. He was still in the city trying to arrange a distribution agreement for his films, and he had been awfully nice to her the night of the party and afterwards. He'd called the house several times, and taken her out for dinner. Despite her evident willingness to be agreeable, and despite their mutual attraction, there had been some constraint.

"It sounds ridiculous," he would say, "but I respect the marriage tie."

"Oh, so do I."

"It makes me uncomfortable to entertain somebody else's wife."

"Even if he's left her?"

"Even then. The whole thing needs thinking out."

"Then think about it."

"I do. I am."

Perhaps his thought processes were very deliberate. He hadn't reached any liberating conclusions, at least not yet, though she kept hoping that the phone would ring. God knows, she thought, I haven't gone from one marriage to the next. She had been married only once, for fifteen years, to Seth. I haven't been promiscuous. We were the idols of the fan magazines, the proof that happy marriages are made in Hollywood. But what do I do for an encore? She was glad that she hadn't said or done anything undignified; she had filed for her decree just as asked, had been a real little gentleman.

She had been widely quoted as saying, "If that's what Seth wants, I hope he gets it." When she had given the press that quote, she had been deliberately ambiguous, had implied right along that Charity Ryan could only be the requital of vice, not of virtue, that in getting her Seth would be getting exactly what he deserved; she'd been widely misunderstood.

Fifteen years with Sir Grishkin, she thought, that's what he turned out to be, just a dirty boy from the Upper West Side, not a knight in shining armour, and anyway I wasn't looking for armour, just justice. She felt that the divorce was somehow her fault, but she couldn't see how. What did I do? What didn't I do? What was missing inside me?

She looked sorrowfully at herself in the mirror, without the narcissism usually present in this act: fifteen years older, ten pounds heavier, lined. In her pictures she was still cast as a girl in her mid-twenties, but soon this would have to stop. "The woman of thirty" had been Madame Sylvie's expression, and surely there was room in society for such people.

She wet a hand towel, passed it over her face and around her eye sockets, and felt refreshed. Two women came into the lavatory, eyed her curiously, and whispered to each other, forgetting that she could observe them in the mirror.

Bzzzz … bzzzz … bzzzz …

Never offend a fan, she thought, and turned and smiled at them as warmly as she could.

"Aren't you Rose Leclair?" She could feel trailing behind this question some qualifying remark like "recently divorced from Seth Lincoln." He was more important than she, Number Two last year, Number One the year before, always in the top five.

"Yes," she said.

One of the women said, "I enjoyed *Sailor Take Warning* so much. You all seemed to be having such a good time."

"That Seth Lincoln," sighed the other, but her companion nudged her and she shut up.

"I haven't seen Mr. Lincoln for quite some time," said Rose, "but I'm sure he'd want to know that you liked the picture. Thank you very much for mentioning it."

They seemed surprised at her cordiality so she added something. "It's always encouraging to hear what people think, you know. Making movies is solitary work; well, not exactly solitary, but isolated. You don't know who you're talking to, not like the stage."

"Have you been on the stage?"

"No, I had no training for the stage. I was a model in California before I went into pictures, and I picked up what I know as I went along."

"Is the stage harder?"

"Yes, I think so, but movies aren't easy. What you need more than anything else in the movies is patience."

The two women said, "Patience?" together, looking at each other. They thought that this wasn't very glamourous.

"You never believe that you'll actually finish the film. You have to wait and stop and try again, and go on trying. Very dull, just like trying to keep your figure." She put her hands under her back hair, gave the heavy mass a toss, shook her head, smiled at the women, and went out on the floor to try again. She was scheduled for half an hour on a stationary bike, and so she walked to a row of them, almost all in use, and looked at the line of sweating, puffing women with detachment. An attendant went by and Rose asked, "Does this really do any good?"

"I have no idea," said the girl negligently.

Feeling pleased to hear a truthful statement, Rose climbed on the nearest free bicycle and began to pedal, slowly and easily at first, and then with a more insistent rhythm. It wasn't like a real bicycle: no resistance from the road. It was like riding a bicycle on the moon, or in some planet where the force of gravity was distinctly less than on earth. A good way to lose weight, she thought, move to Mars.

Around Bristol, Connecticut, as a child, she had owned a bicycle on which she had nearly got herself killed plenty of times on Route 6, riding over to New Britain or even as far as Hartford. Her bike hadn't been in the European style with thin tires and ten-speed gears, but a jazzy American model with fat, hard-to-push balloon tires, red paint, and much chrome. Her father, manager and part owner of a package store, and doing pretty well, had given it to her for her ninth birthday, and he had had to pull a few strings because at that time, during the war, bycles had been getting scarce.

"If you can't be a lawyer or a doctor, the liquor business isn't bad at all," he used to say when one of his more or less doubtful connections did him a favour. The Connecticut package stores were not the property of criminal interests but were not wholly detached from them. Mr. Leclair could remember, or said he could remember—her father had had a romantic imagination—when the highways between New York and Boston and Montreal had been crowded with armed convoys of illicit booze, traveling by night, under the ambiguous obscurity of a series of police payoffs.

"Liquor money," Mr. Leclair would sigh, "I can remember when even beer was against the law." He seemed in some way to yearn after those more colourful years. She was always aware of a radical insecurity in her father; he often spoke of his wish to be entirely respectable. "I didn't finish high school because of the Depression," he would say, "so I don't have a trade or profession. All I have is my connections in the business. Make friends, Rose, and be respectable."

Yet he had allowed her to enter a beauty contest and cross the country alone to look for work in California when she was still in her late teens, a gesture of irresponsibility, or perhaps magnanimity, which she had never clearly understood.

"Maurice, you're crazy. She'll get into trouble, she'll meet hustlers," her mother said.

"Rose is a good girl," he answered, placidly, truthfully, and she had never forgotten that; she had gone on being a good girl in all the senses that lie within personal volition. She had been a faithful wife, if a dull one, had stayed out of the gossip columns until recently, and those recent appearances had not been her choice. It's a good thing he's dead, she thought, pedaling furiously, he would have been disappointed. He hadn't liked Seth at all.

"It isn't that he's a New York Jew, that I don't care about. They're good family men. But you should have got married in church. You're a Catholic, aren't you?" This shocked her. He was no churchgoer himself. "I'd like to have seen you married from church. I guess it doesn't really matter." He had died the next year, and her mother, a nondescript and colourlessly pretty woman, now lived quite happily with a sister in Providence.

If her father had not had some vaguely discreditable associates in the liquor business, she'd have had to wait till after the war for her bicycle, when she'd have been a bit old for such a gift. It was one of the things she had in common with Peggi, early and independent bicycling, but Peggi had had to steal rides in the depressed back streets of Wheeling—her father had been chronically broke, a stationary migrant worker— he'd have been a migrant worker if he had taken any jobs, but he liked Wheeling and staying in one place, and refused to migrate.

"I never stole bicycles, just rides," Peggi said defensively, when they discussed their upbringing, "and I was only ever in night court the once." That had been on account of a semi-orgy at midnight in a gas station, but her sentence had been suspended. Peggi had turned out all right, better than all right, because she had somehow learned to hang on to her dough, and she got parts, not too many, not great, but regular parts, and as long as Rose was in the business Peggi would get supporting parts in her pictures. She was a pretty, plump, good-natured woman who looked stupid, so that she was often cast as a brainless party girl. This vacuity of countenance had kept her from star parts, and from anyone's taking her seriously who didn't know her well. She knew how to be silent, and how to conceal her opinions behind a flow of dumb-blonde chatter. She saved her money. Nobody since Rose's father had been a better friend to her, and like her father, Peggi had an unconcealed dislike of Seth. Years ago, oh, years and years before there was any question of a rift, she had said something.

"I'm not knocking your husband, sweetie, but would you ask him to stop touching me?"

"Touching you?"

"Yeah, patting, pinching, nothing very sexy, he just treats me like a suitcase or something. I don't know, he handles me."

"Seth does?"

"You've only got one husband."

"He doesn't pat me."

"Maybe he's afraid of you. Forget I mentioned it."

"Yes." She hadn't forgotten it, but after years of observation had decided that Peggi had imagined it. Of course she had not imagined it.

She took her feet off the pedals and let them spin. "Coasting," she said to nobody, "just coasting." Her thighs were aching; she decided that she'd had enough. There was still an hour in Goulmoujian's gym to be gotten through, a peculiarly noxious series of calisthenics designed to diminish her rear end and consisting mostly of contortions requiring her to lie on her stomach, grasp her ankles, and rock back and forth with her belly acting as a bearing. It was a taxing regime to which she did not look forward. With a sigh she gave up her bike and her sisterly place in line and went to the dressing room. For an hour she must rock on her belly, and tomorrow she would be stiff. No recourse!

... stiff ... stiff ... she lay in bed that Saturday morning with soft, lovely end-of-April light flickering through the curtains on her still face, stiff dry skin, aching eyes. Somewhere below Macha was operating the vacuum cleaner; the noise groaned and clanged in her eardrums like a dentist's drill. She had that sore, almost feverish, feeling that comes of overexertion, and she didn't want to get out of bed. She hadn't slept.

One good sleep, one good long rest, that's what I need, she thought, eyeing the phone beside her bed and the other bed beyond it. I should move both beds out of here and get a nice big single with lots of room for me and none for anybody else. The vacuum cleaner shrieked; her eyes hurt; another day to get through. Bottles in the glove compartment. Sun in her eyes.

She left her bed unwillingly and went to the big double window, threw back the doors, and looked down onto East-Sixty-first Street. Though it was close to ten o'clock there were few people along the block. They had bought the house in 1959, when their earnings were very high, and to maintain such a house, she now saw, required enormous earnings. It was costing her too much and she would have to do something about it, perhaps lease it to somebody who was really rich. She couldn't afford to live in it. She couldn't afford to live, period. But she didn't want to leave this white elephant to her poor mother, who wouldn't know what to do with it, and wouldn't get the right price.

Seth, she thought, Seth wanted a house in the city, and she was the one who was left to maintain it. She envied Peggi, who had some sense about real estate. She owned none, always leased, and let the landlord take the lumps. She had a two-and-a-half-room apartment on Bank Street near Hudson; there was no upkeep, she did her own dusting. When she was on the Coast she stayed in apartment courts, good but not extravagant, while Seth and Rose, bigger personalities, had to run an establishment on a grand scale wherever they went. "With all my worldly goods," she thought, "I devise and bequeath all whereof I die possessed," and then she saw that she'd telescoped phrases from the marriage service and the standard form of testament.

She decided to give Peggi a call, but the phone rang and rang and Peggi didn't answer. She had mentioned some weekend engagement. A personal appearance, a television interview, a Connecticut holiday? At the other end of the line the phone rang rang rang, No answer. Rose imagined the instrument sounding and echoing in Peggi's immaculate apartment, with the shades drawn and each loved possession in its proper place.

"I'm a clown, it's true," Peggi would say, "but I'm a neat clown. You don't see me leaving my stockings in the bathroom."

She was a strange woman, with a natural talent for self-control and contentment. They had met ten years ago on the set of a romantic comedy called *Next December* in which Rose had played a teen-ager of awesome and even slightly disgusting innocence, adrift in New York at Christmas. Peggi had had the second female lead, a none-too-bright clerk in a department store who takes in the bewildered waif. The dialogue in that picture had been radically banal, and the two young women had amused themselves for years by quoting key lines from *Next December* whenever they felt tired or depressed.

"Golly socks," Rose would say, batting her eyes, "this store is just like a whole world, I bet you."

"That's right, little chum," Peggi would answer with a straight face, "and there's good and bad in it too, like everywhere else."

"Will you watch out for me, Casey?" That was Rose's next line. For some reason a lot of the characters Peggi played had names of indeterminate sex, "Casey" or "Doc," intended to suggest a camaraderie outside of serious sexual relationship.

"You can be sure of that, honey," Peggi would laugh. "The Joan Blondell part," she would say, half angry. "I'm the one who wasn't Joan Blondell."

"You're complaining? I'm the one who wasn't June Allyson. Isn't that awful?" At least they could laugh about it.

"What made me mad about *Next December*," Peggi always said, "was the way everybody assumed that I was ten years older than you." In fact she was four or five years younger than Rose, but their physical types made accurate literal casting impossible. "I mean, you're older than me. And yet . . ."

"I'm just an itty-bitty sing," Rose would say, showing her dimples. "It's stupid, but you're lucky, you aren't stuck at nineteen forever. You could act on the stage. You can do different things. All I can do is stand around like Myrtle in her kirtle in King Arthur-type epics—that and ingénue parts. I'm stuck."

"You won't be nineteen forever."

"I'm not nineteen now, and I'm trying to age gracefully, but can you see me in other parts?"

"Not right now, no."

"But you could play them; you're versatile."

Peggi sighed. "I'd sooner play lovelies, like you."

"Oh, ha ha ha. I'll tell you what I am, Peggi, I'm pretty in the sense that I have a clear complexion and good health, and I'm not obese. I'm no beauty."

"You are, you are."

"Huh!"

People didn't turn around to look at her in the street. Charity now . . .

. . . and Jean-Pierre wouldn't be in the city either; it was that kind of day, probably spending a tough weekend with a banker. She rubbed her eyes and massaged her belly, with the memory of their first date vivid in her imagination, the most important opening date of the year, Easter Saturday, and *Goody* had been spotted in it. You had to give Bud and Danny credit for that at least, and she had a small percentage.

They can pay that to Mama.

She put some money in her bag and told Macha that she and Mr. and Mrs. Ponsonby could have the weekend free. ". . . till Monday afternoon. I'll be back here Monday afternoon."

"What about messages?"

"There won't be any messages, Macha." She passed a hand over her eyes. "But in case anybody should call, note the name and number on the pad by the phone."

The girl smiled dimly as Rose turned away. "Oh, Miss Leclair," she said softly.

"What?"

"I just wondered. Can I get you anything?"

"I'm going out," said Rose with surprise.

"I know . . . I just thought you looked like you needed something."

"A few kind words, Macha, that's all I need."

"Oh, Miss Leclair, I'm so sorry. About everything, I mean."

"Well, don't be."

"'No."

"Tell Mr. and Mrs. Ponsonby to have a nice weekend."

"Yes."

"Goodbye, Macha." She walked west along Sixty-first Street; she didn't want to do it but was unable to resist. She strolled along, feeling the heat of the fine April sun at her back and on her neck and back hair. She had twisted her hair into an unfamiliar knot and wore no makeup. Nobody would bother her. It took two hours to produce the Rose Leclair you saw on the cover of fan magazines, sometimes longer.

She was glad there was a lineup, though the picture had been running over a month. She tried to figure what the New York gross might be. Her pictures had always done well in the East, and in New York especially. But let's face it, she thought, stepping up to buy a ticket, this isn't one of my pictures and it isn't one of Tommy's pictures. It's a Charity Ryan vehicle.

She went inside, feeling very tense, and took an aisle seat well towards the back of the house, a long way from where she'd been at the premiere, right down front. She wanted to take a dispassionate look at the print, if that was possible. It wasn't. From the moment that goddamned song started, from the second the drums took up that boom-boom-boom and the colour went that sickly peach, she stared with frenzied hatred, rage, and self-contempt, at the giant figures, including hers, that towered before her.

She heard again the voices of Horler and Lenehan sitting along the row from her at the opening, and felt the steadying hand of a stranger on her arm, heard him try to calm her. She watched almost all the long film, shutting her eyes when it got too bad, but it finally beat her. She stumbled out of the theatre in tears of anger and naked shame. It was then that she decided to drive out of the city.

3

COMING UP

1

When the orange light came on, Lou Aspinall started to manip-
ulate the switchboard apparatus. He jiggled the hook and spoke
into the operator's mouthpiece, which he held awkwardly in
his left hand. He didn't usually work the switchboard, being the
boss, but the night clerk had taken the weekend off to go up to
Bridgeport to see her parents, and his wife, who normally filled
in, had gone to the movies. When he couldn't get any answer
from 34, he thought at first that he was doing something
wrong, and that his wife would bug him when she came in
for failing to follow her instructions, and annoying the guests.
He grew quite anxious to make a satisfactory connection, so
he went through a series of maneuvers designed to prove that
he was not at fault. He tried everything, but the orange light
stayed on and he still couldn't get any answer from 34.

He was certain that she was in there. Ever since she'd signed
in, he'd been sitting right beside the big window that looked
out onto the court. She'd gone straight to her room and stayed
there; he was sure of that. Her light was on too. He wondered
with growing concern why she had started to phone and then
stopped. If she was anxious to get a call through, wouldn't she
come charging out of her room to cause a stink because of his

mishandling of the switchboard? New York plates, expensive car—what was she doing in the Cresta Corona Motel at nine-thirty on a Saturday night? Why wasn't she off somewhere dancing, or making love, a good-looking girl like that?

He looked at the guest register and this time the name clicked. "Rose Leclair," he said out loud. "She's in the movies; she's even pretty famous."

Everything he had heard and imagined about movie people fell into place, and he guessed what she was doing in his motel. He threw down the register and ran through the door and across the court as fast as he could. Some nearby guests watched, wondering what had excited him.

First he tried to see through the window, but the Venetian blinds were angled down, so he knocked sharply at the door and called, "Miss Leclair, are you all right?"

Three guests came along the walk that ran in front of the rooms, a man from Detroit and a married couple from Rutland, Vermont. They had been enjoying a small party, sharing a bottle of Scotch and watching Saturday night TV, just down the walk.

"Is anything wrong?" said the lady from Vermont. She held a glass in her hand without self-consciousness, and looked smart and capable. Aspinall felt glad to see her.

"I'm not sure," he said, now quite disturbed. "She doesn't answer."

"Call again."

"Miss Leclair, Miss Leclair!"

"Are you sure she's in?"

"Yes, she hasn't opened her door since she arrived."

"Is that the Leclair in the movies, by any chance?" asked the man from Detroit. Suddenly they were all thinking the same thing and knew it. Three of them remembered the recent divorce, and the fourth, the man from Rutland, knew he'd heard something about her recently.

"I think so. I didn't take a real good look."

"You'd better get the door open anyway. Have you tried the lock?"

"Oh, I imagine it's locked, all right."

"Let's just see," said Mrs. Beard, the lady from Rutland. She switched her glass to the other hand, and tried the door. It wasn't locked. She opened it slowly and her head and her husband's and Mr. Aspinall's came around the door like spies in a spoof of a spy movie.

They all said simultaneously, "Oh-oh," and went into the room very fast. The man from Detroit stood in the doorway and talked to the crowd which collected immediately.

"Give them room," he said authoritatively. "Don't crowd around, please."

Aspinall said, "Can any of you run a switchboard?"

"I can," said Mrs. Beard, "in fact I often do, for him." She nodded at her husband, a Ford dealer with a terrific location on U.S. 7 just this side of Rutland.

"Please go into the office and call emergency at Norwalk Hospital; the number is right beside the board with some others. Ask them to send an ambulance in a hurry; it looks like an overdose of drugs." He felt peculiarly unflustered, and was glad he was functioning so smoothly; his wife would be amazed and pleased. "Then call the State Police—their number is there too. Tell them who we think it is."

Mrs. Beard calmly finished her drink, put the glass down on a magazine stand near the door, and went out. She had to push through the crowd.

Aspinall spoke quickly to her husband. "I don't think we have a doctor registered tonight. But you might ask if any of these folks has a medical or nursing background. I'm going to try to revive her. And then you might clear the doorway, so the stretcher team can get in and out."

The Ford dealer obeyed instantly. Aspinall heard his voice, calm and faintly Northern like his wife's, as he spoke to his acquaintance from Detroit and then to some other guests.

"There's been some sort of accident. I don't think it will be too serious." Aspinall felt glad to hear this. The thing to do was to get the whole mess under control. He felt people watching him through the doorway.

Acting much more assured than he was, he pushed back the woman's left eyelid. The eyeball didn't react to the light, and her skin was bluish and slightly cold. He stood up, bent, and straightened her on the bed, loosened her clothes, and went into the bathroom, where he soaked a couple of towels in cold water. He was just improvising but tried to do the right thing. When the towels were icy and heavy with water he came back, sat down beside the woman, and put his right arm under her neck and shoulders, lifting her up beside him. He held her tightly and patted her face and neck with the cold towels. Once or twice he slapped her face lightly, but got no response, or not more than a very faint flicker. In an amazingly short time he heard two sirens approaching from different directions, and in moments both the ambulance and the troopers were in the motel court. There were a driver, an orderly, and an intern on the ambulance crew, and they reacted smartly when they saw her.

"These what she took?" asked the intern. He picked up two small bottles from the bedside table, and then bent and picked up another from the floor. Somebody had stepped on it, and it was split down the side.

"I guess so," said Aspinall, "at least that's all there is around. There's nothing in the bathroom."

They worked her quickly onto the stretcher.

"Is she going to be all right?"

The intern said, "What a drag. I'll never know why they take the trouble."

"You don't think it was an accident?"

"She hadn't gone to bed or anything, and anyway who goes to bed at ten o'clock Saturday night? She didn't bother to undress."

"But she'll be all right?"

"Uh-huh. She isn't too blue yet, so we'll be in time. Better get going." In a few seconds they had her stowed away; then they drove off with the siren going, but not so urgently.

Lou Aspinall's wife appeared in the court. She stared at the disappearing ambulance, the troopers, the crowd along the walk. She spied her husband.

"My God, Lou, what have you done now?" she said.

Aspinall said, "Nothing, angel. I've just got to talk to the troopers."

His wife grew pale. "He hasn't done anything," she said, with the air of someone who lies deliberately out of misguided loyalty.

"Sweetie, they just want a statement."

"I can't turn my back and you get into a mess. Honestly, Lou, I wonder what would happen to you if I weren't around." One of the troopers interrupted her. "Mr. Aspinall's been a big help. He found her. In fact your husband's kind of a hero, Mrs. Aspinall, because he saved the woman's life, I'd say. You can't let these cases go too long."

"Will somebody please tell me what happened?"

Lou asked the troopers to wait for him a second. He led his wife into the office, away from the listening crowd. "We had a suicide attempt. Look, here in the register, Rose Leclair, she's quite well known. I helped to revive her." His wife sat down, amazed, and Aspinall felt superior. "I'm just going over to Norwalk," he said, "to the hospital. I'll hitch a ride with the troopers and give them my statement in the car, and they say they'll bring me back. Don't worry, it wasn't our fault."

"Why did she have to pick us?"

"It won't hurt us. I wouldn't be surprised we get some good publicity. Didn't you hear what the trooper said? I'm kind of a hero because I saved her life. It'll be on television."

The troopers called him and he went out and got in the patrol car. His wife watched him leave, and then began to go over what had happened with some of the guests. They all had different stories.

Riding down to the hospital with the siren going, Lou felt mighty excited as he talked to the officers. The driver said, "Just give us a quick line on what happened. Bert will make notes on it and tomorrow we'll have it typed up and ready for you to sign. Just the essential details, when you found her, what she looked like. It'll help to clarify it in your mind, in case the doctors need some information."

"I think I've got it straight."

The other officer said, "Not too fast now, I can't do shorthand. Maybe you'd better just answer my questions. When did she get to your place?"

"About nine, give or take a few minutes."

"Which way did she come from?"

"She came up from Wilton. I just took it for granted she'd come up from the city—the New York plates, and her clothes."

"How was she acting?"

"Normally."

"Not excited or hysterical?"

"No. I tell you, though, I thought she was mad about something."

"Why?"

"I don't know. She just seemed kind of . . . grim."

Soon the trooper had all he needed. They came to the hospital, got out of the car, and went into Emergency. Just inside the door they passed a phone booth in which the ambulance orderly was talking eagerly. What he said was, "Name your price, and it better be good, because this is real news." He was talking to a stringer for a small chain of Connecticut TV and radio stations that ran a lot of local news from all parts of the state.

"I trust you," said the orderly suspiciously. "We brought in Rose Leclair tonight. Uh-huh. That's who I mean. Looks like attempted suicide, but don't quote me." He went on to give an only slightly distorted story which included everything but the diagnosis and treatment. And because he had acted promptly, Channel 8, New Haven, had the story first, on its eleven-ten roundup of state and local news:

> Movie star Rose Leclair, 34, who recently divorced her longtime husband, top box-office attraction Seth Lincoln, was tonight admitted to Norwalk Hospital suffering from an apparent overdose of sedative and tranquilizing medication. Miss Leclair was discovered unconscious in her motel room by the owner of the Wilton motel where she was an unaccompanied guest. Latest medical bulletins indicate that she will recover.

By midnight the item was on national TV. Horler and Lenehan saw it, and Graham Faiers. Lambert Vogelsang saw it, and wired Seth in Paris. Hank Walden saw it and wondered where his client's interests lay.

Thelma Sloper heard it on her radio, and cried, and was upset for days.

Peggi saw it at eleven-ten on Channel 8. She had been spending the weekend outside Stratford, where some of her friends were preparing a season of Shakespeare. She drove down to Norwalk at once.

Jean-Pierre Fauré saw the same newscast. He had spent Saturday dickering with an exurbanite banker for financing on a projected film; he had a script of a kind to show, not much else. He had to borrow a car because he'd come out on the New Haven, and he and Peggi arrived at the hospital in Norwalk at almost the same time. They identified themselves as Miss Leclair's closest friends, and more or less assumed responsibility for her.

For quite a while they stood together in a doorway to the Emergency waiting room, till they might be able to see Rose.

"I want to phone her mother and tell her she's O.K.," said Peggi, after giving Jean-Pierre a long close look. "I hope she doesn't hear it first on TV."

"Then you'd better call soon. It'll be on all the late summaries."

"Should I just go ahead, without seeing Rose?"

"Yes, I think she'd like that."

Peggi took another good long look at her companion. She liked what she saw, and went at once to the phone booth just inside the entrance to call Mrs. Leclair in Providence.

Press representatives trickled into the hospital, not very many of them. National coverage doesn't require the actual presence of many reporters, as long as the story goes onto a wire. There were three or four men from metropolitan dailies, a Norwalk reporter, a remote crew from a TV station taking footage for network news, and a starved-looking freelance magazine writer. Not a big splash, not a horrifying violation of one's right to agonize in peace, no pushing and shoving. It was remarkable how subdued the whole occasion was. Jean-Pierre heard the doctor on the case give a medical bulletin which was a model of accurate clarity.

The press people stood around him in a congenial circle. "The only problem in a case like this is time," said the doctor. "We always get the happy ending if we have enough time."

"What actually takes place, doctor?" asked an interviewer, sticking a mike under his nose.

"Would you move that thing back a little?"

"Oh sorry, sure."

"When the drug is assimilated into the bloodstream, there is impairment of the circulation. In effect, the capacity of the blood to circulate oxygen is drastically lessened. The result is that the brain cells begin to break down from anoxia. There is this brain damage, and damage to the central and peripheral nervous systems, and unfortunately these effects are irreversible. Once the damage is done, it can't be fixed. So you see it's important to remove the toxic substance at once."

"How much time did you have?"

"I would estimate that she finished swallowing the tablets a little after nine-thirty; there was a margin of about forty-five minutes for assimilation to begin and accelerate. Mr. Aspinall went in to check on her just before ten, and they got her in here very quickly. We were working on her by ten-twenty, by my watch, which might be a minute or two slow."

The interviewer whistled. "That's cutting it pretty fine."

"Yes. Another half-hour and she'd have assimilated a lethal dose. You get a fluttery heart action, progressively inefficient respiration, pale cold skin with a distinctly bluish tone. Deep coma and finally death. You ought to talk to the motel owner; he really did save her life."

"And she's going to be all right?"

"Oh yes, certainly, by Monday she'll be fine. Her stomach will be stiff and sore tomorrow, the pumping has that effect. But there's no physical damage." He thought of a mysterious red welt on her stomach, wondered again how she got it, and decided to say nothing about it. None of his business.

"Doctor, was it a massive overdose?"

"Yes."

"Could she have done it by mistake?"

The doctor's face was without expression. "It's possible."

"Would you care to comment further?"

"Can we have your name, please?"

"I'm Doctor Theodore Sampson."

They had what they wanted and at once went off to talk to Lou Aspinall, who was fidgeting and walking around in little circles at the other end of the room. Doctor Sampson stared at the reporters' retreating backs for a moment, smiled to himself, and came over to Jean-Pierre.

"You and Miss Starr are looking after her?"

"Yes. Miss Starr is telephoning her mother. I'm afraid Miss Leclair led a rather solitary life."

"A recent divorce, wasn't there?"

"Yes. I believe she's alone much of the time, and I'm sorry to say without many close friends."

Doctor Sampson grew sober, almost sad. "That's remarkable, isn't it?"

"It's sad," Jean-Pierre said. "I don't think it's remarkable."

The doctor caught it. "Quite correct. You mean not unusual. All I meant to say is that here we have a woman who is young, rich, famous, admired, but without friends, passed out alone in a motel from an overdose of pills. It's alarming." His face was concerned. He was quite a young man.

"She may have had feelings that we know nothing about," said Jean-Pierre equably.

"Unquestionably," the doctor said, "but it's a reflection on all of us. Is that what we do to our darlings?"

Peggi had come back in time to overhear some of the conversation. She said, "Yes, that's exactly what we do to our darlings. I thank God every night of my life that I never made it big as a star. I'm a big earner, I live a comfortable life, nobody bothers me. And poor Rose . . . I hate to think of her doing that alone." She looked angrily at Jean-Pierre, without meaning to single him out for blame.

"Her mother will be here in the morning."

"We'll stay till we can see her," said Jean-Pierre. "When will that be?"

Doctor Sampson hesitated.

"You said yourself there's no physical damage."

"All right, you can see her when she's comfortably in a room. They'll be taking her up in, oh, I guess forty-five minutes. We just want to observe her heart action for a little while. Routine."

"If I'm any judge, her heart is fine," said Peggi.

"Sure it is, but we have to make absolutely certain. I'll let you know as soon as she can be seen. We'll give her our best accommodation. If you want to go and check at Admissions, they'll give you the room number. Perhaps you could wait up there."

They thanked the doctor and turned to go, but as they moved towards the elevator a reporter identified Peggi, and there was a surge in their direction. Peggi talked it up to the press as though a huge crowd of Rose's friends were pressing against the doors and windows. She felt it inappropriate that just the two of them should be there.

"Do you want to say anything, Miss Starr?"

"I'm not Rose's spokesman, but I think you should remember that she has been under strain, working very hard, and she's had personal problems to work out."

"What about her last picture? Was she disturbed about it?"

"Do you mean *our* last picture?"

"Yes, that's right, you were in it."

"I was in it," said Peggi, very coldly.

"Was Miss Leclair satisfied with the picture?"

"Yes."

"Wasn't her part cut?"

"I'm sorry, I didn't edit the picture. It's doing well and making money for all of us. As far as I know, Rose is satisfied with it."

"Why would she do this?"

"Do what?"

"Take an overdose."

"I have nothing to say about that at all. I haven't talked to Miss Leclair. Look, can't we postpone this till we've seen her? You can't get it into the Sunday editions anyway, so another twelve hours won't hurt."

"Who is this gentleman?"

"This is Jean-Pierre Fauré, the director. If you know anything about French movies, you know his work."

Jean-Pierre seized his cue. "Never mind about my pictures, at least those I've already made. I'm interested in Miss Leclair, and I intend to make her an offer."

"For a new picture?"

"Yes. I think Miss Leclair would fit into European film-making perfectly. She has certain qualities that are perhaps more appreciated there than here. I'm very eager to work with her; she has great charm." He spoke quietly but with intensity, and the reporters grew less strident. It seemed to surprise them that the object of their inquiries should not be entirely without friends.

"Why don't we talk tomorrow, say around noon?" said Peggi. "You'll be doing the follow-up. When we've seen her." She got rid of them by charm and force of will; they went away and began to harass the hospital staff until an intern and some orderlies told them to get out.

"I didn't realize you were after Rose."

"Neither did I, until this minute. You know how you'll carry an idea around in your head for weeks without fully realizing it. Then all at once some suggestion will cause you to act. When you introduced me to those men, I didn't know I was going to say that, but having said it I see that it is true, and I've been thinking about it ever since I met Rose."

"That's not very long."

"At the premiere, you know, I was procured for the job by your producers. I think that's about the last favour I'll do for them. They've caused me a lot of trouble, and I almost didn't do what they asked. I'm glad now that I did. I had talks with Horler and Lenehan for over a year, about putting my pictures into general release over here. I've made four trips for these discussions. I trusted them."

"That's a mistake. Look at poor Rose. Have you been seeing her?"

"Three times. I think we've been getting to know each other."

"She's a very nice girl."

"Yes, I know."

A nurse accosted them. "Miss Starr," she said, "they've taken Miss Leclair upstairs, and she'll be in Room 420 if you want to go up. You'll find Doctor Sampson there, and I'm sure he'll let you see her."

They thanked her. She went away and they buzzed for the elevator, and rode upstairs in thoughtful silence.

He looks okay, Peggi thought, and he talks a good game; he spoke right up to the reporters. She was aware that there was no clear way to guess whether he would be a friend or not. He came from Bud and Danny and was therefore suspect, would have to be checked out. She noticed again the slight physical resemblance to Seth. But his quality, his tone, his personality were all so totally unlike Seth's as almost to conceal the likeness.

She made a mental note to go and see one of his films, if one was playing in the city, or if she could borrow a print and arrange to have it screened. He had a big nose, and eyes like a friendly and rather large animal, an intelligent horse or bear. He wore heavily rimmed glasses, and looked more like a professor than a director. She was curious about his pictures, though she had always considered European producers very small potatoes.

The elevator stopped with a slow whoosh, and after the doors opened they spotted the doctor at the end of the hall by the solarium. He raised a hand and smiled; everything was fine.

Once in a while we have an acute sense of the physical presence of another person, and behind that powerful presence we somehow grasp the reality of that person as subject—the actual life of another self. We really can communicate with others—it's possible though difficult—and Peggi felt, as they sauntered down the corridor, that she was receiving Jean-Pierre's signal, was on his wavelength; she had a clear awareness of how he existed in himself, not as an object. The feeling wasn't exactly that of sexual love or intellectual curiosity; it was what we call "coming across." Like certain other kinds of artists, orchestral conductors especially, the director had an extraordinary ability to project the life of his intelligence and feelings, his soul, to the people whom he met. It's hard to say how this is done, but it isn't simply a trick of the heart, a meretricious device.

This "coming across" or penetration of the trans-objective subject (to change the diction) requires enormous personal reserves of knowledge, experience, and reflection; there has to be something in the person. When we meet such people they are easy to recognize because they radiate understanding and wisdom; they are laden with *esse intentionale*, rich with the being of the people, actions, and things they've known. Peggi sensed this richness in Jean-Pierre; she could see him shine, and wished that for once this kind of action could be directed at her. She saw that she could easily love this man, and wanted to know him much better. But she also knew that Rose had got there first; she would be loyal. And yet she would be as attractive and as candidly friendly as possible, just in case.

The doctor said, "They're tucking her in, and you can see her for a little while before she goes to sleep."

"Has she been sedated?" Peggi asked.

"I gave her very light medication to calm her. This is not a classical case, you know. The pattern is all wrong."

"In what way?" asked Jean-Pierre.

"For one thing you can tell from talking to her that she's a woman of considerable courage and wit, which isn't typical of overdose cases. If you ask me, she's been driven into a gesture out of unendurable irritation. It's a damned good thing she reached for the phone."

"You mean that she won't try it again?"

"I wouldn't have any hesitation about discharging her. I don't want you to think that I'm treating the case lightly. I'm not a psychiatrist, not even a counselor. But I'll willingly discharge her on Monday because I think we ought to treat the matter as a foolish spontaneous gesture, take it lightly and trust her, and our own judgment. I don't believe she'll try it again. I don't believe she really tried it once."

"I don't understand," said Peggi.

"She's terribly strong; her organism is not death-centered, but full of life. As soon as she got that awful junk into her she started to fight it. That's why she went for the phone."

"Consciously?"

"Who can tell? I think the entire organism was involved: she is full of the desire to live."

Jean-Pierre gave a long exhalation, almost a sigh. "That's what I think."

"Then don't think me remiss when I discharge her on Monday. There isn't a thing wrong with her, except the question of sleeping. She's been taking a lot of sedatives and hates them. Can't one of you figure out a way to help her to relax, and sleep in the ordinary way?"

"I'll take her to a Fauré Festival, that should do it," said Jean-Pierre.

"I'll come too, and we'll bore her to sleep," said Peggi.

"Go ahead in then," said the doctor, "and maybe one of you can pick her up on Monday. She says she wants to go get her car and apologize to Mr. Aspinall—they don't often think of that. I suppose you'll be around most of tomorrow?"

They said they would.

"Stay about fifteen minutes," he said, and went on his way.

When they went into the room Rose looked at them and blushed. She said, "Golly socks, this hospital is just like a whole world."

Peggi said with relief, "Yes, little chum, and there's good and bad in it too, like everywhere else. AND yes, yes, I'll take care of you."

"Good," said Rose. "Hello, Jean-Pierre."

"Hello."

"When you talk to the reporters tomorrow, say to them: 'Yes, Miss Leclair tried to kill herself. But then she changed her mind.' That's the important part."

"We'll do that."

"Don't forget, that's the important part. I feel sleepy."

"You are going into a deep sleep," said Jean-Pierre hypnotically, and the friends parted.

The two women in New York who had talked to Rose in the lavatory said wonderingly to each other, "She must have run out of patience."

Late Saturday night, Horler said to Lenehan, "Wouldn't you know she'd miss the Sunday editions."

2

When Doctor Sampson said, "Take the summer off," there was nothing to do but obey. In effect, she decided, she'd been paroled in the custody of Jean-Pierre, which might not be so bad if he was all she hoped. She didn't know whether the police had any grounds for a charge against her; they had no plans to bring one as far as she knew; she decided not to ask about it. When the doctor came by the room Monday morning to discharge her, she decided that one more day on her back wouldn't hurt. She had to emerge pretty soon, but another day . . . another day.

She meant to go straight back to the Cresta Corona Motel to speak to the owner, and maybe give him an extra couple of nights' rent on the suite because of the trouble she'd caused. Then she'd have to face Mr. and Mrs. Ponsonby and Macha, and the image of the somber and ugly features of the young housemaid hovered in front of her and made her uneasy. She would have disappointed the girl by her action, for Macha evidently thought the world of her employer. That she should try to kill herself might make poor Macha very unhappy: things were not as they appeared, Rose was vulnerable. She would have to apologize to Mr. Aspinall, to the Ponsonbys, to Macha.

And there would be men from the papers and magazines, probably not many, wanting to see her, to ask her exactly what she'd intended. Whom had she wished to injure? Had she simply executed a "You'll be sorry when I'm gone" tactic? Could she really be that young? And anyway, who would care, ah, who would care? Seth with his new love in Paris? Max Mars? Her mother would, she thought, and for quite a while, but hardly anybody else. Surely she hadn't tried to kill herself to spite her poor mother; she had forgotten how that lonely and foolish woman would feel. They saw each other only twice a year, but checks went up to Providence every month, and she wrote often. She was no more unfilial than most.

Seth had been brought up by an uncle, a luggage manufacturer, who lived on Eighty-sixth Street between West End Avenue and Riverside, in an apartment building that dated from around 1912. Filiality for Seth had been a semi-annual taxi ride to a superannuated part of town, and for Rose it had been letters and cheques, and the cheques would go on whether she did or not. What was the meaning of what she had done? Her stomach muscles still ached from the pumping, but apart from that inconvenience, the bed rest had made her feel like a freshly minted coin. Another day and she'd be wrestling tigers.

What had she tried to do and why? Had she really desired extinction or had she simply imagined it with insufficient force, and taken it for something else, a sleep, a dream? Why had she gotten over there and knocked the phone off the hook? Who had dictated that action?

She lay comfortably on the firm, flat, hard bed, knees up, thinking vaguely of smoking a cigarette, remembering Saturday afternoon at the movies. She had felt dirty. And she had been planning the attempt.

Before she faced the world again, she would have to try to understand what she had done, to dismiss once and for all the idea of making a second attempt. She hated to give trouble, to derange the routines of others. She blushed fiercely at the thought of becoming one of those tiresome celebrities known the world over for suicide attempts, from whom hotel managers draw back in alarm as they check in, whom private detectives marry for two weeks, who are up to their necks in pill bottles. Such a sad story, such fakery, such childlike exhibitionism. Life was unpleasant, bitter most of the time. She had been badly hurt, had run from the pain, and in running had done something wrong. Self-destruction was not an option, not a legitimate means, and not really within her powers. Doctor Sampson said jovially, "You couldn't kill yourself. Can a cork drown?" He tapped her and prodded her, chuckling now and then and remembering to treat her like a person and not a slab of meat.

"Haw, haw, haw." He had a horse laugh which amused and annoyed her,

"Do you mean I faked it? Why should I fake it?"

"Naw, you didn't fake it. You meant it all right, but you're incapable of it. As soon as your body understood what you were doing, it reacted. You can't kill yourself. Very few people can. In most of us, our substance insists on life. Those who can have often prepared their bodies to submit by drugs or alcohol or opiates of another kind, violence, radical sexuality; or else they don't give the body a fair chance, they hurl it suddenly under a train. That's what I call a cheating suicide; it isn't fair to your body. I once had a man brought into Emergency who had swum twelve miles straight out into the Sound, trying to drown himself. He'd never swum more than four or five miles before and was certain he'd gone too far to get back. When he tried to let himself sink, he wouldn't go down. When he submerged he couldn't force himself to let the air out of his lungs; it just wouldn't go. So he turned around and swam the twelve miles back. Disgusted? You bet."

"Why did they bring him to you?"

"Well, he was pretty tired. But he couldn't kill himself except by cheating, by taking a sudden irrevocable step. The cemeteries are full of people who had no genuine wish to kill themselves. A real honest drive towards self-destruction is extremely rare. Most of us haven't thought the question through. And those who have decide against, in all but a very small minority of cases."

"Have you ever had a case of the real thing?"

"Only once when the man was clearly sane."

"Who?"

"This'll make you laugh. He was a philosophy professor."

"Not very glamourous."

She saw that he didn't want to talk about the case, and let it drop. "As long as you don't think I'm a faker," she said.

"You're not a faker, and you're in wonderful shape. Go home tomorrow and fall in love, so we can use this bed."

"That's an interesting slip," she said. "Will you put through the discharge?"

"Done it already. And that was no slip."

"I just get up and go?" She wondered if he was taking her entirely seriously, and then understood that he wasn't, and why he wasn't. "I'll go quietly," she said.

She did, very quietly, in a cab Tuesday at noon. Peggi had agreed to go by the motel and ask the proprietor to lock the suite she'd had and hold it for her a couple of days. She had told Peggi to offer him double the usual nightly rate, more if necessary, but Mr. Aspinall wouldn't take it.

"My rates don't vary," he said. "How long does she want it for?" He knew whom he was talking to, and was pleased and flattered.

"Tuesday afternoon. Wednesday at the latest."

"She must have made a quick recovery."

"Oh, she's fine, just fine."

"I guess she was under a strain, huh, Miss Starr?"

"Oh, you know me?"

"Sure I do. I've seen you in plenty of movies. I'll go into town with my wife in the middle of the week, nights when the clerk isn't too busy. It's funny, I'd have recognized you before I would Miss Leclair."

"That sometimes happens."

"She's pretty all right, on the screen, but you don't seem to remember how she looks. I didn't recognize her when she checked in, but I knew right away who she was ... after, that is. I guess she was under a strain."

"She's better now, and she'll be along Tuesday or Wednesday. Should I pay you now?"

"That's all right. When she's ready to check out." As Peggi turned to go he said excitedly, "Miss Starr, could you wait a second?" He left the desk and went into the office behind, coming back quickly with one of those photographs you can get in the five-and-ten for half a buck, tinted to look like a colour shot. On it was written "Peggi Starr" and underneath "Appearing in Universal Pictures." She held the shoddy gold-coloured tin frame in her hand and looked at it. She remembered the day in 1960 when it had been taken, when she had been at the very top among the younger featured players, when it had almost looked as if she might make it as a star, if only it hadn't been for that rough-voiced dumb-blonde quality."

She laughed. "Where did you find this?"

"When you phoned I drove into Wilton to the drugstore. I'd be glad to have it."

"Sure. What would you like?"

"Well, my name, if that's O.K."

"What's your wife's name?"

"Dena. With an 'E'."

Peggi wrote: "To Lou and Dena with my very best wishes, April 30th, 1967." She signed it in a big curly hand quite different from the facsimile printed on the photo. He compared the signatures.

"They don't put your own writing on these, eh? I can see why."

Peggi had never thought about it. "She'll be in Tuesday," she said.

"I'll be right here waiting," said Lou. "Goodbye, and thanks." When Peggi left the office he began to look for a place to hang the picture. As he examined the inscription, he puffed out his chest with pleasure and pride. He called, "Deenie, Deenie, come and look at this," looking around for a tack and a hammer. His wife came, and read the inscription. "Isn't that something?" she said. She watched as he hung the picture.

"Over more to the right, Lou," she said.

Rose got there around one o'clock. She left the cab before they were in sight of the motel. "This is far enough," she told the driver, "I'll walk from here." He made a breathtaking U-turn and drove off down Route 7.

It was the second of May, and an absolutely perfect day, just the sort of day to be restored to life and the world. She walked slowly along the shoulder of the highway; twice cars stopped or slowed near her as if to offer a ride. Each time she angled her steps away from the road, and the cars drove on. Soon she came to the motel court and driveway, the big electric sign swinging slowly in the light breeze. CRESTA CORONA MOTEL: LOU ASPINALL PROP. it said cheerfully, in tones of green and brown. She paused in the driveway, took off a shoe, and emptied it. Her car was parked where she'd left it on Saturday night and there was somebody sitting in it. She saw a pair of male ankles propped in the window of the right front door. She hurried over and was delighted to find Jean-Pierre stretched out waiting for her wearing a grin of anticipation.

"I'm very very VERY glad you're here at last. I'm dying of hunger and we have twenty miles to drive to a place I know, that is, if I can find it again. We're going on a picnic."

She saw a basket of food on the back seat, with two bottles of wine sticking out.

"We'll pick up your things and get out of here," he said decisively. They went into the office and were greeted, none too effusively, by Mrs. Aspinall. She let them into the motel room, found Rose's bag, and added up the bill at a very modest daily rate.

Rose said apologetically, "I asked Mr. Aspinall to add on something for the trouble."

"He doesn't want to. He says it's O.K." She conveyed by her attitude what the charge would have been if left to her. Rose paid the bill and they left. Nobody asked for an autographed picture.

As they drove out of the parking lot, Jean-Pierre put the top down, and at no point did he drive fast enough to ruffle Rose's hair. "In France I drive fast," he said, "but I'm a stranger here." He took the car expertly along Route 7 and in a few minutes jogged left on a narrow local road, displaying complete familiarity with the district. In a few minutes more they crossed the state line and came into Westchester County and the beginning of hills and lakes. They turned first left, then right, and drew to a stop beside a pretty and almost countrified little lake, where there were picnic tables.

He walked around the car to help her out, and then leaned into the back seat and caught the handle of the lunch basket. "We're here," he said.

They were certainly ambiguously located.

"Are we in Connecticut or New York?" Rose asked. "I'm lost."

"I didn't think I could find this place. I think it's just about on the borderline."

"Aha."

He lugged the food along to the picnic table he'd chosen—the one nearest the water. There was a green oil drum next to it, for refuse disposal. The view from the table was extremely pleasing.

"I'm impressed by these arrangements, this care for the public convenience." It wasn't really a very sequestered spot; there was nothing special about it, but it was pretty and quiet. There weren't any other picnickers around, perhaps because it was the middle of the week, or because it was almost two o'clock, a little late for lunch. Rose noticed that she felt very calm and very hungry. The sight of the sunlight on the water had for her an oddly soothing, almost soporific effect.

"How do you know about this place?"

He pointed with precision. "I've been staying with people just outside Redding, about half an hour's drive from here. We came here last weekend. I like it even better this time."

"People in the business?"

"I'm afraid so. Finance people. I would sooner eat than talk." As soon as they'd left the car, he'd opened a small cooler and shoved the bottle of white wine well down into cracked ice. "There's no question of its being really chilled," he said regretfully, "but it will be drinkable. I couldn't get it into the cooler when it was closed." They drew the cork and killed twenty minutes putting out paper plates and some red and white checked napkins, and eventually the wine—an inexpensive Pouilly-Fuissé—was cool, though not cold.

"Next time I'll do it right," he said, "and the red is excellent at this temperature." They ate cold fowl and supermarket salad, olives and pickles and slightly messy Roquefort, and other junk, drinking the pleasant wine in friendly silence. When she had had three glasses Rose suddenly noticed that she hadn't thought about her weight. It was a long, self-indulgent; delicious meal. Feeling as though she'd just gotten out of jail, she said, "What about the other bottle?"

"I thought we might sit by the shore and drink it there."

This seemed an excellent notion. They threw their garbage in the oil drum, wiped their glasses, grabbed the Beaujolais, and sauntered down a winding path to the shore, where they sat in the sand, stretched their legs out in front of them and deliberately passed the bottle back and forth: For a cheap wine, it was a sensational success. "This was a very good idea," she said solemnly. She screwed the stem of her glass into the sand and leaned back, supporting herself on her palms. While he watched with intense pleasure she pushed her palms deep into the warm sand, brushed them off briskly and passed them through the heavy warm mass of her hair, lifting it and tossing it over her hands. She had much nicer hair than Charity. He watched her closely; she could hear his slow breathing.

For once she wasn't hungry, she wasn't alone, and she was very slightly drunk She took a long breath, looking at the sky.

"Oh God," she said, "it's good to be alive."

They finished the wine in silence, then went for a stroll along the shore of the miniature lake. She had no idea where he had taken her, or how far, but in a few minutes she grasped his hand, walking along silently beside him. They went to the end of the beach, getting plenty of sand in their shoes, turned and walked the length of the beach in the other direction, passing the bottle of Beaujolais and their empty glasses, stuck upright in the sand.

"That would make a good shot," said Jean-Pierre, breaking the silence.

"Why don't you tell me what you're here for?"

He had been deep in reflection, and blinked once or twice. "I came over first about a year ago, to see about distribution. I own six films which have had no North American distribution outside of Quebec, or virtually none. Two of them have had short runs in the New York area, on a trial basis, and that's all. These films have already earned back their costs in Europe, and if I could get them shown widely in America and reviewed, one after the other, I might make a lot of money."

"Is that what you want?"

"I like to have as much money as possible, but I'm using that as a figure of speech. Most of my profits have always gone into my next picture; that's how I've been able to make the films I've wanted without interference."

"No Horler? No Lenehan?"

"Nothing like that at all, no fraud, no misrepresentation, and no slavery. Did you know that when Truffaut made *Jules et Jim* his star did the cooking for the crew when they were on location in Germany?"

"You're kidding."

"No, I'm not. And I'll tell you another story, how I got into films. When I passed my *bac* I enrolled at the university but spent most of my time seeing movies. I wrote for *Cahiers du Cinéma*. I knew Bazin, and I was an assistant editor on the review for years. My criticisms were always harsh, and all the directors used to challenge me to support my theories by making a film. None of them in the 1950s believed in cinema; they betrayed it, all but those of us who practiced the *politique des auteurs*."

"What's that?"

"Well in sum it's the idea that the director should take all responsibility for the film, should sign it, and leave the mark of his ideas everywhere in it, just as a painter does. Director's cinema. In the early spring of 1957 I inherited some money from my aunt, not much, but in effect her life's savings."

"And you put it into a film."

"Into *Feu James Dean*. That was the year of *Ascenseur pour l'echafaud* and *Le beau Serge* and, I think, *Les quatre cents coups*. Or let's see, no, I think that was a year or so later. But this was the beginning of *la nouvelle vague*, Truffaut, Chabrol, De Broca, Louis Malle and me. Jean-Luc didn't make a feature for a year or two after that. *A bout de souffle* was 1960. I simply took my inheritance and hired a professional crew, and some good young actors whom I knew—two of them are now stars—and made up the shooting schedule, and shot the film in four weeks. I made it in the country around my aunt's farm as a memorial, country I knew well from childhood though I was born in Paris. I wrote it, shot it, directed it, edited it, helped with the dialogue, arranged for distribution, and paid for it. Many people called it the best European film of that year. I think *Le beau Serge* was better, but who am I to disagree?"

"Paradise," said Rose.

"I've made six, all the same way. Each one has done a little better than the last. Now I would like to have international distribution, particularly in North America, and the money that goes with it."

"Why the money?"

"I don't want money for power, but for value, for use, and it's the same with sex. If I had that money, I could use international stars and wide-screen technique, although I'm not sure about wide-screen yet. I could experiment with colour like Antonioni and Godard."

"Value, not power?"

"That's right." "You ought to use my car," Rose said. "You haven't got one here, have you?"

"No."

"If you're trying to get around Connecticut on weekends, you should have a car. Why not drive me back into the city and take the car out to Redding with you? Use it as much as you like."

They picked up the bottle and wine glasses. "I'll do that," he said. "I can take you for rides when you aren't busy."

"I won't be busy. I'm taking the summer off, on the doctor's advice. He claims I've been working too hard, but that isn't what's the matter with me." She followed Jean-Pierre towards the car. "There's nothing the matter with me."

"Evidently not."

They threw the Beaujolais bottle away, got in the car and drove off south and east. In five minutes they crossed the state line, back into Connecticut. They had been poised exactly on the border.

After that, through June and July, they made a series of forays into the Connecticut countryside. They formed the habit of zipping up the Parkway to Route 7 and following that tortuous highway north and west, close to the New York border. As the summer came on they found themselves going deeper and deeper into real country.

The last of these excursions, before they got down to serious matters, turned into one of those gorgeously dreamlike occasions that lodge in the imagination, around which one's most precious recollections may coalesce for the rest of a lifetime. They had come up the highway past many familiar crossroads and turnoffs, past the Cresta Corona Motel, further and further, and with every turn of the road and every mile traversed they felt themselves more certainly lovers, though nothing was said and no embrace achieved at that stage. They were halfway across Connecticut when they stopped to eat at a little Italian steakhouse at the side of the highway. The owner told them that the Appalachian Trail passed along the other side of the highway, crossing it and going into highlands farther south. Where they were, it followed the river.

"What river?"

The owner looked scornful. "The Housatonic, what else?"

They were interested and amused, and after lunch they drove another half mile towards Cornwall Bridge, parked on the river side of the road, and went down a rather steep incline through brush and across rocks till they came to the river. Here the Housatonic isn't a great river like the Saint Lawrence, but it's more than a stream, maybe fifty yards across, shallow but swift, not dammed and sedgy but fresh, enlivening and sweet, no little lost creek but a real strengthening river with rich vegetation along its banks. They were really into the country and the pastoral life, hearing nothing but the calls of wildfowl and the sound of water. They came along marshy banks, stepping carefully on spongy footing, and soon picked up the trail markings. Jean-Pierre told Rose what they were, how the trail ran from New England to Georgia, cleared and marked for friendship's sake by people all along the route.

"Where did you hear about this stuff?"

"I'm a camper," he said, starting to laugh. "Not camp—camping, the real thing." He'd been all over Europe on a scooter in the summers with a companion and a small tent. She didn't ask the sex of the companion.

They moved along slowly in the warm sun. Suddenly there was violent motion in the riverbank grass, a whir of strong wings, and a great bird rose up before them, alarmed at their approach, spiralled into the air and crossed the river to settle peacefully on the other bank. The bird was brown with gray markings and a broad striped tail.

"What is it?" said Rose excitedly.

"It might be a wild turkey." They could see the bird quite plainly at the edge of the water. "There's a nest around here, and she's drawing us off, and she probably feels safer on the other side." They didn't disturb the nest, though they looked for it for a minute or two before they followed the blazes another mile or so to where their path mounted towards the highway and the height of land above. When they came out into open sunlight on a slope fifty yards above the riverbank, they sat down on a log and gazed at each other. Their gaze deepened and they involuntarily moved closer.

The log they sat on was old and rotten in places, split open by successive winters, studded with fungi. It smelt strongly and sweetly of organic matter in decay and was full of congregated insect life. Rose stared down between her legs at a column of ants trailing through the grass. The sun was hot on her neck, the grass green and yellow in a complex, bewildering pattern. Her vision blurred.

"How long are you going to stay here?" she asked.

"Till I finish a draft of a script; a month, two months. I'm beginning to lose interest in American financing, which just means that I haven't been offered any."

"What's the script called?"

Jean-Pierre shuddered instinctively, in a spasm of self-mistrust. "I think you'd like it. It's called *Les honnêtes gens.*" They leaned towards each other, but this time didn't quite touch.

3

August now, high summer. Jean-Pierre stayed in his lair, away from her, trying to collect his ideas and decide exactly what he meant, the possibilities of victimizing her a second time being so real and present. He went on a movie bender, going to three or four a day, looking for images to steal. He'd seen *King Kong* at the Museum of Modern Art last night, and remembered a joke from somewhere.

"You see, all you want to do is marry this girl and settle down, but you can't because you're a gorilla."

And besides, he was too tall for her. They'd had trouble with the special effects in that movie; of course they'd been inventing as they went along, pioneering, and generations of filmmakers had learned from the movie.

The gorilla had kept changing size, relative to his surroundings. Sometimes he wasn't much bigger than a human being, sometimes he was able to grasp an airplane in his hand and hurl it from the top of the Empire State Building. Such a creature would be quite wrong for Fay Wray because too big, too aggressive, too enormous a sexual threat.

Jean-Pierre was staying on East Eighty-seventh on the edge of Yorkville in a small apartment which he'd taken for the summer from a very peculiar rental agent.

"You're gonna love this place, Mister Fauré."

"I hope so."

"Yeah, you will. This is what we call a two-and-a-half-room apartment, the only vacancy in the building. We have a uniformed attendant on duty day and night; there's a closed-circuit monitor in the elevator."

"Why?"

"In case of anything . . . anything, uh, well."

"Is this a violent neighbourhood?"

"Not the people who live here. James Thurber used to live around the corner, the cartoonist, you know."

"I know Thurber, yes, but what's wrong in the elevators?"

The agent writhed. "A certain amount of trouble," he mumbled.

"Killing?"

"I'm afraid so."

"Perhaps I should go elsewhere."

"It's the same all over, violent, everywhere in the city."

"What about the suburbs?"

"You'd have to go a long way out, to get away from it. They have trouble all over Westchester, hubcap thefts, break-ins."

"That's not killing, though. What happens in the elevators?"

The agent said, "I shouldn't be telling you this, but I might as well be honest with a foreigner. They work in pairs. One waits till a single person takes the elevator from the ground floor; then he signals the man upstairs, who stops the elevator and gets on at the second floor. He stops the elevator between floors with the emergency button and mugs the passenger."

"Mugs?"

"Sorry. Grabs him by the throat and half-strangles him. Usually hits him on the head with a sap, rifles his pockets, goes back to the ground floor and beats it."

"How do they get in if the front door is locked?"

"They push all the buttons and somebody always buzzes, thinking its the drugstore, or a pizza coming. They get in any time they want."

"So you have an attendant."

"Three of them, twenty-four hours a day. Ex-cops, big guys. They don't look like doormen, but they can take care of themselves." He sighed. "And at that they're beginning to say that they should work in pairs. Can you imagine what that will do to our overhead?"

"Don't you just pass it on in the rent?"

"Not immediately. A lot of our tenants are on leases, which reminds me, do you want to take the sublet?"

"After what you've told me?" Jean-Pierre burst out laughing. "As you're doing me a favour, letting me have it till the end of September, I think I'd better take it, mugs or no mugs. This is wonderful material, real American violence. I've always been interested in it, but I've never been this close."

"We're not all that way."

"I was exaggerating slightly. I'll take the sublet through the end of September, and I promise to keep my front door locked."

"Double-locked please, building regulation." He pointed out the locks.

"I'll keep my door double-locked and stay home nights. Do you think I should carry a gun, like a cowboy?"

The agent saw the joke. "I don't think that's absolutely necessary, and anyway it's against the law unless you get a license. Just stay off the darker cross streets, and get out to Eighty-sixth and Third quick as you can. Don't loiter."

"It's very small. Could you point out the two rooms and the half?"

"Living room-sleeping room, that's one."

"Pretty damned small too."

"You're right. Bathroom is another one, makes two."

"Oh, you count the bathroom?"

"Sure we do. The kitchen is the half."

"I can see that," said Jean-Pierre. It comprised a small sink and serving counter and two cupboards on one side, and on the other a small refrigerator, stove, and two more cupboards, these components separated by a kind of runway not much more than two feet wide. Frail swinging doors concealed this cubicle. He smiled at the agent.

"It's much worse in Paris," he said boastfully. The agent's jaw dropped. "Oh yes, much worse; this is nothing to it. In Paris you have to *buy* your apartment if you ever want to get one, and it's necessary to apply for it months, years, before the building is begun. Then you wait five years while it's being built; they send you plans and pictures to tease you, and allow you to come in sometimes during construction. It's much worse."

The agent looked slightly crestfallen. "You'll take it?"

"Till the end of September."

And now it was August and his ideas were still confused, and his purposes too. Until last night he hadn't been anywhere near East Sixty-first Street for ten days, because he just didn't know what to do. He loved Rose, unquestionably, but this came so pat, was so convenient for his purposes, that he was continually prey to self-doubt.

He'd been getting up in the middle of the afternoon, going to an evening feature, then perhaps sitting in a bar for an hour watching the late show, then coming home, locking himself in, and watching the late late show, to fall asleep in his chair at four a.m. The New York channels were a mine of film technique from the early thirties onward. He saw Lyle Talbot and Bruce Cabot, Fay Wray and Helen Twelvetrees, Richard Barthelmess, the early films of Howard Hawks, Warner's musicals with Ruby Keeler; he saw Jannings and studied Lubitsch and Lang, and as he stared, rubbing his eyes, he understood why the title of his first film had been *Feu James Dean*. Violence, rebellion, tenderness, innocence, a peculiar blend of moral qualities not to be found elsewhere, associated with the easy purchase of guns and the assassination of great and unsuspecting public figures, the American violence. Who had tried to assassinate Rose?

He sat in the dark, in the oppressively tiny living room, and felt the walls press down on him. It was past four o'clock in the morning and the last of the night's movies had just gone off. The blue light in the screen flickered fitfully before announcing the dawn. Cold light began to filter into the apartment through the slanting Venetian blinds. Jean-Pierre tried to remember if he had snapped the burglar locks on the windows into place. He decided that he hadn't, ignored the chance of an attack, and sat on in front of the television, which now began to tell of startling events at discount clothing stores in Jersey. Crossing the room to turn the sound down, he felt dizzy. When he saw a lot of movies, he often forgot to eat; the experience had something in common with an alcoholic debauch, and with a period of fasting imposed on himself by a hermit in the desert.

The light grew more bleak, and the edges of the furniture took on a hard line. He sank into meditation, and as he went under he saw that he would have to resolve all his dilemmas alone; there was no easy girl here to help him out. In Paris there were always women who wanted to be kind to men like himself, and he had taken his share of their help. Now he felt sorry.

Images swam in his brain, of rape, murder, betrayal, of King Kong at the top of the tallest building in the world, swatting biplanes out of the air like flies. You want to marry the girl and settle down, but you can't because you're a guilty beast. This coupling of monster and innocent woman was a staple in the slick American cartoons, a comic theme or a grotesque one, not tragic.

If he were to seize Rose and carry her off, would he do it like a gorilla, simply violating her, and so subjecting her again to the role of victim? He searched himself, and tried to fend off the foolish images from the old movie, which was simply laughable in the situation. What was the way to treat horror in the movies and in life? The plain fact was that Rose had tried to kill herself in spite of her clear daylight desire to live. Treat horror comically, he thought; that is what they do. King Kong, Count Dracula, Frankenstein's creation, the Addams cartoons, the Teen-Age Wolf Man, the Munsters, the sting drawn progressively with each step towards the trivial—the monster was really lovable and just like us. Mr. Munster *had* settled down and married the girl.

And in a certain sense the monster was innocent, simply wishing to be left alone in his wilderness, idolized by pygmies, crushing a hostile tiger from time to time. Men from civilization had brutalized him, and half-consciously offered Fay Wray for the sacrifice. He laughed; there was no other way to take it. He stood up and unfolded the couch, revealing the crumpled bedclothes. Without pausing to straighten them, he undressed and fell on the bed, sleeping intermittently, with frequent disturbing dreams, until late afternoon.

When he awoke, the first thing he did was look at the papers to see what was playing; then he looked at his watch, which had stopped. He considered going over to the Orpheum to see the new bill, and then decided that he might risk going a little farther downtown. *Kiss Me, Stupid* was playing as a revival at the York, only a few blocks from Rose's house. He could risk it. He didn't want to see her till he had something plain, truthful, and good, to tell her, give her, ask from her.

My nerves never fail me, he thought gratefully, looking at his steady hands. Hunger doesn't seem to affect me. Janine always used to make me eat, but I should have resisted the meal.

He admired Billy Wilder immensely and hadn't seen *Kiss Me, Stupid* when it was first released. He didn't even know that the title was the tag line of a famous American sex joke.

He went down to the York as innocently as could be, and what he saw when he got there intensified his depression and bewilderment terribly. He saw a story about a rich and famous lunatic satyriast, a rampant, eager cuckold, a wife who would comply with anyone for convenience or money, and a prostitute (but a nice girl really) called "the Pistol." The whole conception oppressed him, it was so bitter.

Once upon a time, this director had done light entertainment; later he had made *Sunset Boulevard*, a tale of murderous lunacy and fantastic self-deception. Finally he had added the lunacy and the self-deception to the recipe for light comedy, shaken well, omitted the murderous except here and there, and offered the result to his public, ostensibly as comedy: *Some Like It Hot, Irma la Douce, The Apartment*, and now this, and how should you react to this? He sat through the picture twice, marvelling at the technical dexterity, the way the director moved people through the principal set, from living room through bathroom to bedroom and back to bathroom. Wilder had chosen to spend thirty minutes showing the audience how easily he could have been a stage director if he'd wanted. Nothing to it, says Billy Wilder. No tricky angles, no stop-action gags, no overindulgence in low comedy close-ups, simply marvellously detailed black and white, and the unobtrusively speedy camera movement.

Jean-Pierre found himself feeling pretty ashamed of the tricks he'd tried in comedy. He had parodied silent movies, used chases, wipes, iris-in, iris-out jokes, and in short had compiled a little anthology of tried-and-true devices. Wilder didn't do that. He used no devices, or invented his own, and his camera was always working. When Felicia Farr walked away into the bathroom, the camera recorded the grain and feel of her slip over her hips and thighs with ferocious sensuality. It's astonishing what can be done with black and white and gray.

The movie was a drawn-out hymn to hatred, mutual contempt, and the use of other people as instruments for lust, conveniences. You use a woman as you do the toilet, to discharge offensive matter from your body, and you do this daily as a matter of necessity. There is some fleeting pleasure in the act, the excitement of two membranes brought together and rubbed, and that is all. Decent people. Decent music master, decent little wife, decent gas-station attendant, and Polly the Pistol.

Smart talk, smart sex, smart low-cut cowboy costume barely retaining the star's breasts, as a concession to decency. The prostitute is the good one, and all the rest are vapid brutes. If you sat too long over repeated screenings of this film, you would begin to feel profoundly unhappy. But nobody would do that, and Wilder knew it, and Jean-Pierre, and a few other people, not many. The movie had been damned when it came out, but afterwards played fairly successfully on its sex quotient. He got up to leave, feeling overstimulated and sick, and went out onto the sidewalk, where he paused and put his hand into his coat pocket. There were six small glossy shots of Rose in an envelope in his pocket, which he'd been carrying around for weeks; he'd begged them of her on a specious plea of research, but he really wanted them to gaze at lovingly when he was away from her. They were from each of the phases of her career, the dreadful ingénue, the clean-cut girl chum, the young married, and none of them were sex shots . . . he felt that he was getting closer to her.

He leaned against the wall of the theatre, swallowed a mouthful of bile, remembered that he should eat. As he riffled through the pictures, he almost started towards her place, but restrained himself.

"Why don't you want to see me?" she'd demanded fearfully.

"I want to think about you, to imagine you."

"You wouldn't go away suddenly?"

"I'll see you in three weeks and I'll have something definite for you, a story idea. I can do something with you. I want to do something for you. I want to decide what to do."

"In the film?"

"In both ways."

It was dark; he'd been in the theatre for five hours and had learned much, but not what he wanted. They meshed. Their needs and desires meshed too perfectly; she needed a director; he needed a star. He looked around him on the sidewalk and inadvertently swayed back on his heels, and a passer-by said suddenly, "What's the matter, Mister, you sick?"

"I'm all right, thank you," he said, shrinking from the strange voice. I'm afraid, he thought, I'm afraid of this city. He hailed a cab and told the driver to take him through the park and up to Broadway and Ninety-fifth, to the Thalia, where *Feu James Dean* was showing for a single night as the last of a "Festival of French Film."

"You want out here?" the driver said at length. He sat up and saw that they were in front of the Thalia; the last show had started and the lights were dark, the box office closed and a single door open to admit late arrivals. He went into the theatre and an usher accosted him at the door.

"The last show is on."

"That's all right," he said, feeling in his pocket for the price of the ticket. "I've seen this one before. How long has it been on?"

"You've missed the first three sequences," said the usher knowledgeably, taking the money. "There's a single on the aisle, two rows down." He pointed, and Jean-Pierre sank into the seat with relief and a sense of coming home.

Even after ten years the soundtrack was very good, he thought. On the screen, a solitary bicyclist made his way across difficult roadless terrain, empty country, the haunt of many wild birds, and you could hear the birds' cries very distinctly, an effect that everybody had used afterwards, wind, birdcalls, the crunch of the bicycle tires over stony ground. He recognized his aunt's country with joy; he had spent his summer vacations there for more than twenty years. He remembered the excitement of making the picture, and the comradeship, mixed with almost intolerable tension, he had shared with Michel and Claude as they worked. They had counted so much on the picture, and later their hopes had been so generously fulfilled that the tension seemed in retrospect acutely agreeable.

On his bicycle Michel came to the last ridge of the lonely hills, straddled his machine and gazed, the audience over his shoulder, down into the valley with the straggling stony village at the bottom. A cart track began to define itself in the grass, and turned itself, as the camera trucked along, into a hillside road. Michel pushed forward and began coasting down into the village faster and faster and the camera watched him go. Change the shot.

He came along at immense speed and leaned back in bravado, first waving his arms, then putting both long legs on the handlebars, bumping perilously over ruts and stones as he flew down into the village. The sky was gray behind and above him and he was a black silhouette. Close on the inn door where Claude stood sullenly, watching him come on.

"*Salut, salut, je viens, j'arrive.*"

"*Oh, ça.*"

Jean-Pierre laughed, remembering the dolorous tone in which Claude had first read the line. There had been half an hour of discussion while they tried to clarify the character.

"James Dean, yes, I see that," Claude had kept saying, "we're talking about loss and rebellion."

"But you mustn't simply sulk, or you won't be taken seriously."

"What exactly has happened to me?" Claude wanted to know.

"You've come apart, like a clock that's been broken, and you don't know why. You could have gone to school like your friend, but he has had the strength, and you haven't."

"Am I glad to see him?"

"At first, not afterwards. Later on you beat him badly, when you're drunk."

"I wish I knew why."

"Who knows why some come apart and some don't? I think that we can show it happening." They went back to work, and Claude said, "*Ça, alors*," and "*Oh, ça*," and numberless other things, and began to get the right tone. In the end he had given a great performance, and Michel had been just as good. The scene of drunken violence struck the New York audience forcibly; they were silent and attentive, and the film was applauded enthusiastically as the FIN came over the broken, slowly spinning bicycle wheel.

He left quickly. Outside there were men on ladders, re-lettering the marquee. Somebody bumped against him, a woman gave a sharp exclamation and her hand took his arm. He peered at her, and saw with mixed feelings that the woman was Peggi Starr.

4

On Bank Street it was deathly still and quiet and dark. Going into the hall of Peggi's apartment building, Jean-Pierre tripped over a low rise in the floor just at the doorway. As he came inside he saw with faint distaste that a pale greenish light gleamed in the halls; it was like a bomb shelter, the walls crossed and recrossed by rectangular lines, the edges of cement blocks.

When Peggi opened the front door of her place, it was black dark in the living room, and they both stuck their arms out in front of them. Involuntarily they clasped hands and held on for an instant, before Peggi found the light switch and flipped it.

The room was pleasant, plain, severe, almost conventual, which he hadn't expected. The kitchen smelled of baking and, suddenly starving-hungry, he walked straight in and began to sniff around. There were long rows of spice bottles in little racks, copper-bottomed pans hanging in descending order of size, spatulas, serving forks, all precisely arranged.

Peggi came into the kitchen behind him, and in the full yellow light from above he could see her more clearly than he ever had before. She was wearing a thin blouse which emphasized the solidity and sturdiness of her shoulders and arms. She wore glasses, which he hadn't remembered seeing before, and her face was plump but firm. Something that surprised him more was an impression she gave of ready sexuality, though she didn't come close to him.

She said, "You look awful, and where have you been? Rose is worried about you and so am I."

"I've been working," he said. Nobody ever believed that his bouts of film addiction had anything to do with work. "I've been picking up ideas here and there, stealing them, if you want the exact truth."

Her face relaxed. "You're not a drinker, and you're not a chaser, as far as I know."

"That's right. You haven't got any evidence. I'm certainly not a drinker."

"What about the other?"

"I'm considerably over thirty."

"And I suppose that's all you have to say." She went to the stove and lighted a burner under a coffeepot. "Don't do anything we'll all be sorry for. I've seen two of your pictures this week, and it hasn't been easy."

"Why?"

"They're almost impossible to find; they don't play." She measured out coffee from a bright yellow-and-black can of Medaglia d'Oro.

"They play all right, only not here," he said, a little annoyed.

"Do you like it very strong?"

"I need it strong. Could you give me a piece of cake?"

"Yes. You ought to eat if you're really working."

"I really am."

"Go and sit down then." But he watched her as she prepared a tray. She moved quickly, with control, and he admired her self-containment. When the food and the coffee were ready they went into the living room and sat side by side on a divan and began to eat. The coffee was awfully strong; he could feel it stimulating him, and quickly ate some salami on dark bread. Soon he felt better.

"Very strong coffee."

"Mmmmnn."

"What did you think of the pictures?"

"A reaction? You certainly are interested in what goes on between men and women."

"Between friends, just between friends."

"And they mostly end sadly, don't they?"

"I'm afraid so."

"This one tonight," she said, "that was the first, wasn't it? I couldn't understand why they fought, why one boy got drunk and beat up his friend. Was it just because the other had left him and gone to the university? It was so sad."

"I'm only beginning to understand why. He felt betrayed and useless. Let me try to express it better. Sometimes people find some obscure blank obstruction inside them, which stops them, beyond which they can't force themselves. They grow to a certain height and stop, and no matter what they do they can't go any further. Once in a while such a person is sprung free, long after he's decided that his life is over. But that can never be predicted, and by the time we approach early middle age the rails are fixed; we run on them in our course. It drove him to violence. He couldn't surrender and couldn't get free. Do you see?"

"There's more to it than that."

"Yes but I can't talk about it. I can show it in pictures." He bounced up and down on the divan. "I suppose this turns into a bed."

"It does. Why?"

"So does mine; there must be millions of these in New York, in little rooms. I hate solitude. I've had enough of it."

"What are you going to do?"

"Make another film about it." She glared at him. "Yes, with Rose, in Europe. Somebody always suffers; there's always somebody left behind." He put his arms around her; she was submissive and felt warm and he held her against him for an instant. "I love Rose," he said softly.

Peggi turned her face to him sorrowfully. She made a small choking noise in her throat. "You'd better," she said.

5

So Jean-Pierre came back down to East Sixty-first, one dark night a few days later in August, to tell Rose his sad story. She greeted him joyfully at the door, standing beside her somber servant Macha, their arms linked in a sisterly pose. The luxurious block was silent, still, almost deserted in the intensely hot blackness. He thought of the premiere party and laughter surged in his heart.

"Come inside; it's cooler. Could we have something to drink, Macha? Ask Mrs. Ponsonby. Then you can go as soon as you like." She turned to Jean-Pierre. "Macha's off to see *Une femme mariée*. She wants to see her namesake."

"Oh movies, movies. You'll enjoy it," he said to the quiet girl. She nodded, and went to get them a drink. She'll be left behind too, he thought; there is always loss.

"We won't go upstairs," said Rose.

"Certainly not."

He followed her into the little conservatory off the hall, and they sat down and looked happily at each other. Macha came into the room in a few moments and when she saw them broke into laughter. She handed them glasses containing an icy fluid, clear but with a faint cloudiness, vodka with a little lemon.

Jean-Pierre said, "Why are you laughing?"

"I wish you happiness," said the girl, blushing. It was the first time he had seen colour in her face. "I'm very pleased."

"Thank you, Macha," Rose said gravely, and the girl turned and almost ran from the room.

"We have to seize it, when it's offered," said Jean-Pierre, "and we'll see that Macha's all right. Now listen to my story."

"Go on."

"You are a young American woman about twenty-seven years old and you've been in one of the provincial university towns—I'm thinking of Aix-en-Provence—about four years, perhaps a little longer. You came to France to study, perhaps history, a serious subject but not a technical one like philosophy or law. You aren't an intellectual, but a simple woman, intelligent but not aggressive. I think you probably came from somewhere near New York, but not the city itself. You've never been rich. You are almost plain; your hair is much brushed and extremely clean and shining and you wear almost no makeup."

"An innocent."

"But not a fool. By this time you've learned the language as well as anyone does who isn't a language specialist, and instead of going back to America you have lingered from year to year, made friends, mostly woman friends, and now you know the university town, the countryside; you know the language well enough to work in a small bookstore with a younger girl who is your apartment-mate."

"Will I be able to handle French dialogue?"

"Oh yes. For one thing I want to keep the American accent, which sounds charming if the French is correct; two or three American actresses have done this. I'll keep your dialogue very short and simple—there's never much dialogue in my films anyway, and I want to pay a lot of attention to your face in repose and silence, without makeup, just for the bone structure and the spirit underneath. I think that the American accent and the hesitation in speech will show your defenselessness, something that will have to be clear."

Rose looked very pensive at this.

"It's a film, not reportage. The girl in the film has no defenses, she's trusting, unable to imagine that anyone would want to hurt her. Very good. In the bookstore are the *patron*, who is a retired professor, yourself, and the girl who shares your apartment. The *patron* is a shrewd, kindly old man who takes care of you as though you were his daughters, and you are his favourite. He's helped you with the language and trained you, made you half a Frenchwoman. You are his work of art and he is very fond of you. The younger girl is perhaps twenty-four and she isn't clever. Not stupid. Hardly anyone is stupid. But she is less intelligent than you are, a little frivolous. You're very good friends and when the shop is empty or closed you chatter, and make plans for your evenings and weekends and vacations."

"This is very thorough," said Rose.

"Wait, just wait. There are men, of course, whom you see in various places, the tennis courts, cafés where you dance to phonograph music, sometimes perhaps in ciné-clubs. There is quite a lot of this towards the beginning of the picture. At one point you and the younger girl are seen dancing in your favourite café; we see the reflection of the disk mirrored in the jukebox glass, spinning round and round as you move to the music. Often you ride on the backs of scooters and in small, broken-down Citroëns, but never in anything more powerful or imposing. The pace of this part of the film will be leisurely, with many shots of the people around and behind you, giving us a sense of your life and the life of your friends: you go to the *charcuterie*, you have small quarrels, you share your money and your men, and we have the sense of kindness and decency among you. It is a small, kind, quiet life. You have a man for a friend, who is small, a mouse of a man—I have the actor in mind for this—and we understand that you are good to each other, but that there is no passion."

"You should be a writer."

"I am a writer. I've written all my scripts. I have a better sense of story and character than I do of technique. I'm not much of a technician, but then neither is Truffaut. Story is the great element, story and character. So anyway, your man friend will sometimes come to the window and look in, to show you that he is waiting, but *le patron* won't let him come into the store while business is being done, unless to buy something. He shoos him away with a great show of comic authority, which you all accept. Now we begin to establish close-ups of the two young women's faces. Yours has a graceful oval quality, and you have very pretty frightened eyes. The younger girl has a soft, almost sleepy expression, very contented. In fact," he said slowly, "you are both waiting for love."

Rose didn't speak.

"Very well. We go back to long shots of you walking in the streets, sometimes right at the edge of the town, and now from time to time we see passing in the background a big American car, which stands out because it's about the only one in the town. Some of your friends always describe it as '*la belle Américaine*' and then they look at you and laugh, and you laugh with them gently. But this car is not a rich man's car, not a Cadillac. It's a Chevrolet, about five- or six-years-old, two-toned, what would be a workingman's car in America. In Aix-en-Provence it seems enormous and eccentric. First it passes you on the street and the driver makes a noise and a gesture of some sort, not necessarily directed at you. Later on, we have some shots of the car driving along country roads in darkness, immediately recognizable and slightly out of place.

"It gradually becomes clear that the driver of the car is insinuating himself into your background or that of your

friends. One night you come along the street very late with
your girlfriend and you see the Chevrolet parked a short distance from your door. You stop and giggle together as you
look at it; it shines gloriously and has much extra equipment
hanging on it, with large red reflectors studded here and
there. You and your friend stare at each other, then back to
the car. You laugh and shrug and go along home to bed, rather
pleased by the incident. As you approach your door you hear
the car's horns, and the sound of its engine, just around the
corner. You both smile, and you close the door.

"Later on, the mousy little man comes to the store to see
you, hovering outside the window until you feel impelled
to do something definite. You ignore *le patron* and rush
out into an alley beside the bookstore. He joins you, and
we have a very slowly paced but short scene between you.
He asks about tennis, tonight. You say no, casually at first. He
wonders why, gently, not insistently, and you really have nothing definite to tell him. You lean your head against the frame
of the door, with one arm above you. I can see this shot very
vividly. Medium-close to close. You are silent and we insert a
quick little shot of the man, from above. He tilts his head and
says one or two words; he is hurt. Cut to you. You don't look
at him; you look down and away from him and say nothing, a
very still, very feminine pose. I want to show the line of your
neck, and I want to be able to see the motion of your eyelashes.
The silence continues for some seconds. We cut to the tennis
court where your sect, group, coterie, often meet in the evening. There is a great deal of laughter about everyone's poor
play. Shots of flying balls and swinging rackets against the sky.
There is no cruel joking, the men teasing the girls or handling
them roughly in these games. We still have that sense of active
friendships."

"And the man who owns the Chevrolet makes his bow."
said Rose.

"How did you know?"

"I'm beginning to see how your imagination works."

"I'm very glad. Have you guessed the end of the story?"

"I have an idea."

"This stranger appears and asks for a game. He's French, by the way, not American, and we see immediately that his car is the greatest thing in his life. He picks up the joke about '*la belle Américaine*' at once and we suddenly realize that he has his eyes on you most. of the time. We see your spirit quicken and your eyes gleam more brightly, but you don't say much directly to him; you wait. It's your habit, by lifelong training, to wait passively until somebody takes action towards you."

"In the film."

"In the film."

"I see."

"You all leave the tennis courts together when it begins to get dark. I should say that the motorist plays a very powerful game of tennis, much better than the other men in your group, with a big serve. He's quite short, not much taller than you, but powerfully muscled. On your way home, as you take leave of him, you notice that he wears a very rich-looking, expensive driving coat, very warm, an *imperméable*. He works constantly at tuning up his car, and we soon learn that he's the wild son of the town's principal *garagiste*, and not a student or a university person. He has a name, quite an ordinary name, I think. I haven't chosen it yet. It shouldn't be too unusual. When you see him, after the tennis, you notice the richness and warmth and costliness of his coat, which he carries with him even though it's summer. You don't seem to notice that his shoes are worn out, and his other clothes shabby and uncared for. There's something disjointed about him. A quick series of close-ups of the two of you looking at and away from each other.

"From now on you are lovers, not sexually, you never become his mistress, unless in a very unusual sense, as you'll see. In the next sequence, he takes you for your first ride in his car, and we establish one of the most important visual points in the film. When you get into the car, you are astonished to see that its entire interior is covered with photographs clipped from American magazines like *Life,* and from *Paris-Match.* Pictures of motorcycles and folk singers, the Beatles, racing cars, movie stars, shots of crimes with people lying dead on the streets, pictures of guns and of cowboys. All over the inside of the car. Sitting beside him on the front seat, you show your surprise, and we see his lips twitch slightly as though he were keeping back a laugh. You crane your neck, looking around into the back seat. More and more photographs, in a bizarre montage, a collection of images of modern life. You are half-alarmed and half-captivated by this show because it makes you remember where you came from. In a sense, you are *la belle Américaine,* just as the Chevrolet is.

"Then we see you all over the little town, and the surrounding country, on narrow side roads, among trees, in sunlight, at night. He drives and you sit beside him, closer and closer, with your hair blowing in your eyes, breeze from the open windows. Here we find most of the camera tricks, some amusing dissolves, perhaps some impressions of speed, shot from the hood of the car, the road speeding underneath you, half-perceived images of the other traffic. A comic attempt to park in a too small space. Your friends are worried about you, but you are ecstatic, you are in love. He is subtly evasive about himself, but always terribly strong, charming, pleasing. He takes you everywhere that he can afford, completely away from the quiet of the bookstore and the university. He's very generous, and we see that he loves you.

"One weekend he takes you for a long excursion in the country. I haven't chosen the exact location, but there should be a lake or a river, some woods, and nearby a restaurant or café, perhaps in a village, where he takes you for lunch. While you are eating, he tells you quite quietly that he loves you; then after a few moments of silence while you smile at him happily he begins to act very exuberantly. He does little tricks with his napkin, making a rabbit's ears out of it. He blows enormous smoke rings. After each trick he gives a whoop of laughter, and you smile. He is in a state of intense elation. We begin, faintly but unmistakably, to realize that all is not quite right with him.

"After lunch he quiets down and you walk through the woods and along the river, then into woods again. There's tremendous tension between you, each waiting for the other to make a sudden gesture. All at once you shiver as if with cold, and he wraps you in his fine driving coat. You walk before him to a grassy slope in the woods and throw yourself down, and he falls on top of you in agony. We cut to a peasant walking along a road through the woods, a man who looks like Bourvil, that type. He sees the big Chevrolet parked at the roadside and stops to walk around it admiringly. He looks around him and puts his hand in the window to touch the horn ring. The horn sounds and he jumps guiltily. He'll remember the car.

"Quick cut to a very tight close-up of your face and neck; silence; he strangles you. The only sound on the track is a very faint choking noise from your throat. Cut to your roommate's face as she sits in a café with the mousy little man who likes you. A jukebox begins to play and they get up and dance. Her face is dreamy and absorbed as she dances slowly. Cut to the glass in the front of the jukebox; the music gets a bit louder and we watch the record spinning round and round, and that's the end."

6

At midnight they stood close together just outside the front door, on the steps leading up to the sidewalk. "*Le métier, c'est tout,*" said Jean-Pierre thoughtfully. "Renoir used to say that, when I worked with him. '*Restez toujours fidèle au cinéma.*'"

Rose lifted her head from his shoulder. "What does that mean? It's your favourite word."

"*Métier*?"

"Yes."

"Professionalism. No. Devotion to craft. No. Seriousness, calling, vocation, technique, all these things. Expertise is a part of it, but not the whole, which is where Americans can go wrong, thinking that technique and expertise can storm the gates of heaven. You have to have devotion too, love, consuming ambition to use the medium properly." He laughed ruefully, knowing that he couldn't really translate the idea. "*Métier, c'est tout.*"

"Do I have it?"

"You? You're an amateur."

"After thirty-five pictures?"

"Oh my darling, I know that you can walk and stand and wear clothes and speak, and that you are a star. The rest I can supply. Cary Grant has it, I suppose, and Bette Davis, and plenty of directors, Hawks, Wilder, Aldrich, Lester. Film, pure and simple."

"I see what you mean."

"So what about it, will you come to Paris with me? You have something that has been in none of your pictures, and with this script I can deliver it."

This was very shrewd, Rose thought. "I know a little French," she said, "and I could read dialogue off a board." Jean-Pierre stroked her cheek with loving attention. "It's a very strong story and a wonderful title. You don't think I'm too old?"

"Don't be silly," he said. "I'm going to pay you a great compliment. Did you see *La Dolce Vita*?"

"Uh-huh."

"Do you remember the girl in the sports car? She played his wife in *Otto e Mezzo*. And last year she was in *Un homme et une femme.*"

"I remember her vividly."

"Isn't she beautiful? Anouk Aimée, an absolutely marvellous woman, with that quality of goodness. That reminds me of you, and if I can get it across you'll be marvellous too. You are marvellous anyway, but it'll be on the screen and the public will see. You don't have to have breasts like melons to be a woman."

"I hope not," she said. They joined hands and climbed up to the sidewalk It was still very warm, but clear and not humid, starry, intensely dark. A policeman idled at the end of the block. He stared curiously as Rose and Jean-Pierre embraced. They might already have been in Paris, they drew so close, held on so tight, and were so obviously, profoundly, lovers. They moved in towards one another, pressing hard and clinging dizzily, bathed in the warm night air, kissing as though their lives depended on it.

"Aahhhh," Rose gasped, "aahhhh, my life isn't over."

"Just getting started."

They noticed the shocked policeman, laughed and defiantly kissed again, longer than before, enchantingly. He drew back only to gaze at her enraptured. "You'll come?"

"Oh my dear love," she sighed, "I will follow you anywhere."

7

You can't set up long-term European residence overnight; it takes weeks and even months to do the thing right. You have to close your house, store the furniture or sell it, get a passport, your shots, any necessary visas. Your car goes up on blocks in a garage, or is sold. You need letters of credit or transfers to foreign banks of American funds at (unhappily) official rates of exchange. There's much to be done.

For Rose and Jean-Pierre there was the further complication of their marriage ceremony, where it should be performed.

"I'm sure you're perfectly free," he'd said. "I don't believe you've ever been married in any real sense."

She had invited an even closer embrace. "I haven't thought about it. I just want to be married to you."

They decided to aim at getting over to Paris around the beginning of October. Jean-Pierre was used to doing business by cable, so he stayed in New York to help Rose arrange her affairs, working on the script of *Les honnêtes gens* and helping his girl compose confused lists, conventionally headed "Things to do."

He bought a portable typewriter and a supply of stationery and came every morning to East Sixty-first Street, happy to get out of his apartment. He spent part of the day roughing out the proportions of the movie, and the rest of it giving Rose advice, sometimes of dubious practicality, and kissing her assiduously and lovingly.

"Again," she sighed, much stirred. "Why don't we get married here, right now?"

"No, we'll be married in the parish church of Saint-Merri, with organ music, banns, everything. We'll take our time and do it right."

"At least set a date."

"You're reversing our roles. It's the bride's affair to set the date, once she knows the ground rules. As soon as possible."

"How long will the arrangements take?"

"Not very long. Perhaps till around Christmas."

"It's only August," said Rose unhappily. She saw immense delight, final contentment, looming up before her, and wanted to make certain that it was not a mirage. "My lawyers are checking the marriage records in Palm Springs. They'll have full information in a few days."

"There'll be no trouble about that; it was a straight civil ceremony. Did you write for your baptismal certificate?"

All this made her feel forgetful and cared for. She was entranced by the formalities, foreseeing that once married in this way there'd be no getting out. She knew that she would never want to get out, and like a sweet good girl she went dutifully through the preparations, for travel, for marriage, getting birth and baptismal certificates and photocopies of the records of her first marriage, a passport, her shots. How wise it is, she thought, to surround the really important choices with ritual and formality, to assure us of their meaning and value. It gave her great pleasure to leap each small hurdle.

When she'd married Seth it had been a casually convenient arrangement, settled quickly and without reflection. She'd been sleeping with him for several months, and he had apparently gotten to like her particular ass, so to speak. Lovemaking had been inconvenient in many ways: they had to drive for miles looking for motels; they couldn't use the same motel too often for fear of being identified. After one of these sessions Seth had, one early afternoon, raised himself on an elbow beside her and said, "Rose, for Christ's sake, we'd be better off married." And she'd agreed.

Neither had thought through what they were doing. They certainly had some kind of strong mutual attraction, and later on a solid emotional tie; but it didn't seem to her, thinking it over after it was finished, that the insides of the relationship had been there, the essence, the whatever it was that filled an affair out. Something had been missing that left them connected mainly by good-natured irony and a strange passivity on both sides. "We'd be better off married, Rose." But they hadn't made it.

This time around, with her marriage postponed for three months or more, and her flight to Europe to arrange, she wanted very much to sleep with Jean-Pierre, and at the same time felt a counterbalancing strong wish to put off the consummation until all the formalities had been gone through, at which delightful time their love-making would be sweeter because waited for. Her contemplations, imaginings, wantings, hesitations, the waiting, the strongly reviving sexuality of her nature, all conferred enormous benefits. After the first marriage there is no other.

She began to enjoy dropping into an office-supplies store and Xeroxing everything imaginable, in a dozen copies or more.

She said to Jean-Pierre, "I have photocopies of my vaccination and of the monogram on my underwear."

"You're a wonder." He went on with his script.

"*Ça va?*"

He looked up with a grin. "*Ça va, m'amie.*"

"When do I get to see it?"

"When it's finished, naturally, not before."

She wasn't used to that answer from a writer. Usually writers rushed pages to her hot from the platen, so as to get a commitment on which they could then raise money at a bank. The thought of banks and bankers made her laugh.

"What is it?"

"Nothing," she said smiling, "a little surprise."

"For me?"

"Partly, partly."

"I suppose I'll have to wait."

"I'll see you for a cocktail," she said, and went out, over to Fifth and up, to the French Consulate for the next in a series of appointments.

She was royally received at the Consulate; they knew her well by now and were used to her sometimes confused requests. It's surprisingly complicated to transfer even quite modest capital holdings to a new country. People kept saying, "Are you sure you want to do this?"

Apart from banking technicalities and the problem of finding a place to live in Paris, these later visits were pleasant formalities. On this next-to-last trip the staff bowed her into the Vice-Consul's office immediately, where a big-boned marvellously dressed blond young man with an eight-centuries-old name rose to greet her: De Rohan? La Tremoïlle? Guermantes? The exalted descent stuck in her imagination, but not his precise rank and name, except that it was ancient and revered. He bowed, saw her comfortably seated, and started to chatter wildly about the French film industry, of which he was an enthusiast and connoisseur. He'd helped to finance films and admired Jean-Pierre's work. He'd been overjoyed to find that Rose would now be a luminary of the European screen rather than of the American.

" . . . a work permit? Purely a technicality. Your financial responsibility is clear, and your work will not take opportunities away from French actresses. I imagine you'll play American girls."

"At first. But I hope to learn French as well as Eddie Constantine or Jean Seberg."

The Vice-Consul was pleased. "You're thinking of adopting French citizenship?"

"I will adopt my husband's citizenship, naturally."

"You would have to choose one or the other after the lapse of a certain time, in order to enjoy full civil rights."

"I know that. I think I should accept the civil responsibilities of the country where I live."

"You have great faith in Monsieur Fauré."

"I love him. I trust him." The Vice-Consul felt ashamed. "Will it be necessary for me to see the Consul?" Rose asked, winding up the interview.

"Not necessary, but it will be his pleasure. He has asked me to arrange an appointment at your convenience, after Labour Day if that's agreeable. He will be in Washington all next week, and will be back after the holiday."

"That would please me very much."

"Then I'll telephone your home for a definite appointment at the end of next week. Your papers will be ready for your meeting with the chief. I know that he'll want to hand them to you personally."

He escorted her out of the building and she had the impression that he'd have bowed her all the way out of town if politeness had suggested it. She thought the young man would go far, and wondered why he wasn't in Washington himself. They stood in the doorway of the consulate long enough for a female columnist to spot them as she cruised on her daily patrol of Fifth Avenue. Next morning there was an item in her column:

Glimpsed Rose Leclair on the doorstep of a friendly (?) European consulate this P.M. Does the petite sweet plan a flight to the City of Light with the new love, or a brute pursuit of the old? Where there's Seth, Rosie, there's Charity.

How many children you had, their legitimacy, your diet when well, and the frequency of your bowel movements when *in extremis*, anything was appropriate for the publicity mill. The lady columnist had thought that Rose would be glad of the exposure.

Bud and Danny saw the item and quickly looked over their contract with Rose. As they saw it, she couldn't leave the country without first discharging her commitments to them. They had an option on her services for a second picture, and she owed them a publicity tour which she'd run out on when she tried to kill herself. The attempt had earned her some public sympathy and they hadn't wanted to press for immediate fulfillment of the commitment; but now that she was getting around again they thought they should take some action. Maybe she could be forced to do some promotional work or coerced into paying a sum of money to get out of the option. They phoned the house, and Rose—all compliant innocence—agreed to come into the office and talk things over. They made an appointment for the Wednesday after Labour Day, the sixth of the month.

They preened themselves on their enforcement of the strict terms of the contract. After all, they had their rights.

"I knew you'd see it our way," said Danny agreeably, talking to her on the phone. He'd suspected she might try to make trouble. His idea of human life was that of perpetual war, where you screw others before they screw you. He often asked himself why he trusted Horler, and found no answer. There were no grounds for such trust, except that the need to confide in at least one person was inescapable. It seemed to Danny that if he couldn't trust Bud, he couldn't trust anybody, even himself, and he would therefore be utterly alone in the world. That way, he sometimes guessed, lay total paralysis of the will, if not lunacy. He trusted Bud as a kind of necessary moral postulate, much as the Kantian postulates God, freedom, and immortality as the grounds of human action—indemonstrable but necessary hypotheses of the moral life.

"Come along any time, sweetie, what's a good time for you?" He was casually, insultingly, nice to her, knowing that he had the ascendancy in the relationship. "We'll work out something together. Huh? What?" He turned from the phone and muffled the transmitter against his pants. "Bud," he said, puzzled, "she wants to bring Peggi, and that French fellow."

Horler crossed the room and stuck his head out the door. The switchboard girl was busy doing her nails, and her intercom key was down. He wrote a note on a piece of paper and shoved it across to his partner.

"Hold on, love," said Danny. He read the note, then crumpled it and put it in his pocket, nodding at Bud. The note read, "Be careful what you say; just make the appointment." He spoke into the phone. "All three of you? Do you want to have lunch or not? Why not?" He seemed annoyed. "In the office then, right, we'll be waiting, darling. Goodbye."

He looked somberly at Horler. "That was a strange chat," he said, obscurely worried.

"We'd have paid for lunch."

"She just said she wouldn't eat with us."

"Was she unfriendly? Threatening? What?"

"Bud, she was funny. She wasn't anything. I felt like I was talking to the wall."

"I don't understand that."

"I can't explain it any better."

"She'll do what we tell her; she has no choice." Horler too looked puzzled and vaguely disturbed. "It's getting so you've got to have a club in your hand at all times. I never thought Rose Leclair, of all people, would try to run out on a contract—it isn't like her. If she ever got away to Europe, we'd have a hell of a time trying to collect, especially since we don't want her for a picture."

"What should we ask for the release?"

"Substantial indemnification, that's the phrase. They haven't sent over a figure yet."

"Do we want lawyers in the room while we talk?"

"That fucking Solomon," said Bud, really furious. "No, we don't, not the way we have to do business."

Jean-Pierre said, "You should have a lawyer with you."

"Not this time. This time we're going to use the house rules, and we'll murder them."

"There's something you haven't told us," said Peggi.

Rose smiled smugly. "Right!"

"Aren't you going to?"

"Wait and see. I'll fix Danny Lenehan good if it's the last thing I do in the good old U.S.A."

"I've got some news for you," said Peggi. "You won't find Lawyer Solomon at the conference table. He's left them."

"You're kidding."

"I'm not. I had lunch with him a week ago. He said he had to look out for his reputation . . . and he's been with them eight or ten years."

Rose said, "I'm glad. I never thought he was quite as bad as the others. I ought to get him to come with us. Wouldn't that be a switch?"

"I don't think he would."

"I guess not. Let's get back to work." They were flipping through the script of *Les honnêtes gens*, which Jean-Pierre had finished over the holiday weekend and had brought to the house the day before their appointment with Bud and Danny. This smoothly dovetailed development seemed almost providential to Rose, and made her feel that her transition was going ahead exactly as designed: she had a script, a director, European distribution, a terrific part. She was still in business. *Les honnêtes gens* would cost less than a tenth of what *Goody* had; it would be in black and white, with a male star who wasn't widely known. But it was going to be a good picture, and would play, and she was doing something she really could do, in expert hands. They hoped for an award winner.

205

Peggi knew no French at all, and they had spent most of the morning getting the idea of the picture across to her. As they did so, it grew more and more plain to all three that leaving Peggi behind was going to be painful, involving their feelings in complex and unexpected ways. It seemed to each of them, as they argued out the implications of the new script, with its subtle moral ideas, that a final break between old friends would be effected when Rose went, and there was nothing to be done about it.

Peggi couldn't quite get the title.

Jean-Pierre said, "It's a joke with a double reference. In France for centuries that phrase has described a special group of people, good or bad depending on how you see them. If you approve of them, it means the class between the nobility and the *bourgeoisie*." He could see that Peggi wasn't following him; she didn't know what the *bourgeoisie* was. He tried again: "Between the aristocrats and the middle class," and realized that Peggi couldn't understand or take seriously such conceptions of class because she had no experience of them whatsoever, and virtually no formal education. She had a formidable natural moral intelligence, but no learning beyond simple literacy.

"Then again," he said, floundering, "if you disapprove of them it means 'The Hypocrites' or something like that. 'The Pharisees.' I don't think that I can make myself clear."

"Well if you can't, I don't see how the title can make its point."

"It will in France," said Jean-Pierre, jealous for his script.

"Not internationally. Maybe that's why your pictures haven't played here, maybe they're too special."

She had a point. "That's the way my mind works," he said.

"Would that title translate? Would an American audience get the joke?"

"What audience?"

"The big audience. My folks in Wheeling."

"I can't make films for your folks in Wheeling, Peggi. I don't know them."

Peggi shrugged, looking at Rose, and Jean-Pierre tried to think of the right translation. "Let's see? 'The Good People' is too literal. 'Right-Thinking People' is inexact."

Rose said, "What about 'People Who Count'?"

"Too cynical."

Peggi was thinking hard. Finally she said, "I think 'Decent People' is what you're looking for." She was right, and they all knew it.

"Exactly," said Jean-Pierre. "I promise you that'll be the North American title, and I'll send you a royalty."

She looked at him forlornly.

"Oh, Peggi," said Rose. "Oh!"

"Honey, you've got to do what's best for you."

They sat looking at one another unhappily.

But when they landed on the Horler/Lenehan doorstep next day, they didn't betray their feelings. They were determined not to be put down by the producers. Bud and Danny had nothing on any of them, except perhaps Peggi, who would still be working in the U.S. and was therefore in a slightly exposed position. Jean-Pierre and Rose had urged her to stay away from the meeting so as not to get involved in a fight.

"Ho ho ho," she said, "nothing would make me miss this."

"But they might want to use you again."

"I wouldn't let them . . ."

"Makes it unanimous," said Rose.

She wasn't going to do anything for them at all, and was especially determined not to let them exercise any coercion over her, of any kind. She'd had all that.

But they didn't open the ball with her; they went after Jean-Pierre, with Danny leading off.

" . . . depriving us of the services of our star by running off 207 with her just when we need her. Is that wise?"

Jean-Pierre had resolved to keep his temper. "I think so. We plan to be married in Paris, at Christmas, when we've completed some private arrangements. We'll be doing a picture together till then."

Danny pricked up his ears. "Who's producing?"

"My own company, Films Vinteuil."

"A low-budget production."

Rose said, "A sane production, sensibly budgeted for a change."

Danny ignored her. "What will you have going for you internationally?"

"My star, my direction, and my script, which is a very good one."

"It really is, Danny," said Peggi. "It's a shame they won't let you read it."

"Just stay out of this, Peggi, it doesn't have anything to do with you."

Peggi looked slightly frightened, and Jean-Pierre began to forget his resolutions. "That's enough of that," he said.

"I don't think so," said Horler from behind his desk. "Do you want us to forget all about distributing your pictures?"

"You've done nothing whatever about distributing my pictures, and I'm withdrawing them from your office today."

"I don't think any distributor will handle them, without consulting us."

"That's a lie, Jean-Pierre," said Rose. "They have no influence with the distributors; it's the other way around."

Jean-Pierre said calmly, "I know. Those are empty threats and I don't know why they bother to make them."

"We'll see if they're empty," said Lenehan. "I think I can guarantee that none of your pictures will get North American bookings without our say-so."

"Except in Quebec," said Horler cheerfully.

"How do you enforce your blacklist?"

"This is how it is. We have our producers' association, don't you see?"

"They're all at each other's throats," said Rose scornfully.

"Maybe on domestic matters," said Danny, "but just let a foreigner come in and try to break a contract we have with one of our own stars, and listen for the screams. This has been tried before, you know. You're not the first who ever tried to run out on an option. Do you know what happened?"

"What?" asked Rose. She didn't seem very alarmed.

"None of that man's pictures ever played the domestic market again. I don't need to remind you what that did to his star status. Inside of two years he didn't draw flies at the box office; we had solidarity; we told the distributors, 'Don't book his pictures. If you do we'll stop supplying you with our product.' They backed off. You know who I mean, and what he's doing now."

"He's one of the ones who built the industry," said Rose bitterly, "and you people screwed him without a second thought. But you won't screw us, not this time."

"Yes we will."

"I don't think so. Don't worry about a thing, Jean-Pierre. When we've got a print to market we'll be able to go right across the street and book it all over North America, because we're going to have next year's top picture."

"You'll fulfill your contract first," said Horler.

"Then you'll pay us 'substantial indemnification.'"

"I'll pay you ninety-eight cents."

"We're thinking in terms of two hundred thousand."

"Don't be silly, Bud. Was I worth two hundred thousand when you edited me out of *Goody*?"

"You helped *Goody*. The courts would see that."

"It isn't coming into court. I'm not going to pay you off for the option, not any more than ninety-eight cents, that is, and I'm not going to make any publicity tours for you, and when I'm interviewed I'm going to have nothing but harsh and libellous names for you, you pair of shits." She grabbed Horler's hand as it moved under his desk. "Don't bother to switch it on. You won't want a record of this next part."

"I don't know what you're talking about."

"Don't you? Then let me fill you in. It's a common practice to tape conversations like these, business discussions, just in case anything comes up." She paused, every inch the experienced actress. "Have you ever heard of a man called Callegarini? Paul Callegarini?" The partners looked at each other with surprise. They couldn't remember offhand how much Rose knew about their financing.

"I may know the name," said Horler.

"I think you may," said Rose, enjoying herself. She drew a stiff piece of paper from her bag. "I've got a letter from him right here. He says he's the bank officer who approved your loans for *Goody*. That's so, isn't it?"

"I guess it is, isn't it, Bud?" said Danny.

"Yes."

"Uh-huh," said Rose. "Seems that Mr. Callegarini is one of my fans, isn't that sweet? He says here that he sees me as one of the great ladies of the screen, and he's not happy about the way I was treated by you boys, not too happy, no."

"So what?"

"He tells me that he has tape recordings of his conversations with you about the first of April 1966, when you were arranging the financing of *Goody*. This is one of a number of photocopies of his letter—I've been passing them around for opinions. I can let you keep this one." She passed it to Horler, who hastily scanned it. "As you see, he says that on these tapes your voices are perfectly recognizable, and that you conspire to induce my husband, I should say my ex-husband, to have an affair with another actress while still married to me, for publicity purposes connected with the exploitation of *Goody*. And he's willing to testify about other, later conversations tending to the same purpose. I don't think you want this statement made public, do you?"

"No," said Danny.

"And I don't suppose that you'll be wanting to hold me to any contractual obligations, real or imaginary, will you?"

"I guess not."

"I'll be running along then. I'll put a check for ninety-eight cents in the mail to you, maybe even a dollar. In return, I want a piece of paper waiving that option, for value received, just in case."

"You needn't worry," said Danny, who seemed to be taking it well.

"But I would worry," Rose said, "I'd worry about you and Bud. I'd sooner have the piece of paper, if you don't mind, for a souvenir, after you get my cheque in the mail tomorrow."

"If that's what you want," said Danny reluctantly.

"All right. Goody-bye now." She took Jean-Pierre's hand and they sailed out of the room laughing. Peggi turned to follow and Danny stepped silently across the carpet and put his hand gently on her shoulder. "Just wait one moment, will you, dear?" he entreated. Peggi paused, looking after her friends as they went out. Danny's grip tightened on her shoulder.

8

For some reason Danny and Bud kept their New York conference room very badly lighted. Perhaps they felt that the murky atmosphere intensified the aura of trickiness and half-offered bribery in which they felt most at home. The lighting may have been nothing more than a calculated prop, but as Peggi turned back into the center of the longish narrow room she felt real fright, for she wasn't immune to threats. She was not a star, and who would protect her? She was a scrambling featured player whose last four or five parts had been found for her through Rose's help. She'd been certain of a part in any Rose Leclair picture if she wanted one, but couldn't count on that any longer. She understood that Rose had had to make her move when she did, if she wasn't to slide downhill very fast. And yet she knew that she could hardly afford to lose Rose's help and Horler and Lenehan too. Her last credit had been just fine; a lot of people were talking her up for an Oscar nomination for *Goody*, but nominations and awards didn't necessarily keep you working; sometimes they had the opposite effect.

"Peggi, do you know what that just cost us?" said Horler.

She shook her head silently. The narrow room seemed to confuse her thoughts peculiarly. She said, "I'm leaving. I've got a date."

"Stick around for a minute," said Lenehan brusquely, "we've got things to talk about."

"I'm late."

"Oh, you're not going anywhere, is she, Bud?"

The situation was exaggerated; surely they wouldn't hurt her. She was in a midtown office building with a receptionist next door. Her imagination was carrying her away. "What is it?" she asked.

"Peggi, do you want to go on working in pictures?" Horler stood up and tried to look mean and threatening, but didn't achieve much more than a comic English Peter Lorre effect. "Do you know what we can do to you?" His ineffectual menace made her giggle, and then stop, as they both began to gesture spasmodically in what now struck her as a shared murderous rage. For a second time she thought that Horler was going to hit her.

"Don't you threaten me," she said bravely, "I'm just as important as you are." She knew as she said it that it wasn't true; she didn't have the leverage they had. "Why would you want to hurt me anyway?" She saw that both men were in frenzied pain, they were so angry.

"It isn't the money," Lenehan got out.

"It is and it isn't," said Horler. "We might have got two hundred thousand out of her."

"You're out of your mind," said Peggi, and Horler came up to her and almost seized her collar; she saw his hand tremble with the repressed movement. "Don't," she said.

"Don't tell me I'm crazy," he said, "you're the crazy one. You put her up to it, didn't you? Actors!" He said the word as you might exclaim: "*Ordure!*"

"You introduced her to Jean-Pierre," Peggi said, "and you thought you might as well use him, the way you use everybody else. It's time you learned that you can't pick people up and drop them, just like that. Look how you treated Rose! She's going to come back and haunt all you little Hitlers who think sex is a matter of big tits. I'll bet you in five years she's set for life, bigger than she's ever been over here. This fellow she's got now, he's smart and he's good, not like you. I know you're supposed to be smart, with your hidden microphones and your cutting-room tricks, but you're bad people. I mean wicked."

Horler took a last step towards her and slapped her face very hard.

"Oh," cried Peggi, "that's it. You're going to shut me up with a slap or a punch, you big producer, you. All your money and all your reputation doesn't make you any better than the bums who used to shove me around when I was a teen-ager in Wheeling. Worse, because they had no chance to be anything but what they were, slobs, punks, little nothings; and you're worse. Horler and Lenehan, the columnists' delight, beating up a woman in their office. You really are out of your mind."

"Better keep your hands off her, Bud," said Danny. "All right, dear, time to go. I'll just mention this one thing: we don't like actors tampering with people under contract to us."

"I didn't tamper with her. I never suggested anything to her."

"Everybody knows you're her best friend. Now go on, beat it. We'll get you on the blacklist if it's the last thing we do. Producers don't like mouthy actors. I mean, Christ, who are you? It wasn't as if you were anybody. You need work and we're going to make it awfully tough for you to work. Remember that!"

Taking her arm, as gently as ever, he turned her towards the door.

9

"If Antonioni hadn't existed, it would have been necessary for Fellini to invent him."

"Oh, shut up," said Seth.

Hank Walden paid no attention. He said, "The one baroque, the other classically pure. The one all ornament, the other essential intention."

"God."

"I'd have thought Antonioni would be your idea of a director, wouldn't he? He thinks actors are puppets."

"I'm no puppet," Seth said, "and I won't talk to you when you're in this frame of mind. What's got into you anyway?"

"I'm following the Antonioni retrospective at the MacMahon."

"The MacMahon?"

"In the seventeenth. You must have been to the MacMahon."

"On MacMahon?"

"You can see it from here, just the other side of the Arc. You're right in the middle of things here, aren't you? I never heard of this place before."

"Charity wanted to stay at the Georges-cinq. She said all her friends stayed there, can you beat that? Five minutes off the Redlands campus and her friends stay at the Georges-cinq. She'd never even been East before *Goody*."

"How did it do here?"

"It did good business . . . and you should have seen her when the titles came on; she kept wriggling. It was sensual."

"How long is it now?"

"What?"

"Since you got married?"

"Eons."

"No, really?"

"Rose had her decree the beginning of March, around there." He grimaced when he spoke of Rose. "I guess it was just before *Goody* opened in New York, around six months." He stood up and crossed the carpet of gray and dusty pink, going to the balcony and looking down at the Avenue Kléber; you could see for miles. "She's gone to Saint-Cloud on a picnic for the day. She went out of here in a wide-brimmed hat and one of those chaste little-girl dresses she's been buying, and a straw basket with wine and strawberries in it. Strawberries. I don't know where she learns these things, but sometimes I have the impression that she's climbing all over me."

"How did they like her here?"

"Pretty good. It isn't indigenous American opera, Hank, but it'll play."

"It's doing very well at home."

Seth kept his eyes averted, looking at the sky and the roofs and the Etoile up the street. "Why do we have to be in the six-teenth anyway?"

"You couldn't not."

"People would say I was slipping. So how did you like the Antonioni retrospective, I mean do you really think he ever had anything? All that hemming and hawing, and do you love me—I don't know, I don't know. The last one I saw was *Red Desert*. Red trees and gray sky, Jesus. At first I thought the process was off, till I saw he meant it."

"He doesn't get big grosses."

"None of them do, do they?"

"I haven't got any figures with me, but none has ever grossed over three and a half million, except perhaps *And God Created Woman* and maybe Fellini."

"Yeah, Bardot."

"Ten years, eleven years, it doesn't seem that long."

"Boy, I remember when that came out in the States; the colour was the end, and the scenery."

"Yeah, the scenery." Walden snickered.

"Who else? Godard, Fauré, Truffaut, Chabrol?"

"Oh, no. You've got to have saturation bookings and an international name or two. Truffaut, say, makes a good pic-ture; it wins a couple of awards, and that boosts the star to the point where she's usable internationally, to tie up the European market. But she doesn't mean a thing in Waukegan or Singa-pore, and she isn't a star like you're a star. What happened to your deal?"

"You're my agent."

"I work for your agent."

"Same thing."

"No, it isn't. When are you going back to work?"

"You know when."

"You're a foolish idealist, a thing like that helps a picture. Look at all the fuss over *Cleopatra*. That didn't hurt it at all."

"I believe it did."

"Who can tell?"

"I can tell. I've been in this business twenty years, Hank, and I can feel it when a picture isn't going right. If I came out with a release around Christmas, they'd be saying, 'Him, remember?'"

"It could have been worse."

"You mean she could have died? Yeah, boy, that would really have packaged things up nice. Boy, when I think."

"Seth, you can release a picture any time you want, and you better get busy and make one. You can't sit in Paris and wait for them to come to you."

Seth gave his representative a very dirty look.

"Do you know what Jean-Pierre Fauré's doing this fall?" asked Walden, following up his advantage.

"I've heard rumours."

"The rumours are true, lover."

There was a long silence as Seth stretched his legs; back and forth he walked across the beautiful carpet, while Walden squinted at him through beams of afternoon sunlight. Shutters creaked on the balcony, and there were sounds of leaves and breeze.

"It isn't that I haven't tried to line something up. As soon as I came over I went into the question of finance, with the idea of setting up a Swiss coproduction deal—for the tax situation—and retaining real ownership of the property. I own a number of scripts, as you know."

"I wish you wouldn't bypass us like that."

"Hank, in Europe you don't count; this is another world. Anyway the banking looked sound, and I started looking for a director. I even considered Fauré, but he was in the States."

"Minding the store," said Walden, and they both laughed.

"But the thing is, I don't own a property suitable for both of us, Charity and me. She's basically a musical-comedy type, and she'll never be anything else, at least I can't see any dramatic potential there. A smart director might shoot around her, but she'd still be in the middle of half the frames, bouncing and jiggling and moving her arms and getting up on her toes, the way people do in musicals."

Walden thought that this didn't sound like a six months' bridegroom, but he didn't mention it. Seth scraped the carpet with his foot; the room seemed full of dusty pink and gray light, and he was framed in it, storklike and angry. Walden remembered the first time they'd met, in the Lyricart offices. Seth had been bullying his personal representative into demanding a bigger percentage of the package. Later on, Seth had picked him out for that difficult spot, and had taught him much.

He thought of his predecessor, Vogelsang, without pity. "Rose left us," he said suddenly, implicitly blaming Seth, "almost as soon as she came to. Must have been the first thing she did."

"I'll bet Vogelsang misses her."

"Vogelsang cried," said Walden contemptuously, "but it was really us she was hitting at, you and me."

"She hated you, Hank." Seth came across the room and took his agent by the lapels. "You think I don't know what they're saying in New York? 'He drove her to it.' That's what they're saying and they're probably right. It doesn't look good, and what's more I feel it. I could always make a picture with Rosie. We made four, and one was perhaps the worst movie ever made, but it made money. None of them lost a nickel, and *Sailor Take Warning* grossed twelve million on a very small investment. *She* isn't just a musical-comedy star. Sure I drove her to it, doesn't everybody?" He was very disturbed. "I've never made a picture with anybody like Charity."

"Wasn't there something at Universal with Piper Laurie?"

"For Pete's sake, that was close to twenty years ago, and don't kid yourself, Piper Laurie wasn't a bad actress at all. She just got into a rut, one that I was lucky to get out of."

Walden ruminated. "I can see you and Charity together. Might be quite a switch for you."

"She doesn't listen to anybody else's lines."

"At home or at work?"

"Anywhere. What is the kid, twenty? Nineteen? I tell you Hank, she scares me. I'm not exactly in my grave, you know. I'm thirty-eight, and I mean, I really am thirty-eight."

"We've got a photostat of your birth certificate in your dossier."

"I love the way agents talk about dossiers," Seth grumbled. "Like the secret police. 'Pull Lincoln's dossier from the files' But don't forget, somebody somewhere is keeping a dossier on *you*."

Walden shrugged. You're twice her age, he thought, what did you expect?

"I'm in real good shape," Seth complained, "I play a lot of tennis and I swim when I can, but she wears you down. I'm too old for the Olympia. I will admit, she's a terrific dancer."

"That's a major sector of the human experience."

"It is if you're in musical comedy." He looked at Walden desperately.

The agent was pitiless. "You know where she was really terrific, don't you? In those titles. Guys all over America must have envied you."

Seth looked ready to cry. "It was my idea," he said, "I suggested it to whozis-you know, Faiers."

"I thought it must have been."

"It was me all right. I said to Bud and Danny, 'Build her up. Cut Rose down' And they obeyed me, to this day I don't know why. I've been wrong often enough." That was correct. He had made a number of very bad guesses about scripts. But somehow or other his most inartistic choices of story had a way of turning out well at the box office. He had no taste, or not much, but was extremely prudent commercially, and this paradox confused his life continually. His pictures were mainly artistically unsuccessful money-makers; once in a while, when he had good direction and a good script, he made excellent pictures that made money. Either way, he made money, and was therefore a great star. He felt awfully uneasy, as if somebody was about to knock him off. Not Rose, who had never really been in his class, but somebody out there somewhere.

"You'll be in the top five for 1967," said Walden, "but not for 1968. Nothing in release."

"I will have two pictures in release for 1968."

Walden suddenly showed his anger. "It's as simple as that, is it? If you want two pictures in release next year, neither can be a musical. Do I have to spell it out for you? You should go into production this afternoon, like right now, and you should keep working for eight months, and you can't make a musical because there isn't time, which leaves Charity out on a limb. Do you want to risk her in a straight part, at this stage, of the size she'll demand? She may be your wife this year, but she's in pictures permanently. Christ, she's tampered successfully with you; how does she know somebody else won't? Do you want to go into production on a film where you can't work with the other star because she plays in a different style, in a medium you don't understand? Or do you intend to try and fit her into your style? I can't really see her in light comedy, musicals apart, or in serious drama, and I sure to God can't see you in musicals. You're a valuable property as far as Lyricart is concerned; that's why I'm here. If you want to work in Europe, that's great; everybody works in Europe these days. Just so you work."

"I'll work."

"With or without her?"

"Without, if necessary. I'd like to try one with her, but she's so completely corn-fed, fresh-faced heifer; how could we cast her? I haven't seen a story that makes sense for us, and I've been reading scripts for months."

"You need a light comedy script with a part for each of you, producible over here. Shouldn't be too hard to find."

"So find one; you're so smart. God, that girl is insistent."

"Something to cost around three and a half million, with your percentage off the gross, if we set it up that you aren't the producer of record?"

"Yeah," said Seth. He brightened up a bit. "Rose never worked off the gross."

He thought of his first sight of her, up at Lake Arrowhead sixteen years ago. She had been modelling sportswear for a teen magazine, being then at the end of her teens, just Charity's age. She's smarter than Charity, he realized suddenly, though not as stacked. At nineteen, without makeup, she had been fresh and alight, alive, a perfect ingénue, and had been picked up to do a series of clean American-girl parts at Metro. That was all she could handle for a long time, ingénues and fan-magazine layouts, where she wore girlish prints and shared the space with an animal, a horse or dog.

As he stood talking to Walden, the voice of his superego, whom he had always disliked intensely, Seth felt more and more certainly what he had suspected all summer, that his taste had betrayed him again. Perhaps, he let himself reflect for the first time, perhaps a man is entitled to only one nineteen-year-old girl per lifetime. Perhaps he can't handle more than one. Rose danced mistily in his imagination, rather short, with pretty dark brown hair and clearly drawn features, no raving beauty. Her big weapon had been her diction, which was naturally clear and precise and which recorded beautifully; she had never needed a voice coach, while he, Seth Lincoln, big star, had been working on his speech for years after they were married.

"Don't worry about it, it's just phonetic geography," she used to tell him. "Nobody cares about it but smart-ass reviewers."

"Dis, dat, dese, dem, dose," he would say worriedly.

He remembered her smile. "What are we doing this crazy thing for? Who would cast a kid from Bristol, Connecticut, as the Lady Aminta, with a boy from the Upper West Side as Sir Grishkin? It's loony, no?"

"Sir Gawain," said Seth. "Spell my name right."

That had been an awful movie in almost every conceivable way, except that it had earned back its production costs in the neighbourhoods and had gone on earning afterwards. Kids loved it, and it still ran and ran, all over the States. After that, when Rose wanted to be specially nice to him, she called him Sir Grishkin.

"I've come a long way," he would tell her:

"Sure you have. Let me hear you say, 'THis, THat, THese, THem, THose.'"

"THis, THat, THese, THem, THose."

"Very good. Let me give you a kiss." Where had she got her clear diction and her fresh face? She was a nothing and so was he; but she hadn't become as big a star; he'd outgrown her. She'd never really learned her trade. After they were married she'd been content to go on doing solid leads in not quite top productions, while he had acquired a lot of prestige.

I could have stayed king of the teens, he thought, but I wasn't able to accept that. I improved myself. I didn't do television. I cleaned up my diction, and it wasn't easy. I worked for good directors and associated myself with the best people, and I got better. Rose depended on my reputation, and on me personally, and I just got tired of carrying her. I'm no kid. I'm almost forty.

One nineteen-year-old to a lifetime, was that the regulation? He had used up fifteen years of Rose, would he get as much of Charity? He remembered some idiotic debutante's line to the press: "It's wonderful to be getting married for the first time." This had always seemed to him comically corrupt, but how was he any better? He added fifteen years to his present age, and wondered if he would catch another youthful virgin at fifty-three. *Maybe I won't need them any more, wouldn't that be wonderful? Fifteen years of Charity* . . .

"What is this stuff?" said Walden, picking at the wall with his fingernails.

"Ormolu. *Or-moulu*. Ground gold, powdered up and brushed on. Actually it isn't gold, it's bronze. Don't pull it off; that's real authentic inlay and they couldn't replace it."

Walden picked up a white and gold clock that stood on the chimneypiece. "Really works," he mumbled, listening for the delicate tick. "Pretty nice place for a West Side boy."

"That's the real West Side story, Hank, from slavery to ormolu. I've worked hard to get where I am. Listen, let's go have a couple of drinks. I told Charity we'd be in the bar or the restaurant, and I think we'd better try to come to some kind of agreement about script possibilities and a director before she gets back."

"Too bad we can't get Fauré," said Walden. "He's really a virtuoso, working with inexperienced people. He may be able to do something with Rose; there's plenty there to start with."

"Ah, she never liked you."

"What do they call this place again?" asked Walden vaguely.

"The Raphaël, but I'm no archangel." They went in search of drink.

10

"She'll be here tomorrow; she might be in full flight at this moment."

"And I suppose I'm not," said Charity, with explicit nastiness.

"Oh, you. I don't give a damn who you eat strawberries with, as long as you do it on your own time."

"That jerk never laid a hand on me. I'm famous and I've got a reputation to protect. I'm going to be above suspicion and gossip, like Rose."

"How can you, of all people, talk about her to me? It was you made me betray her."

"Me?"

"Who else?"

"You were making eyes at me before I ever spoke to you. I remember how it was. I never even looked at you till she introduced us."

"Who was that?"

"Your wife."

"You are my wife."

"Like hell I am. I'm your whore."

"Don't be silly; we're married."

"I'll never get you away from her; you've got her in your bones and you'll never get her out—I'm not talking law, I'm talking feelings."

"How old are you, Charity?"

"Never mind that, you've been telling me how young and insignificant I am for a year. Why didn't you leave me alone?"

Seth took a step backwards.

Charity said, "I didn't want to be just another Hollywood tramp with five husbands. I wanted to get married."

"We are married."

"Oh, I could kill you if you don't stop saying that. You know what I mean. You don't even like me very much."

This was so accurate that he could think of no reply.

She went on bitterly, "I could have got out of being a sexpot. I don't want that; it just makes you silly. I want to be a real person, like some of these French stars we've met around. I don't want to be a joke. If there's anything in the world I don't want to be, it's a dirty joke with my big ass and my big front, and every little masturbator in the U.S.A. thinking of me instead of his wife."

"Where do you get these ideas?"

"God damn you, Seth! Can't you get it through your head that I'm not a dumb bunny even though I look like one? I'm no brood mare, not an animal. I know how all you people look at me and what you're thinking. You've never looked at me as anything but furniture for your bedroom."

Unfortunately this was nearly true too. In the beginning, Seth thought, I may have harboured some vaguely protective feelings towards her, and I may have been pretty bored with Rose. Like a traveler in the Alps who ascends a range of mountains which he takes to be the highest, Seth now began to discern new ranges, new heights.

He saw that there might be a kind of life, a system of personal morality, in which you did not discard your wife as soon as you had grown bored with her, but instead studied with her the ways in which to dissipate the boredom, which was after all a product of your mutual relations. Perhaps if one was really married, the union was indissoluble.

I thought Rose was mine forever, but apparently she belongs to this Fauré. This was the first time these questions had occurred to him. He saw Charity move before him in the beautiful room and was aware of matters that were wholly unfamiliar. He saw the girl clearly: young, in magnificent health, bewildered though not malicious, with nothing in her mind, not vicious but unformed. And he began to see himself: a fool, a deluded man. I ran away from what I had, he thought, and now I have nothing. This child doesn't know me, or care about me. What can I do?

It's wonderful to be getting married for the first time.

"Look," he said, advancing on the frightened girl, "don't shrink from me, I'm trying to help us. Look, we made a mistake, that's true. But we can fix it. We don't have to give up on ourselves, just because we pretended we were in love. I see what we wanted. I was looking for fresh sex and I guess you were after some free advertising."

Charity looked at him with round eyes and nodded mutely.

"Either we get a quick divorce and start all over again, or we can try to save what we've put into this." He felt exhausted and didn't know what to do. "I don't know that I've ever loved anybody," he said, "I don't know what it feels like. Isn't that awful?"

Charity began to cry. "Me too," she said.

"Well Christ, we're not helpless. You're beautiful, and I'm rich and famous. Surely we can make something out of that."

"I'm famous too," said Charity, crying, "and I want to make a picture. I haven't worked all year, and Rose is going to make lots of them here."

"Don't cry, Charity. I own scripts. I have Walden out at work, lining things up. You'll be working in six weeks."

"Really, Seth?"

"That's a promise. And between the two of us, we'll kill them." He put his arms around her and kissed her with passion. He thought possibly I can get to love her, and vice versa. He felt that something had been rounded off.

11

Going out to Kennedy in the early morning for a departure, you catch the sun coming up out of the Atlantic, tipping Long Island with an extraordinary orange brilliance, and it was into this bursting light that Peggi drove, the trunk of her car loaded with hand baggage, and the back seat with the absorbed lovers, ready to go. It was the last day of September, a Saturday, and Jean-Pierre had promised to take Rose to Mass with him at Saint-Merri the following morning. They were going to start the picture in ten days, the sooner the better, because they meant to have it in release by next spring.

Taking the eastbound jet at this hour would get them into Orly in plenty of time to dine with a fine leisurely hunger; they had a dinner reservation *au grand Véfour*, made for them by the Paris office of Films Vinteuil (an assistant director and a secretary), and they talked away behind her like kids going to a birthday party—of dinner, wines, the future, finance, their film, which grew into shape as they talked it over.

It seemed to Peggi that Jean-Pierre made his films the way a kid makes a snowman, starting with a small hard centre, patting and adding here and there, sculpting, shaping, accepting any solid new substance brought to the work by others, working freely and flexibly without a vast overload of economic structure weighing him down.

At the end of this intensely free process there appeared a brilliant, almost improvised imitation of an action. Hearing them talk about their picture, and remembering that part of it, the title, would be her contribution, Peggi grew silent and glum. She would have liked to work as freely as that, but nobody did so here. She felt like asking, "Aren't there parts for me in Europe?" But the situation didn't allow it; for that kind of part they would naturally use European character people. She thought if I were only a star.

She was sure that they'd never come back.

Following an airlines bus which had slashed around her and in towards the turnoff, she began to circle nearer and nearer the main building, coming across the flat between the parkway and the airstrips. The sun mounted. The clouds that had formed just before dawn grew wispy and were shredded as the air moved and warmed for the day. Later it would be very fair. The clouds were streaked pink and orange, and between the streaks was a variety of soft rich grays. Pink, brownish-gray, pink-to-orange, fleecy gray, then behind sheer deep blue. Morning.

All at once the car shot up a ramp, which turned and allowed them a grand perspective of distant Manhattan, shrouded in mists that rose and drew off as they watched. In spite of herself, Peggi's heart lifted. She'd seen this sight a hundred times, arriving by jet from the Coast, and it never failed to move her, the fragile shapes so distant, yet so sharp and clear.

The parking attendant slid into the driver's seat, as the three of them superintended the movements of the baggage. They had to pay for a lot of weight over the allowance, and then they moved on to the Air France board to check the departure time. All was ready; they could line up, check in, and go aboard.

"I told you I'd get you here at the right time," said Peggi.

"You're a sweetie," said Rose. "Listen, what are you doing in the next while, that you haven't told us?"

"I'm guesting on Crossword next week. I may do some television this season."

"If you ever come to Paris . . ."

"Of course you've got to come, the sooner the better," said Jean-Pierre, giving her a hug.

The flight was called, interrupting their embrace. She followed them to the boarding gate, then crossed to a window and watched them go aboard in the middle of a crowd. At the stairs, predictably, two photographers and a stewardess picked them out of the throng and drew them to one side. When the plane had filled, as the jets began to whistle, Rose and Jean-Pierre posed on the stairs, waving, smiling, embracing. Peggi saw it all through the wall of glass like a silent movie. Rose spoke, laughed, called out to one of the photographers, whom she seemed to know. The jet whistle grew, penetrating the thick glass. Peggi could hear nothing else; it made her dizzy.

The stewardess went inside, the stairway was withdrawn, the door drawn up and locked electrically, and the plane turned away.

She noticed that she was holding the claim cheque for her car crushed into a moist ball in her fist. She unfolded it with difficulty and went briskly off and handed it to the attendant. In a surprisingly short time, the car appeared. She tipped the attendant and climbed in, and followed the arrows slowly towards the exit.

Halfway back to the parkway, she saw the Air France flight go by on the takeoff, so she stopped her car and leaped out, standing by the side of the service road and shading her eyes. Even at this considerable distance she could pick out the sound of that particular plane, a high forceful whoooooo-oosshhhh and whine. The windows looked very small. Nobody would see her from there, but she lifted her hand anyway and waved, turning her head to follow the plane as it lifted off.

The plane rose into the intense blue, the clouds all gone now. It gained altitude at that peculiar angle the jets always seem to hit, a more acute angle than one expects; it seemed to hang for a moment without forward motion, rising straight up in a very slow climb, hanging . . . hanging. The sound diminished. The plane receded; its image grew smaller, as it turned eastward and headed out over the ocean.

It was now the middle of the morning. The light had stopped changing so quickly, and the Manhattan buildings seemed fantastically sharp-edged in the clear air. Peggi drove away fast, towards the dangerous city.

Hugh Hood (1928–2000) was a Canadian novelist, short story writer, essayist and university professor. Hood wrote 32 books: 17 novels, including the 12-volume New Age novel sequence (influenced by Marcel Proust and Anthony Powell), several volumes of short fiction, and 5 of nonfiction. He taught English literature at the Université de Montréal. In the early 1970s he and fellow authors Clark Blaise, Raymond Fraser, John Metcalf and Ray Smith formed the well-known Montreal Story Tellers Fiction Performance Group, which popularized the public reading of fiction in Canada. In 1988, he was made an Officer of the Order of Canada.